THE CURSED

THE
COVEN OF BONES
SERIES

THE
CURSED

HARPER L. WOODS

BRAMBLE

TOR PUBLISHING GROUP
NEW YORK

THE CURSED

Copyright © 2023 by Harper L. Woods

A Bramble Book
Published by Tom Doherty Associates / Tor Publishing Group
120 Broadway
New York, NY 10271

www.torpublishinggroup.com

Bramble™ is a trademark of Macmillan Publishing Group, LLC.

The Library of Congress Cataloging-in-Publication Data
is available upon request.

ISBN 978-1-250-35894-3 (hardcover)
ISBN 978-1-250-34429-8 (ebook)

Our books may be purchased in bulk for promotional, educational, or business use. Please contact your local bookseller or the Macmillan Corporate and Premium Sales Department at 1-800-221-7945, extension 5442, or by email at MacmillanSpecialMarkets@macmillan.com.

First Hardcover Edition: 2024

Printed in China

0 9 8 7 6 5 4 3 2 1

For those who love them murderous.

TRIGGER WARNINGS

- Dubious consent
- Forced feeding
- Graphic on-page violence and torture
- Rough and explicit sexual content
- Forced proximity and captive scenarios
- Betrayal
- References to past abuse and traumatic reactions to triggering stimuli
- Knife violence
- Graphic depictions of blood
- Physical harm inflicted upon the main character
- Ritualistic murder
- Rape of a minor by an adult (off-page, historical context)
- Self-harm/cutting for magical purposes
- Blood magic

LEGACIES OF CRYSTAL HOLLOW

CRYSTAL WITCHES (also known as Whites)
House Petra
House Beltran

COSMIC WITCHES (also known as Purples)
House Realta
House Amar

EARTH WITCHES (also known as Greens)
House Madizza
House Bray

AIR WITCHES (also known as Grays)
House Aurai
House Devoe

WATER WITCHES (also known as Blues)
House Tethys
House Hawthorne

SEX/DESIRE WITCHES (also known as Reds)
House Erotes
House Peabody

FIRE WITCHES (also known as Yellows)
House Collins
House Madlock

NECROMANCY WITCHES (also known as Blacks)
House Hecate

THE CURSED

PROLOGUE

LUCIFER MORNINGSTAR

Fifty years prior

Loralei Hecate wandered the halls, her deep ebony hair swaying as she moved. The piece of onyx held in her palm would do nothing to protect her from the creature hunting her, but that didn't stop her from clinging to it like a lifeline as I followed in the shadows. Her best friend was a White who had given Loralei the gem to protect herself against that nagging feeling of being followed that she just couldn't seem to shake.

The only protection she would have found was safety in numbers, and she'd been foolish enough to leave the haven of her bed at night. It hadn't taken much for me to lure her away, just the quiet whisper of a call so subtle it didn't activate the amulet around her neck.

I followed her, keeping to the shadows to avoid her notice. It would take the right place for her death, because as much as she needed to die, I didn't want her to suffer. I didn't have any need for her final moments to be filled with fear and darkness.

Her death was nothing personal. In fact, her death was a sacrifice designed to bring everything to fruition.

Centuries of planning depended on this moment and relied on the ceasing of her heartbeat, but the role she had played in the years leading up to this had earned her a token of my respect.

Loralei stopped suddenly, spinning to look back at me. The vivid blue of her eyes shone in the darkness, shimmering like moonlight with a faint purple tint that was so reminiscent of her ancestor Charlotte. Her forehead twisted as her mouth parted in a silent scream while she moved, dropping the onyx crystal to the floor.

The protection of the stone lay forgotten when she found me stalking after her. She didn't know the truth of who I was, of *what* I was beneath the meat suit I called home, but nothing good could come from a Vessel stalking his prey in the night.

I took a single step toward her, coming to a halt suddenly when a mismatched stare looked in my direction. A woman stepped into the dim light shining in through the windows, approaching Loralei hesitantly. There was something unreal about her body, as if she were there but not, and if I reached out to touch her, I wondered if I would find flesh or only the faintest whisper of a half-forgotten memory.

Loralei ran, sprinting forward and heading for a bend in the hall as the woman searched the shadows I called home. She saw nothing, her eerie multicolored stare darting all over and searching as if she could *feel* me but not see me.

But I saw her.

I felt her. The moment those purple and amber eyes landed on mine, I knew exactly what she was—who she was. Her inky dark hair fell over her shoulders in soft waves, the slight burgundy tint to the bottom reminding me of the finest merlot. Her body was curved and soft with thick thighs that I could just imagine wrapped around my head and breasts that would bounce when I fucked her.

My intentions for the daughter of two had never been to make her mine. They'd never been to keep her, but simply to use her for what her unique combination of magic could offer me.

That all changed when a growl rumbled in my chest, sinking through my body. The floor shook beneath my feet with the force of it, the windows rattling in the wall as the pieces of destiny clicked and clacked together in an endless symphony like the clatter of bones swaying in the wind.

Loralei clutched the bag of bones at her hip as the young Hecate witch turned and followed after her aunt, the ghost of her visage flickering in the moonlight. Her gaze dropped to that bag of bones as if she felt the call, part of her recognizing that they would one day be hers.

She wanted them, and all I wanted was to take what was mine. *Her.*

"I don't have what you seek," Loralei said into the nothingness. Her stare remained fixed on me, her body flinching with each step I took. The halls pulsed in recognition of what moved through them as I released the little bits of power I could access in this form, filling the university with my presence.

The younger Hecate witch, the woman who hadn't yet been born, faltered, catching herself with a hand on the wall. Both witches' breath fanned before their faces as the temperature of the hall dropped so low it burned.

"Loralei!" the younger witch called in panic. Loralei snapped her gaze to the side as if she, too, saw the strange witch, her eyes widening with recognition. She dropped her hand away from the bag of bones that gave her power, her body stilling as I watched something arch between them.

"Run, Charlotte. Run!" she screamed as the other witch moved closer to help her aunt.

Charlotte.

There was a certain familiarity in her, pulsing off her in waves that reminded me of the original witch. Of the one who had called to me in the woods that night and begged for the tools to seek her revenge.

But the name was all wrong for her, as if the part of her that remained independent of that familiarity rebelled against the notion of being so thoroughly tied to the ancestor who had started it all.

I struck, a clawed hand slipping out of the shadows so quickly that I doubted the new witch even saw me. Loralei's chest erupted into red, three deep slash marks tearing her open as blood splattered against the younger one's face. Loralei reached out as she fell to her knees, grasping her niece by the arm as the floor shook beneath her. I took a step closer, ready to take what was mine even if it ruined everything.

My body moved as if in a trance, as if she'd used the bones she didn't possess to command my body.

"Wake up, Willow," Loralei whispered as her eyes rolled back. *Willow.*

That name was right. I stepped closer, my attention riveted not on the witch I'd come to kill but the one I planned to own one day.

I swept my claws across her shoulder in three sharp, fast movements. Willow screamed as her blood sank beneath my nails, covering my fingers and making me feel complete for the first time in centuries. I raised them to my mouth, earning my first taste of my future.

She moved to look at me, and I wondered if the curious creature would see me standing there. I wondered if she was already mine as I leaned forward, dragging my nose through the hair on the back of her head and inhaling her scent.

"Wake up!" Loralei screamed.

The ground shook beneath me as my rage heightened, the witch bleeding out doing everything in her power to take my witchling from me. Willow fell, her knees ready to crash against the stone.

Until she vanished.

1

WILLOW

I gasped the moment those strange, glowing golden eyes found mine without hesitation, His stare latching on and pinning me to the spot. My hand trembled against His chest as I blinked back the sting of horrified tears.

What had I done?

I swallowed, pulling my gaze off His slowly and glancing to the archdemons watching our interaction with far more interest than I cared for. I tugged at my hand where it was still pressed against His chest, His skin crackling and peeling where it had burned against mine. Nausea stung the back of my throat at the scent as I tugged again, revealing raw red flesh in the shape of my hand.

The handprint was a vivid red against the gold of His skin. My breath shuddered in my lungs as I fought to pull free but didn't dare to do so quickly. He watched me, His eerie golden stare assessing my every move as I tried to quell the panic in my body.

His hand moved quickly as I pulled away, tearing more of the burnt, charred skin from Him. He grasped me around the wrist, His grip solid as I struggled to get free. Moving slowly, He sat up in a smooth, fluid glide that didn't betray a hint of how long His body had been vacant and neglected. I moved with Him as He left me no choice, slowly swinging His legs over the side of the cot. The archdemons had raised it up, laying it atop the arms of the Tethys throne so that He was level with me as I stood.

The cot didn't shift as He moved despite the precarious position, His movement so carefully controlled that it was unnatural. His heated stare never left my face to look at the others in the room as His other hand lifted from his side, reaching beneath my free arm to settle at my waist. His fingers grasped the fabric of my top, bunching it against my skin as He jerked me forward to stand between His spread legs.

He held my stare, ignoring the trembling of my hand and bottom lip as He leaned forward, pressing His forehead against mine. A deep sigh left Him the moment our skin touched, His grip twitching against my wrist as His eyes finally drifted closed.

I swallowed, pulling back to glare up at Him. He ground His back teeth together as His hand dropped from my waist, and He raised it to slide it beneath the curtain of my hair and touch my jaw. Sweat slicked my skin at the contact, His body so warm it felt like it might burn me. It was such a contrast to the way His Vessel had felt, to that striking chill that had always permeated the air around him.

"Don't look at me like that, Witchling," He murmured softly, His grip tightening around the curve of my head when I tried to flinch away from His touch.

Those ethereal eyes hardened into a glare, glimmering like molten gold when I used His moment of distraction to tear my hand from His chest. I tried not to look at the perfect handprint that marred His skin, at the way it didn't seem to show any sign of healing in the way I would have hoped.

He tilted His head to look at the mark, His lips tipping into a cruel smirk. "You marked me," He said, gazing at me through His lashes with the hint of white teeth peeking through His parted lips. It was a look of smug satisfaction, purely dominant— a predator who had won His prey.

"I did everything you asked," I said, shaking my head as I tried to pull away from His touch. He grasped my hand in His, raising it to stare at the burnt remains of flesh that clung to my skin. When He touched a single finger to it, I watched in horror as the remnants melted into blood, sliding away from my hand and dripping onto the floor at our feet. It was the same way He'd melted the new flesh off the Covenant's bones to form Charlotte, and the memory was far too fresh in my mind.

"You did," He agreed, trailing a finger through His blood and dragging it up to where my wrist peeked out from the sleeve of my sweater.

"So let me go. You have no use for me anymore," I argued, keeping my voice quiet. His finger stopped that slow, traitorous trail over my skin, freezing in place as His nail seemed to elongate in the sudden anger that pulsed off Him in waves.

It pierced my skin, my own blood welling as I gasped at the sensation of the warmth of His slipping into the wound and entangling itself with my own. It shouldn't have felt that way, shouldn't have flooded my veins with tingling heat that set me aflame.

But it did.

"You want to leave me," He said, slowly turning that animalistic gaze to my face once again. There was no warmth in the hardness of His rage, only anger I didn't want to contemplate as I flinched back from Him.

"What reason would I have to stay?" I asked. His face fell immediately, the anger from a moment before disappearing so suddenly it gave me whiplash. Somehow, the vast emptiness and lack of all emotion on His features were worse than His anger.

He released me, allowing me to stumble over my own feet at my sudden freedom. I backed away another step as He stood smoothly, this form of Him so similar to the Vessel He'd occupied for centuries. But that had been a hollow imitation of the real man before me, of the dominant, masculine beauty that prowled toward me with slow confidence.

He'd been beautiful before, more handsome than any human I'd seen, but now, in this form, He was somehow *more*. His hair was thicker and darker, a deep brown so close to black that only the lanterns overhead showed the difference. His bone structure was deeper somehow, more sharply tuned and distinctly masculine. His golden eyes seemed to sit deeper in the structure of His face, making His brow more pronounced. In spite of the delicate fullness of His mouth, the tense line of it was menacing and ruthless as He stared at me. He seemed bigger than before, not just His height but the width of Him. His muscles were carved into His lean form as if He were a sculpture that belonged in one of the churches in Rome.

Because they'd been based off Him.

Even His forearms and hands spoke of strength, of the ability to crack my spine in half if I looked at Him wrong. His very essence filled the room, plunging us into darkness as the air turned sickeningly warm, the taste of apples coating my tongue.

"I achieved what I came here to do and things I never would have wanted," I said in an attempt to remind Him that I'd always had an agenda in coming to Crystal Hollow. In my ideal scenario, this town had always been a pit stop, if I managed to survive it anyway.

The latter seemed unlikely given the unfortunate turn of events.

Like being stabbed by the man I'd somehow allowed myself to fall for like the naive little girl he'd accused me of being.

Even I knew I stood no chance of fighting my way to freedom. My magic was distant, overused in the opening of the seal and with no earth nearby for me to call on. I glanced at the Madizza throne from the corner of my eye, the black-tinted rose petals fluttering in an invisible breeze as if they felt the faint call of my magic.

I stepped back once more, hoping to get just a little bit closer and avoid the death Lucifer promised in His stare. I bumped into something massive and hard at my back, tilting my head up to look at where Beelzebub stared down at me with disinterest—his leathery black wings twitching as they curled around his shoulders.

He reached around the front of my body, capturing my chin with a hand as the other touched the back of my head.

The breath caught in my throat, the realization of what he intended flashing through me faster than I could react. Gray wouldn't even give me the courtesy of killing me himself, allowing his minion to do his dirty work in the end.

Lucifer's eyes widened, His expression turning horrified as His mouth opened suddenly. "No!" He commanded as Beelzebub snapped my head to the side sharply.

A crack resounded through my skull as Gray rushed forward, catching me as I fell. He stopped me from crumpling to the ground as my head hung at an unnatural angle that I couldn't right, my lungs compressing as they expelled a final breath.

His hand slammed into my chest, an ache spreading from the heat of his touch when all that surrounded me was cold.

But inside, I burned.

2

LUCIFER MORNINGSTAR

Willow dropped, her legs crumpling beneath her as her eyes glazed over. Beelzebub released her as if she'd burned him the moment I shouted my protest, as if that would be enough to undo what he'd done. My body moved more quickly than I remembered, leaving me to stumble slightly as I adjusted to the feeling of my own skin wrapped around my soul.

I caught Willow before she could hit the floor, sliding an arm beneath her to offer support. I winced at the odd angle of her neck, at the way it hung limply with nothing to support it. The shape of her reminded me of Susannah, of the grotesque way her death had clung to what remained of her even after Charlotte and I raised her from the grave.

No.

Her eyes rolled back in her head as her soul severed from her physical form, the ghost of her spirit rising from her chest in a faint mist.

"I'm sorry," I murmured, even though I knew she was past hearing me. The Willow I knew could no longer sense those trying to reach her, her spirit lost to the call of Hell in her soul. What I would do would bring her pain, would torment her and likely make her hate me even more than she already did.

I pushed my hand through that mist leaking free from her heart, slamming my palm against the bare skin of her chest. Inky tendrils of dark, forbidden magic spread through the mist that could have brought her to peace if her soul hadn't been damned by her ancestor's actions, wrapping around what remained of Willow and clinging to her.

Her skin split beneath my hand, cracking open as if she were made of porcelain. Darkness spread over her skin like the vines she loved, creating a hollow in her body as I focused my magic on gripping every last wisp of her soul. I wouldn't let any part of her escape me, wouldn't let any bit of the woman I'd come to crave more than my own freedom sever from what made her *her.*

The tendrils latched on, caging her in a brutal, cruel embrace as her body shuddered in my arms. My free hand inched up her back, slipping beneath her top and touching the mark I'd put on her shoulder. The one that made her *mine.*

The one that enabled me to bind her to me in a desperate bid to save her.

Her back arched involuntarily as my nails sank into the center of the triangle I'd marked her with, elongating into black talons that pierced her flesh. I knew the pain she'd feel when she awoke would be crippling, that she'd remember bits and pieces of what had happened in the aches that plagued her body.

Cradling her in my arms, I leaned forward and touched my forehead to hers, holding her in position as I shifted my hand on her chest, sinking my fingers between the cracks I'd created in her skin.

The dark magic I'd used to trap her soul here returned to me, surrounding my skin and tugging her back into her body. Only when her soul had returned to her, wrapping around her heart and making itself at home in the useless, dead flesh of her body, did I pull my fingers free and stare down at where the mist tinted with the slightest green and black wisps swirled inside the crevice I'd made.

She hung limply as I pulled back, holding up my forearm to Beelzebub, who stared at it and swallowed. "Lucifer . . ." he said, his voice trailing off as he looked between me and my wife.

"Do it now," I commanded, watching as he unsheathed his favored dagger from the strap crossed over his chest. He pressed it into the vulnerable underside of my wrist, dragging it up my vein until he reached the inner part of my elbow. What I aimed to do would require far more blood than any mortal could easily give, only the true immortality of my form offering her salvation.

Blood flowed freely over my skin, dripping onto the floor beneath me as I shifted to place it over Willow's mouth. She was unresponsive as I pressed it to her lips, smearing her lips and skin with my blood and allowing it to pool in her mouth. The archdemons were silent as we waited for it to drip down the back of her throat, for her body to consume what would fix the wrong done to her mortal form.

A ragged breath filled her lungs, her neck shifting and snapping back into place as the bones mended. I hung my head forward, pulling her tighter into me and drawing comfort from the rise and fall of her chest in an even, natural rhythm. It was the same one she had when I watched her sleep, the same heartbeat that echoed with her breaths.

My blood dripped onto the floor as my flesh worked to knit itself back together, straining as I stood with Willow in my arms and headed for the door. Her screams of pain began, tearing through my eardrums and making me wince. The pain in that sound was unimaginable; to think of what she must have been feeling to make noises like that even in the depths of sleep . . .

"Lucifer, we need to know what you want us to do. The plans have clearly changed," Asmodeus called behind me.

"The plans can fucking wait," I snarled, leaving the archdemons to wreak whatever havoc they wished upon the Coven. None of them mattered. None of *it* mattered.

Only the witch in my arms.

3

WILLOW

One moment, there was only darkness. Only a hollow where light had once been. The vague vestiges of flames burned the backs of my eyelids, taunting and teasing me as if my spirit readied itself for the pyre.

Then there was air, sharp and painful as it filled my lungs. My eyes flung open as I drew in a ragged gasp, sitting up so suddenly that my vision swam with dizziness. My lungs burned with the air that filled them, as if they'd been frozen in time, waiting for me to wake.

My mind was a mess, a maze I couldn't find my way out of. My chest heaved with exertion as if I'd just run a mile, my breathing labored in the panic that consumed me. My hand crept toward my throat, grasping the skin there as I fought to remember how I'd come to be in Gray's bed.

The moment my fingers touched my skin, the crack of my neck snapping burst through my memory. The darkness that came after and then the complete and blinding pain that overwhelmed my body.

I scrambled from the bed, getting tangled in the blankets as I flung my legs over the edge. Falling to the floor with a thump, I fought to free myself from the distinctive mess of them in my panic. Kicking and clawing at them as I shook my head from side to side, I crawled toward the bathroom on the other side of Gray's room.

"Willow!" he yelled, but I couldn't bear to turn my eyes to him. I couldn't stand to look at him even as I felt him step into the open doorway to his private living area. I grimaced as I tried to stand, resisting the urge to scream when I couldn't seem to get my legs out of the fucking blanket.

My chest throbbed with pain, and I touched my palm to it as a strangled noise clawed its way up my throat.

Gray moved, carefully avoiding my legs as he pulled the blanket free and dropped it on the bed. My legs were bare, only a black nightgown covering my intimate areas as I squeezed my thighs together. He lowered himself beside me, sitting on his haunches as his face came into view. "You're all right," he said softly, his voice deceptive and soothing. It called to me like the softest melody, a teasing taunt of magic that hadn't been there in his Vessel form.

Sin wrapped up in skin, a body meant for luring humans to a place of endless suffering.

Tears stung my eyes at the notes of it that still reminded me of the man I'd known, of the one I'd somehow, foolishly, allowed to deceive me into falling in love with him.

The man who had never even existed in the first place.

I wrapped my arms around my stomach, my mind a whirlwind. I couldn't make sense of all that had happened. I couldn't understand the implications of what he'd done, of how *long* he'd been planning this.

"How did I get here?" I asked, swallowing as I pinched my eyes closed. I wouldn't have willingly come to his bed, not after everything he'd done. There was this hole in my memory, a gap where I couldn't remember anything.

I'd opened the seal and put Gray back into Lucifer's body, but there was very little after that. "You need to rest," Gray said, reaching forward to slip his hand beneath the curtain of my hair. His fingers brushed against my skin first, then his palm cupped my jaw as he turned me to face him. His golden eyes shimmered as he stared down at me, his thumb brushing against my skin in a soft caress.

The sound of my neck cracking again pulsed through my mind, sending me scrambling back, away from the Devil Himself.

I drew in a deep, shuddering breath, trying to quell the rising nausea in my stomach that came with the realization.

"I died," I said, my voice barely a whisper as I stared at Gray, at *Lucifer,* I forced myself to think, giving Him the name he'd always owned. Separating the being who stood before me from the one I'd thought I'd known.

"Briefly," he said, as if that absolved him of any guilt. His demon had snapped my neck, taken me from the world that I'd barely even gotten to know. But the acknowledgment was enough to know that he'd done something even worse to bring me back.

"What did you do?" I asked, raising my hand to cover my mouth as my nausea worsened.

"Come back to bed, love. Your body needs more rest," he said, ignoring the question entirely.

I groaned, rushing for the bathroom as guilt struck me in the chest that was already throbbing. My legs slipped beneath me, feeling as if they weren't my own. There was something so *off* about the body that had always been mine, something so strange about what I'd always called my home on this plane.

"Willow," Gray repeated, following after me with slow, measured steps. He wrapped his arms around my waist, helping me get my balance as he brought me to the bathroom and let me drop to my knees in front of the toilet just in time for my stomach to purge itself.

Soft, gentle fingers coaxed my hair back from the sides of my face and from where it threatened to fall forward, gathering it into their grip at the nape of my neck as I vomited. "You're all right," he murmured, and I wondered if the words were more to convince me of it, or himself.

My stomach continued heaving long after I'd finished vomiting, my body seizing as it tried to expel what was no longer there. I raised my hand, wiping my mouth with the back of it before placing a hand on each side of the toilet and rising to my feet weakly. Flushing the contents down, I tried not to panic at the sight of the red liquid filling the toilet and moved to the sink to furiously rinse out my mouth.

"Don't worry, Witchling. It's not your blood," Gray said, ever helpful, as the sink stained with pink. As if vomiting blood was my biggest worry right now.

The reflection I saw in the mirror when I finally raised my gaze looked exactly as I remembered, no sign of the ways I'd changed so drastically. The only jarring difference rested on my chest at the top of my cleavage, where a black circle stained my skin. Tendrils of darkness bled out from the center, carving through my skin like cracks in a windowpane that hadn't yet shattered.

My amulet hung just above it, the rose gold stark against the black tourmaline and the mark. My bottom lip trembled as I stared at it, trying not to let my fingers touch the stain. "Will it go away?" I asked, sinking my teeth into my bottom lip. It was such a stupid thing to care about, when the alternative was rotting in Hell.

But I didn't want to spend the rest of my life marked by the fact that he'd sacrificed to save me.

"No," he said calmly, handing me a bottle of mouthwash. I took it, refusing to thank him for it as I sipped and rinsed my mouth more thoroughly.

I glanced at him in the mirror when I was done, holding his eerie golden stare. His hair was more disheveled than I'd ever seen it, his torso still bare. The line of a single scar was raised in white from his wrist to his elbow, and I felt certain it hadn't been there before I'd . . .

I swallowed.

"Who?" I demanded, turning to face him. He stepped closer

as I spun, trapping me between his body and the vanity as he leaned forward.

"It doesn't matter," he said simply, shrugging lightly as he raised a hand to touch a single finger to the darkness blooming on my chest.

I swallowed, trying to gauge my best course of action. Gray had been strong when I'd thought him to be just a Vessel, but this form must have infinite power at its disposal. He'd been the one to create my ancestor. To give her the magic that she then shared with all the witches. That kind of power made what I held at my fingertips look like child's play. "It does to me," I said, not knowing how to proceed.

My instinct was to punch him in the throat, knee him in the balls—to curse him into oblivion, and judging by the smirk on his face, the bastard damn well knew it.

"Don't look at me like that when I can't bend you over the sink and remind you exactly what you really want, Witchling," he growled, taking me by the hand as he guided me out of the bathroom. I stumbled over my own feet, my steps uncoordinated. He tore back the covers that he'd dropped on the bed when he helped me untangle myself.

"All that I want to do to you is slit your fucking throat," I snarled, wincing when he reached into the nightstand drawer and pulled a blade free.

He held it out for me, turning it so that he gripped the flat sides of the blade between two fingers and gave me the hilt. "Go ahead then, love. See what good it does," he said, his voice fading into a condescending laugh.

I took it, gripping the handle and finding no comfort in it. I could slit his throat, but I knew it would do no good. He would bleed all over the floor, but life would never leave him from a wound of the flesh. "Surely you know this will not go well for either of us. How exactly do you see this ending?" I asked, slamming the tip of the dagger down into the nightstand at the bedside.

Gray paused, placing a finger beneath my chin. "End?" he asked, his voice going mystified. As if I were the one who had lost my sense, as if I were the one who needed a reality check. "There is no end for you and I, Witchling."

I took a step back, the mattress behind me pressing into the backs of my thighs and giving me no escape unless I wanted to make myself vulnerable by attempting to climb over it. I paused, raising my chin as I stared him down. "Everything ends, Lucifer. Even you," I said, forcing my bottom lip to remain still. The task seemed daunting, *impossible* even, but I would find a way.

"Do you remember when I told you that I can afford to be patient? One day, everything you know, everyone you love will cease to exist. I will be all you have left to turn to," he said, the words striking me in the chest. "It would be such a shame if you were to fight this—*us*. It just may motivate me to assist the natural course of life and death and rid us of all those who you would turn to for help."

I swallowed, staring up at him with a furrowed brow as I tried to grasp the meaning of his words. Surely he couldn't mean—

The memory of him quickly and efficiently killing the twelve other new students to join Hollow's Grove forced me to close my eyes.

He could. He could and he would.

"Lucifer," I said, the quiet plea in my voice making me feel weak. I hated him for making me reduce myself to begging for the lives of the few friends I had.

"That is not who I am. Not to you," he snapped, cupping my face gently and brushing his thumb over the front of my cheek.

"Gray," I said, the word coming out choked. I didn't want him to be Gray anymore. I wanted to remind myself of the evil that lurked beneath his skin.

"It doesn't have to be this way," he said, the words a reminder of how it had been between us so briefly. I didn't answer, unable to find the words to remind him that he'd *made* it this way. No one had forced him to manipulate me, to use me for his own purpose. He leaned forward, touching his lips to mine softly. He pulled away before I could even protest, his mouth warm where I was used to feeling him cold. "Get some rest."

I looked at the bed over my shoulder, shaking my head. I needed to see Della and Iban, to know that they were safe. "I need—"

"You need to sleep. Your body came back from death, no matter how brief. Sleep, my Willow," he said, pressing down on my shoulders until I had no choice but to sit on the edge of the mattress.

"No. I need to know who paid my price. Who you killed in my place to satisfy the balance," I said, attempting to push to my feet.

"Hell help me, Witchling. You are going to rest even if I have to put you in this bed and pin you down myself," he argued, the warning lingering in the air between us. I didn't want him in the bed with me, not when I couldn't trust myself around him.

Even hating him, even wanting to gut him and send him back to the pits of Hell for what he'd done to me, part of me remembered the way he'd felt when I thought I cared for him. "I'll rest," I said, offering an olive branch for the moment.

One battle at a time, I reminded myself.

"If you tell me who," I said, watching as he clenched his teeth in frustration.

"A witch. I don't know her name, nor do I care to. Beelzebub made it quick and painless, just as he did with you," he said, the matter-of-fact statement feeling like truth. Gray didn't bother to acquaint himself with the witches who couldn't offer him anything in return.

I nodded, hoping he would have at least recognized Della or Margot or Nova as my roommates. I could only hope they hadn't been harmed because of me, unable to live with that on my conscience.

I slowly lifted my legs into the bed, ignoring the ache in my bones as it felt like my very being shifted with the movement. Like my body couldn't adjust to the strangeness of coming back from the dead. I lay back awkwardly, wishing I had more clothes and hating the thought of Gray changing me while I'd been unconscious. Gray covered me with the blanket the moment my head hit the pillow, taking up residence in the chair beside the bed.

I sighed, staring at the ceiling.

Who could sleep while the devil was watching them?

4

WILLOW

Light trickled in the window at the edge of the room, the faint hint of sunshine fading over the horizon as I slowly peeled my eyes open. A soft grumble crawled up my throat as I forced myself to sit, cradling my forehead in my hands as a piercing headache seemed to split me in two.

Drawing in a few deep breaths, I glanced toward the chair that Gray had occupied when I'd somehow fallen asleep. My sense of self-preservation was severely lacking if I managed to rest at all with the devil watching me, because I clearly couldn't trust any of his motivations or plans.

Let me love you.

Those haunting words rang in my ears as I took in the sight of his now empty chair, shoving the blanket down to my feet and freeing my legs. He'd closed the bedroom door when he left, and I walked slowly on unsteady feet to test the knob. It barely moved, the lock keeping it stationary as I turned too quickly and stumbled.

What the fuck was wrong with me?

I shook off the unsteady, tight feeling in my body, moving toward the window, where the last rays of daylight shone in. Looking down at the courtyard beneath Gray's rooms, I swallowed as I searched for any hint of a Vessel or archdemon below.

I found none, glancing back toward the door to Gray's office. I couldn't imagine abandoning the others to the fate that I'd played such a key role in causing, but I couldn't help anyone if I remained locked in the devil's bedroom.

My eyes drifted closed as I flipped the lock on top of the window pane, only opening it as I steadied myself against the guilt I already felt.

I'd come back, I promised myself. Promised *them,* even though they couldn't hear me. Only a few weeks prior, I'd come determined to destroy the Coven and everyone in it. I'd been intent on getting the vengeance I'd been raised for, even if it meant my own death.

So why did I hesitate to leave them to their fate now?

I grimaced as I shoved the window up in my anger at my own hesitation, wincing when the force of the window sliding into place cracked the glass. I touched my trembling fingers to the spiderweb-like cracks, staring at the hands that didn't look any different from what I remembered from *before.*

Before I died.

Swallowing, I climbed up onto the windowsill. I knew my time would be limited, and that Gray would never leave me unattended for long. Surely he knew escape would be the first thing on my mind, so he must have simply not expected me to wake so soon.

I managed to get my legs out over the windowsill, feeling as awkward as a newborn deer as I maneuvered my way through the small space. The stone building was like a cliff, with no shorter parts of the building in this section to get me closer to the ground. Glancing down to the courtyard, I closed my eyes and drew in a breath as I called to the part of myself that was as vital to me as air.

The earth below answered, the vines of the trellis that scaled the sides of the building twitching as they came to life. They grew slowly, extending toward me until I could reach out and grasp them. Wrapping one around my hand and gripping it tightly, I sucked back a deep breath.

Green witches were not meant to fly, and the knowledge of

the impact that awaited me if I fell was almost enough to send me back into the bedroom that had become a prison.

Petty spite drove me forward. I jumped, content in the knowledge that if I died in my attempt, at least I would go out having ruined Gray's plans.

He didn't get to win. Not after what he'd done, not after the way my entire life had been a wasted manipulation for his own selfish gain. I didn't want to think of who I might have become if it hadn't been for the suffering he caused through whatever connection he and my father shared.

I bit back my scream as I plummeted toward the ground, moving slowly at first, as if time itself stopped the moment my body left the windowsill. Air rushed up to meet me, forcing my nightgown up around my waist as I fell into the gentle embrace of the vines that shot forward to catch me.

I closed my eyes as the ground came closer, sure that the vines wouldn't be able to stop me from the death waiting for me. Curling into the fetal position, I winced when I crashed onto something soft that shoved me back into the air the moment it caught me.

The momentum took some of the force from my collision, making the second thump against something plush more uncomfortable than painful. Relaxing my body, I let my legs drop from my chest as I opened my eyes finally and glanced down at the pillow of flowers that had risen up from the garden beds to cradle me.

They rose up higher, pushing me to my feet before they retreated back into the earth. The vine that I had wrapped around my hand coiled tighter, thorns sinking into my skin to take the blood required for the aid.

The bones around my neck clinked together as I took a step away from the plants, reminding me of their presence with every step. I considered the driveway and the road that cut a path through the woods that I knew would probably deliver me to certain death, but I knew sneaking out of Hollow's Grove would be far more difficult if I did it in plain sight.

I swallowed as I headed for the woods and the Cursed that waited for me there, determined to take my chances with the beasts over the archdemons. The Cursed could be killed.

I wasn't so sure about the archdemons.

The vine unwound from my arm slowly as I walked, separating from me with longing. It knew as well as I that I was the best chance this land had of true restoration. I refused to acknowledge the goodbye in that longing touch, promising that I'd help it when I returned to bring the Coven back to what it always should have been.

Blood dripped down my arm as I made my way to the woods slowly. My steps grew steadier with each one, less uncertain of the way my body worked. Whatever had changed within me when Gray brought me back from the dead couldn't be seen, but I felt it in the corded lines of muscle beneath my skin. I felt the strange, unfamiliar strength in each of my fingers.

My steps gained momentum, increasing in speed until I sprinted toward the woods. Normally, I'd have detested running from the onset. Hell, I'd have hated that I had to run before I even moved my legs.

This took no energy, surging me forward with such little effort that I nearly tripped. A massive figure stepped out of the shadows of the woods just as I reached them, his leathery wings spreading from where he'd curled them in front to shield him from sight. Beelzebub's hair was shaggy, framing his square jaw as he stared down at me.

"You're meant to be sleeping, Consort," he said as I skidded to a stop in front of him. He didn't so much as flinch as my awkward attempt to control my limbs sent me sprawling forward, crashing into him and smacking my hands against the gleaming bronze skin of his chest.

He'd tattooed himself with runes that glowed the same gold as Lucifer's eyes, the Enochian symbols seeming to writhe beneath my hands as I panicked and shoved myself back. I fell onto my ass on the grass, my fingers instinctively digging into the earth beneath me.

Grounding myself against the unknown, against the fear of the archdemon in front of me.

"You fucking killed me," I said finally, my voice dropping low in warning.

The bastard shrugged, his wings spreading behind him as if they needed to stretch. "I apologize. The last time Lucifer and I spoke, you were meant to die. I wasn't aware of the change of plans."

"You *apologize*?" I asked, my voice as incredulous as I felt. "Do you think that is enough for what you did to me?"

He trailed his gaze down my body, bringing it back up to my face with nothing but disinterest on his features. "You look fine to me."

"I'm not *fine*. Do you know what it is to be trapped in the darkness between life and death? Do you have any fucking idea how disorienting and terrifying it is to be aware that I died and somehow still be fucking trapped in this Hellhole?" I screeched, lunging forward.

I planted two palms on his chest, shoving him with all my rage isolated in the movement. Beelzebub's eyes widened in shock for a brief moment before the sound of my flesh slapping against him erupted through the courtyard. He stumbled back, barely catching himself with the tip of his wing on the ground behind him as we stared at one another.

His gaze narrowed as he righted himself, dropping down to my palms where I wiped them against the silk of my nightgown. "Go back to your husband, Consort. He'll not be pleased to find you out of bed just yet."

"He is not my husband," I snarled, my nostrils flaring with the constant reminder of something that had been done to me while I'd been *sleeping*.

He stepped closer, towering over me as he glared down.

"Whatever helps you sleep at night. I don't know what spell you've cast, but it serves you right that the very trap you set to make him love you is what imprisoned you in the end."

"You think I enchanted him?" I asked, scoffing as I sidestepped him and made to stride away toward the woods.

Fuck this.

His hand wrapped around my bicep, pulling me to a halt as he held perfectly still beside me. "I think you wanted him wrapped around your twisted little finger, and you got exactly that. He left friends in Hell rather than risk losing you to the seal. If that is not an enchantment, then I do not know what is."

"Perhaps it was simply my glowing personality that attracted him. Did you think of that?" I asked, pulling at my bicep. Beelzebub's grip slipped, his fingers bruising me harshly as he fought to keep hold of me.

He dropped his gaze lower and trailed it back up before huffing a soft, condescending laugh. "I see you, Willow Hecate. I'm not impressed."

My anger grew, coiling in my stomach with a strength that took my breath away. I couldn't see past the tint of red to my rage, past the tunnel vision as I stared at the demon who was so willing to underestimate me and accuse me of ensnaring the devil all in the same breath.

The branches on the trees shifted, moving as if they blew in the wind, but there was no movement to the air that could be responsible for such a thing. In fact, the air went unnaturally still as I stared up at the purple-eyed demon.

He seemed unaware of the rustling trees that I felt in my blood, completely ignorant of the way they slowly inched toward him with my anger.

"That's enough, Beelzebub. Unhand my errant wife," Gray said from somewhere behind me. I sighed, trying not to wince when Beelzebub slowly released my bicep and stepped away. I paused, trying to calm the humming in my blood but keeping the life around me at my disposal in case I needed the help.

Swallowing, I turned on my heel and faced the man who had quickly gone from too good to be true to my worst nightmare.

He'd changed into a suit, having foregone his jacket so that only a white button-up covered his chest. The sleeves were rolled up to reveal the golden skin that was so at odds with how fair he'd been before getting his body back. His hands were clenched at his sides, the only physical symptom of his anger, and it made the muscles in his forearms tense and visible. He tipped his head to the side, letting his gaze trail down over my body, which, in my haste to escape, was still only clad in the silken nightgown he'd changed me into. "Going somewhere, Witchling?"

5

WILLOW

I'm leaving," I said, drawing in a deep breath as he lowered his chin ever so slightly. A week ago I might have missed the subtle change, but some part of me recognized his movements for what they were.

A threat. A promise.

He sighed, walking slowly toward where I stood beside Beelzebub and closing the distance. He didn't speak a word to tell me that I wouldn't be allowed to leave, but he didn't really need to. I pivoted slowly to face him more fully, leaving the other archdemon to finally step away and walk toward the school. His wings twitched as he walked, and I had the sinking feeling it was a sign of his irritation with the male who had approached me.

He raised a hand slowly, grasping me in that sensitive space where my jaw met the side of my neck. "Don't make this more difficult than it needs to be, love."

I jerked back from his touch, wincing when his fingers trailed over the front of my throat and his jaw hardened. His golden eyes flashed, such a horrific contrast to the blue I'd grown used to seeing staring down at me. "Don't make this difficult?" I asked, my words coming out slowly as the pit of anger that existed within me threatened to swallow me whole.

I'd had a target for it all, had a *purpose* for all the ugly and the bad in my life. There'd been a way to channel it before, whereas now . . .

Now there was just rage, and there was only *one* logical target for it.

"Willow—" he said carefully.

"You fucking stabbed me!" I screamed. "And you have the fucking *nerve* to act as if I am the one who is the problem?"

His hand dropped to his side slowly, clenching into a fist as he opened his mouth and closed it once before speaking. His own anger lingered beneath the words, hidden beneath something soft and vulnerable that I didn't care to take the time to think about. "You were trying to leave me."

My lips spread into a cruel, disbelieving smile as I turned my head to the side and winced at the bitter laugh that crept its way up my throat. "Of course I want to leave you." I sounded more the demon and he the victim, when the reality was the opposite.

I'd believed every manipulation. Believed every lie and twisted truth.

"Again," I said, pausing as I turned my attention back to him. My smile dropped, my laughter stopping suddenly as I leaned toward him. "You fucking stabbed me."

"To save your life!" he yelled, snatching my hand from my side and tugging me toward him. My chest collided with his stomach, sending a ripple of tingles through me in spite of the clothing between us. I'd always been hyperaware of his body and felt the charge of attraction between us, but it had been more extreme since waking. "Everything I did in that Tribunal room was to keep you alive."

"No," I argued, shaking my head. He didn't get to rewrite what he'd done as if it were for my benefit. As if I'd asked him to kill all those witches.

I'd have sooner died.

"Everything you did in that tribunal room was for *you*. It

was so that you could have your body on this plane. Everything you've done for *centuries* was so that you could end up right here, and fuck the consequences and the people who've been hurt. If it was for me, you never would have gone through with opening the seal."

He paused, taking my free hand in his and touching it to his chest where his shirt was unbuttoned at the top. My finger brushed against his bare skin, and his eyes drifted closed with a pleasured sigh. He held my wrist tight, keeping me pinned there as he tipped his head to the side, and a tiny smile curved his lips upward as he opened that golden gaze to stare down at me.

"You're right. I did what I had to do to be here in truth, to feel *this*," he said, pressing my hand tighter into his flesh. "That was for me and me alone, and I have waited centuries for it to come to pass. But if I hadn't taken the rib from you, you would have given your life to the seal. I couldn't allow that."

"And why not? That was always the plan, wasn't it?" I asked, waiting for the confirmation of just how far his deception had gone. If it was as intense as Charlotte had implied, if I really was the cost of her bargain, then I didn't see any other way.

He had the decency to look ashamed as he pursed his lips. "That was before."

"Before what, exactly? Before you fucked me? Before you told my father to raise me to believe I would be getting revenge for his sister, even though you're the one who killed her?" I asked.

"Before I saw you the night I killed Loralei," he said, stealing the breath from my lungs.

"That's impossible," I said with a scoff. "That was decades before I was born."

"And yet it is the night that I marked you as mine," he said, releasing my wrist finally and touching it to the top of my shoulder. His fingers brushed over the bare skin, the very tips grazing the devil's eye I'd woken with after my nightmare.

"Loralei had been dead for decades by that point, Gray," I

argued, refusing to admit what I'd seen in my nightmare. It was too unfathomable to even consider.

"For you," he admitted, conceding that point. "But I gave this mark to an apparition who appeared at her side when I murdered her fifty years ago."

"I don't understand how that's possible. I don't have that kind of magic," I said, trailing off. There was no way to deny what he had said though, not in truth when I knew what I'd seen.

What I'd felt.

"You channel your black magic through the bones of your ancestors. Even without them, their blood runs through your veins. There's a connection there that none of your relatives have thought to consider, but it seems maybe you could walk through their lives in your dreams if you tried."

"I have no interest in using anything related to the Hecate line," I snapped, knowing that every bit of it, every moment of my life that led me here, had been so that I could die.

Charlotte wanted me to fix what she'd done. I just wanted to go home.

"You'd be a fool not to. You'll need it if you're going to take the Covenant's place here," Gray said as I pulled back again. I couldn't think straight with his hands on me, with that charge between us that defied all nature making my skin prickle with awareness.

"I have no intention of taking anyone's place. I'm leaving Crystal Hollow." I swallowed as I said the words, knowing it was the only way for me to regain any of my humanity. For me to salvage who I wanted to be in the face of all that I'd lost through my life.

I wouldn't be the devil's puppet any longer.

Gray sighed as I stepped away, moving toward the tree line waiting for me and the Cursed who would hunt me down if they could. Even that would be far better than a life as a prisoner. The trees swayed as if they could welcome me home, taking me into their embrace as I put my first foot into the woods.

"Please, don't make me do this to you," Gray said behind me. I paused mid-step, putting my foot down slowly as something in that voice made my heart sink. He approached slowly as I turned to watch him, rooted to the spot like the tree at my back. "Stay with me, Witchling."

"Or what?" I asked, glaring at him. I took a step back as he approached, his steps casual and easy, as if he didn't have a care in the world.

"Or I will take back what I have given," he said, reaching me finally.

He touched a single finger to my chest as I tried to call to the earth around me. A whisper from the trees came back, an apology in the wind, but nothing struck out at him. Nothing defended me this time.

His fingernail elongated into a talon, the sharp point of it pressing against my skin. I gasped as it broke through, a slow droplet of blood falling from the wound. It wasn't the cut itself that stole the breath from my lungs and made my body seize with pain.

It was the suffocation of my magic, the sudden silence as the trees around me quieted. For the first time since I turned sixteen, they'd ignored my call.

"Gray," I gasped.

He clenched his jaw, dragging his nail down through the center of my chest. The gash he drew bled little for how deep it was, a green mist coiling as it emerged from the cut. He twisted his hand, letting the mist settle in his palm as it slid free from me.

"It didn't have to be this way," he said, his face sad as I raised my eyes to meet his. My hands trembled as I grabbed his in both of mine, holding them tight to my chest. Everything inside me was empty, the lack of buzzing in my head making everything . . .

Silent.

My bottom lip trembled as tears stung my eyes. "Don't," I begged, hating the plea in those words. "Please." Black mist followed the green, gathering in his hand as he stole what he'd given to Charlotte and the first Madizza witches. "I don't know who I am without it," I said with a strangled sob.

His face twisted with what I would have called sadness if he hadn't been the one to cause me pain. He raised his free hand to cup my cheek, leaning down to touch his forehead to mine. "You're mine," he said as tears stained my cheeks and dropped down my chin onto his hand, which I refused to release. "I cannot allow you to keep the magic you would use to leave me."

"I'll stay," I said, my voice turning frantic as that silence grew in my head. Nausea churned in my gut, the distinct feeling of being alone in my body overwhelming me. I couldn't remember a time when I'd felt so disconnected from everything around me, when the loneliness threatened to swallow me whole. "I'll stay, just anything but that, Gray."

He sighed, touching his mouth to mine softly as I cried. "I wish I could believe you. I wish I could trust that you wouldn't leave me, but you tell such pretty lies, wife. I can't believe a single one of them," he said.

The bark at my back felt strange and unfamiliar, nothing like the warm comfort of earth. "I'll do anything," I said, choking as I tried to will that magic back into me. As I tried to take back what was mine.

"Then make a deal with me, love. There is something that I want, and that is the only way you will leave this place with your magic," he said, his golden eyes flashing as the devil beneath his skin wanted to come out and play. I couldn't stand the knowledge that I was trapped in truth, that there was no way around the deal but to become used to being alone.

"What do you want?" I asked, even as the potential answer terrified me. He already had his body; surely that was the extent of his sick, twisted plans.

"I want to finally consummate our marriage," he said simply, tucking a strand of hair behind my ear.

My confusion compelled me to question everything. "But

we already . . ." I trailed off, unable to complete the sentence. I couldn't believe I'd been so fucking blind that I'd given my virginity to the devil.

"I was wearing a fake meat suit," he said, the softness of his voice fading away as he laid out his desire. "You had sex with my Vessel, and yes, it was me inside of it. But you are not the wife of a Vessel, Willow. You are the wife of Lucifer Morningstar, so you need to consummate with *me*."

I sank my teeth into my bottom lip. It was only sex.

"Now?" I asked, trying to still the tremble in my hands. "Here?"

"No," he said with a bitter laugh. "I have no interest in fucking you while you cry. So you are going to run, and if you make it through the woods, you're free to go."

I glanced over my shoulder as the mist held in his palm began to recede, sinking back inside me and slowly filling me with the hum of magic. My relief over it drowned the fear I should have felt about what would happen if he caught me, but the opportunity for freedom—for a life with Ash—was too great for me to ignore. "And if you catch me?"

"If I catch you, then you'll give me the fight I've come to crave from you. If I catch you, we will go to war in the way our souls already know—until my body recognizes every inch of your skin by touch. *When* I catch you, I will fuck you, and we both know you'll love every goddamn minute of it," Gray said simply, leaning in to whisper the threat in my ear. His teeth nipped at the sensitive spot below my ear, all at once a tease and a torment of things to come.

"What does that change? Having our marriage consummated?" I asked, glancing down at where the last of the mist had faded into my body. Gray withdrew his hand, and I watched in horror as the wound healed over on its own.

My body was not my own anymore.

"You let me worry about that, love," he said, taking a single step back. He stabbed his talon into the tip of his finger, touching it to my chest as his consent to the terms of his deal.

A deal with the devil.

Black spread across my skin, tendrils of darkness sparking over my body before it faded. He held out his talon for me, letting me reach out with a trembling, furious hand to prick my fingertip on the sharp point before it receded back to a normal nail.

I touched the bloodied finger to the hollow at the base of his throat, watching as my own darkness spread over his skin before it too faded.

He closed his eyes, a sigh leaving him before he opened them to stare down at me. I lingered awkwardly, not knowing when our game would begin. He answered that unasked question with a single menacing word.

"Run."

6

WILLOW

I took a deep breath, staring into the eyes of the Devil Himself. Trying to sink into the feeling of the noise in my head, of the shifting of each leaf on a tree branch as my magic filled every crevice of my body. It might have been a gift from the devil centuries ago, but it was a part of me that I couldn't bear to part with.

I didn't want to think of who I might be without it. Even if Lucifer's manipulations had caused me so much pain, the beauty of the earth around me had filled those hollow places that my life had created within me.

Without the magic flowing through my veins, all that was left was the empty shell of a woman who had suffered.

"You'll never take my magic from me after this," I said instead of running. The distinctive scent of apples filled the air, accompanying our bargain as I spoke the words. I watched the tendrils of darkness spread over his skin once again when he nodded, accepting the addition to our bargain.

"Contrary to what you may believe, I do not want you weak, Witchling. I want you to embrace just how powerful you are and rule at my side. The others of your kind may be beneath me, but you?" he asked, reaching forward to tuck two fingers beneath my jaw and raise my chin higher. "You could be my equal. You're the only one standing in your way."

"If you don't want me weak, then why do you want to chase me through the woods before you fuck me? Fear is weakness, is it not?" I asked with a glare. My fingers dug into the tree bark at my back, sinking my magic into the wood and using it to build my connection to the forest all over again.

Stalling. Buying time.

Gray chuckled, releasing me with one last nudge to my chin. "But are you afraid?" he asked, tilting his head as he knowingly looked at where I'd burrowed my fingers into the base of the tree, melding the wood around me so that I could become one with it. "Or are you just pissed?"

"I'm *always* pissed," I snapped, clenching my teeth together as I sank into that anger. Into the feeling of being so fucking tired of being somebody else's puppet. If I'd been stronger, I'd have let Gray take my magic and walked away as soon as I had the chance, but I was too afraid to live with the hole inside me. "You wanting to fuck me when I'm afraid doesn't exactly put me in a good mood."

"I don't want to fuck you when you're afraid, *wife*," he said, stressing the word. I flinched, as I suspected I would do every time he called me by the term that I was so certain couldn't be possible. I didn't pretend to know the intricacies of demon marriage rites, but it seemed like even for the evil creatures from Hell there should have been some level of consent involved. "I want to fuck you when you're so mad you try to claw my eyes out. I want to fight you, and *then* I want to fuck you while you direct all that anger toward me."

"You want me to fight you? Why?" I asked, chewing the inside of my cheek in disbelief. There was something so primal about the way he stared down at me, in the way he watched every twitch of my body as if I might flee mid-conversation.

He knew I was stalling for time, and that I would leave as soon as I felt I was able to get a head start without being unprepared.

"Because that is who you are," he said, stressing the words he'd given me the night I showed him the vulnerable, jagged edges of me. The parts that no one else had seen, that had been so very hidden in the depths of my soul until he'd somehow managed to work his way beneath my skin and make himself at home. "Because you're the only one who is brave enough to even try."

"Lucky me," I said, swallowing against the rising emotion that swelled in my gut. I didn't want to remember the nights when he'd made me think I was more than just a pawn in his game. They'd been a lie, just like everything else. Pain was messy and chaotic and everything I couldn't allow in the moments leading up to my only shot at freedom.

Anger was safer.

Gray laughed, the sound soft and quiet as I withdrew my fingers from the tree finally. I searched for something to say, waited for him to continue the conversation so that I could catch him off guard. But he only watched me knowingly, shoving his hands into his trouser pockets with that infuriating smirk on his face—as if he knew every thought inside my head.

"I don't even stand a chance, do I?" I asked, grinding my teeth together. I'd known there was a slim possibility of escape when I made the deal, but his assurance and casual ease made a pit in my gut.

"Only a fool would dare to underestimate you, my love," he said, leaning toward me as I shoved off the tree and sprinted into the tree line.

I didn't dare to look behind me to see if he'd followed, unable to hear anything beyond the pounding of my own heart and the desperation filling my veins. As I ran, I waited for the familiar sound of him following behind me, for the sound of his rapid footsteps as I leapt over a tree root and kept going.

I rounded a fallen tree, glimpsing the clearing behind me for a brief moment before I spun forward and focused on the path to escape.

Where the devil had once stood was empty.

Gray was gone.

7

GRAY

Willow ran, sprinting through the trees. The feeling of her magic washed over me, her connection to the land pulsing through the forest with a strength I hadn't felt in centuries. Susannah's daughter had possessed magic like this, that deep connection that went further than anything I could give.

This was the magic of love, of mutual respect that came from a symbiotic relationship that could not be taught. Willow was one with the earth around her, in a way that would have been a tragedy to take from her.

Which was why I never would have followed through, if she had chosen to reject our deal.

I might have kept her locked in a room on the upper floors of Hollow's Grove and sealed off any windows so she couldn't escape, but I couldn't have taken this part of her away.

Not knowing just how severely it would have broken her. Where others might have wanted to control the fire in her veins, I only wanted to watch her learn how to embrace what it was to burn.

I strolled through the woods, keeping my pace casual so that I could give her a fighting chance—or the illusion of one. Her anger would reach an all-time high when she *thought* she could make it.

When victory was just outside her grasp, I would snatch it away from her.

Willow needed to know that I was her only home. That her future started and ended with me. I would tolerate nothing less than an eternity with her by my side, guiding her along the path that she'd always been destined to walk.

I listened, hearing the crack of each and every branch she stepped over. Listening to the rustling of the leaves at her feet and using them to place her. The Cursed kept their distance as I walked among them, having learned their lesson previously when they came upon the corpses of their dead. The witch was mine, and I would not allow them to hurt her for the crimes of her ancestor.

Immersing myself in the place that Willow felt most at home, I tried to sink down into that part of the magic that I'd shared with her ancestor. Even recognizing the call of the magic, the love that Willow felt for the earth wasn't what resided inside me. The love she had was missing from my very being.

Perhaps it was because I'd spent so many centuries separated from it, unable to touch any of my magic. But to me, it was a tool to be used.

For Willow, it was a part of her—a part that she would miss every day of her life if it were lost.

A smile drifted over my face as I continued on my path. I ran my fingers over a leaf, feeling it crumple beneath my fingers while I waited for the witchling who would have felt that loss as if it were her own.

Feeling her approach the center of the woods, I ran forward. With the same speed I'd used that day in the woods outside her childhood home, I sprinted through the trees with ease. I quickly passed Willow, standing in the path she would need to cross if she wanted to reach her freedom.

Freedom that did not exist for her.

Leaning my back against a tree, I waited for the witchling

to reach me. For the moment that her hope faded into nothing. She'd unknowingly come to the perfect place for our final battle, a clearing where the sun drifted through the canopy of trees to illuminate the ground in soft sunshine and warmth. I enjoyed the feeling of it on my skin, the comfortable warmth that was so at odds with what this body remembered in Hell.

How long had it been since I really felt the sun?

A figure appeared in the distance, walking toward me slowly as if she didn't want me to hear her. She knew how keen the hearing of a Vessel was, but Willow had no understanding of my abilities in this form. She was very much a witch who liked to know her opponent before a battle, but in this she knew nothing and it showed in her awkward gait. She made far too much noise as she stumbled through the autumn leaves on the forest floor, shuffling toward me. The changes in her body were evident from the way she struggled, and I knew it would take her some time to learn to control her newfound strength and what that meant for completing the simplest of tasks.

If she wasn't careful, she could crack her teeth when she tried to brush them. She could snap a pen when she simply tried to grab it.

It wasn't until she stepped into the sun shining through the trees above that I realized what the clever, deceptive little witch had done.

The creature, which was not my wife, had been crafted from fallen branches, and she'd somehow managed to bind them together, spelling them to shuffle forward on two tree stumps for legs. She'd tied grass to the head, making it mimic her hair from a distance but, as the sun landed on it, sharing none of the shine of her deep raven tresses.

The noises I'd heard had been this thing, stumbling through the woods without eyes to see. Animated only by the blood she'd smeared along the bark to share her magic.

"Willow!" I yelled, spinning in the woods to listen for her as I swiped a hand through the wooded creature and sent it collapsing to the ground. I'd expected her to be lost to her anger, to fight back with panic and fury.

Instead, she'd met me with calm, lethal cunning.

She'd behaved as a queen, when I'd still been expecting a girl.

Without the louder creature to distract me, I heard the much quieter sounds of her moving through the woods. She'd gotten past me, approaching the edge of the woods on the opposite end far more quickly than I found tolerable.

I sprinted forward, racing through the woods as my own heart raced. Blood pumped in my veins more quickly than I ever remembered, so at odds with the way my body hadn't had such functions when I'd been a Vessel. It wasn't the physical activity that made my heart race, but my blinding panic at what I would do if Willow *left*.

If she made it out, I'd have no choice but to honor my end of the bargain. I'd have no choice but to let her leave Crystal Hollow—to let her leave me.

It was unthinkable to go back to being alone in such a way.

I raced forward, colliding with her back and tackling her to the ground. Light shone through the trees that formed the tree line just ahead, her freedom so close I could practically taste it.

Willow snarled as she struck the ground, throwing her head back into my face with a scream of frustration. I felt the pain of that, the rage, echo through my bones.

She'd been so close. *Too close.*

My nose throbbed with what would have been a crushing blow to a human, or even a Vessel, the tingle of pain letting me know just how harshly she'd struck. Her body trembled in my grasp, her fury making each and every one of her muscles tense as she prepared for the fight we both knew was coming.

I'd expected it, expected war when I caught her and tackled her into my arms.

I'd just planned to be farther from the tree line and able to toy with her more, to allow her the small victories that would make our battle all the more pleasurable when I finally rolled her beneath me, tore her nightgown down the center, and fucked her in the dirt.

My cock hardened with the thought, twitching in my slacks. It had been so long since this body had felt the pleasure of a woman, but even if it had been satiated yesterday, my need for Willow would have overwhelmed it.

She thrust her arm behind her head, jabbing the knuckles of two bent fingers into my eye and forcing me back slightly. Her body twisted beneath me as her torso was freed, her teeth bared as she glared at me and bucked her hips.

Gripping her around the waist with one arm, I forced her to bend slightly. Tugging her up at the waist so that her ass rose toward me, I pressed against her as that black nightgown slid up her thighs and exposed the curve of her.

"Let go of me!" she screamed, continuing her struggle. It only shifted her nightgown higher, until the full swell of her ass was bare for me to see.

"We had a deal, Witchling," I said, reminding her with a chuckle. I'd caught her, trapping her in my embrace even if she'd come close to escaping it. "Now hold still so I can fuck you."

"I am going to rip your cock off while you sleep and feed it to Beelzebub, you dick," she snapped, twisting her body to try to free herself from my iron grip on her hip. I let my fingers slip lower, to the part of her that was bare beneath me. She flinched as my fingertips grazed the top of her slit, dipping in and circling her clit before lowering and teasing her entrance. The involuntary movement of her hips that came next pressed her closer to the hard length of my cock in my pants instead of away, seeking out the pleasure only I could give her.

The first touch of her wet heat against my skin, and I found home. I would live in her pussy, live in the haven of her body for the rest of my days.

"You can yell and scream and curse me out all you want, but nothing will change the fact that you *agreed* to this. You chose this, and now?" I paused, dragging the wetness I'd gathered from her pussy up and using it to apply the wet heat of my fingers to her clit. I leaned in, whispering the condemning words that showed just how well suited she was to me. How dark and depraved her twisted little soul was, a soul that I'd claimed as mine. "Now we both know just how much you're going to like it."

"If only the rest of you were as pleasant as your cock," she growled, bringing a chuckle from me. She'd never even had this cock, only having been with me in my Vessel form. It didn't seem natural for me to feel jealous of my other form, for me to possess feelings of rage that the other version of me had been inside her.

If it weren't a useless pile of mud now, I'd have killed it for knowing how she felt on the inside.

I dropped my hand to my pants, freeing myself as Willow squirmed beneath me. She stilled as I guided myself into the space between her thighs as she pressed them tightly together. I let her feel all of me as I slid through, touching her pussy and gliding through the wetness there until I bumped against her clit.

My hand dragged up to her nightgown as I made shallow thrusts through her, tormenting her with what was to come, and she moved with me in tiny pulses.

I tore her nightgown down the back, craving her bare skin to trail my fingers over. I dragged them up her spine, taking far too much pleasure in the goose bumps that rose on her skin in response to my touch. "If my cock is my only redeeming quality," I said, shoving her hair out of my way so that I could wrap my fingers around the back of her neck. I used that grip to press her toward the ground, letting her turn her head so that I could see her profile. I pinned her, holding her perfectly still as I shifted my hips and pulled back. "Then I expect you to spend most of your time sitting on it, wife."

I drove forward, sinking inside her in a fast, hard thrust. She gasped, the sound getting louder as her lips parted and her eyes drifted closed. The groan that escaped me was torn from my soul as her gasp increased into a sharp whimper of pleasure, making me all the more determined to make her scream.

To fill the forest with the sound of her pure, unrelenting pleasure. To make her feel exactly what I felt as it filled me, sliding up the ridge of my cock and up my spine, enveloping me with the feeling of her warmth. She was so fucking wet as I pulled back and drove deeper, spreading her open for me. The magic of our marital bond snapped into place with it finally consummated in truth, that warmth all-consuming.

Willow's eyes flew open, a flash of black bleeding over, consuming them. That stare flicked to mine, shock and disbelief lurking beneath the black stain that marked her as mine. It faded eventually, returning her eyes to the mismatched stare I'd fallen in love with as the magic sank into all the corners of her soul and body.

Still, she continued to hold my stare, a challenge in her gaze and her body tense. I pulled back, thrusting forward and fucking her quickly. Not because I wanted to rush my time with her, but because I couldn't imagine anything else.

My *need* to fill her with my cum was undeniable. My need to watch it leak out of her swollen pussy like something I'd never known. And when I got her back to our room, I'd fuck her all over again and feel how wet she was when she was already filled with me.

"Gray," she said, her whimper like music to my soul. It was the plea of a woman on the edge of oblivion, of a woman who couldn't deny the orgasm that was coming to pull her under. I released her, pulling out of her as she leveled me with a glare.

"Take what you need, love," I said, kneeling and waiting for her to move. I wanted there to be no doubt in her mind that she'd wanted this. I didn't want her to be able to rewrite history to say that she'd been unwilling when I took her, and I knew her well enough to know she would attempt to deny the darkest part of herself that she wasn't willing to come to terms with.

She wasn't ready to dance with the monster beneath her skin. To acknowledge that while I might be the devil, she'd made her home in my soul and felt comfortable there.

She maneuvered to her knees, her breathing deep and focused as she stared at me. I was still fully clothed except for my open fly, and her languid stare trailed over me briefly before it landed on my cock for the first time. She reached out with a single hand, shoving me backward with a force that managed to knock me over. I fell onto my back on the forest floor, shifting to get my legs to a natural angle as Willow stripped her ruined, torn nightgown off and stood. She stepped over me, staring down at me as she gave me a perfect, flawless view of her in all her glory.

She sank to her knees quickly, far too quickly for a human, and she seemed to realize it as she slowed her movements, straddling my hips. She lifted just enough to slide her hand between us, putting my cock at the angle she needed so that she could lower herself onto it as her eyes drifted closed.

"Fucking Hell," I groaned, grasping her by the hips as she started to move. The way she rode me was like a dance, a fluid roll of her hips back and a sharp snap forward to take me deep, grinding her clit against me with every movement.

She grabbed the sides of my shirt in a hand each, yanking them apart so the buttons flew into the air, and she touched her bare hands to my chest for balance. She hesitated only for a moment when the handprint on my chest came into view, settling her hands down on top of it finally to block it from her line of sight. It had healed somewhat, the bright red fading into a white scar. I'd hoped it would never heal, that it would stay with me forever.

I watched her, holding off my own pleasure long enough to allow my wife to use me in a way I'd never thought to enjoy.

But I enjoyed everything that brought Willow pleasure.

"That's it, love," I murmured when she tossed her head back. Her nipples strained toward me, begging me to take them into my mouth and love them the way every bit of her deserved.

Later.

We had centuries together. An eternity for me to worship every part of her.

She sought her release, the rolls of her hips becoming less rhythmic and controlled. Her body turned to chaos as it consumed her, her whimpers threatening to make me come. She went silent as the orgasm consumed her, her mouth dropping open on a silent scream as the center of my chest burned.

Black filled my vision, shadows surrounding her hands where she touched me as she came. The burn was like nothing I'd ever felt, hotter than the flames of Hell itself. The white scar tissue beneath her hands shifted, forming something new entirely— something unique.

She'd fucking marked me.

The thought brought me more joy than it should have, knowing that she'd claimed me as her husband. Even though I knew it hadn't been intentional, I couldn't help the grin that stole over my face as I reached up and pulled her toward me. Sealing my lips to hers, I devoured her mouth as I flipped her onto her back and hiked one of her legs high so that I could fuck her.

"Wicked little witch," I said with a laugh, feeling her pussy tighten around me with every thrust. She was still in the lingering throes of her orgasm, her body spasming as I plowed into her as hard and as fast as I could manage.

"Fuck!" she screamed, the sound filling the silence of the forest as I drove her toward a second orgasm right on the tail of the first. Her pussy clamped down on me, holding me prisoner and stealing the cum from my balls. I filled her in shallow pumps, roaring my own release as I dropped toward her and bit her shoulder. There were no fangs to draw blood, and I missed the sensation of that part of her within me.

When I pulled back, the witchling's gaze dropped to the circular maze of labyrinths she'd imprinted on my chest.

Hecate's maze marred my skin, the mark of my necromancer wife burned into my flesh like a brand.

Willow swallowed, staring up at me as she floundered for words.

"You're mine now, Willow Morningstar."

8

WILLOW

That mark on his chest held me captive, a swallow throbbing the entire way down my throat as I tried to come to terms with what I'd done. I hadn't meant to, hadn't even wanted to claim him in any way, but the magic pulsing through my veins now felt wild—uncontrollable.

"What have you done to me?" I asked him, refusing to allow him to see the emotion that clogged my throat. My connection to the earth had always been strong, our relationship intense because I loved it more than any other part of me.

But now . . .

Now it felt like the magic itself was alive within me, like it writhed and coiled beneath my skin. There was a darker tint to it, like shadows following the light, that I could only assume was what I'd inherited from Charlotte and the bones hanging around my neck. That was the part that scared me the most, the pulsing threat that craved death and decay, the cycle of life that demanded payment.

I couldn't be the one to deliver it. I couldn't be the one to make choices of life and death.

"I know you were a virgin before, but we've done that enough times now that I know you're aware of what an orgasm is, my love," Gray responded, quirking an eyebrow at me as that infuriating smirk tried to make light of the situation. As if he hadn't turned my entire world upside down.

"What am I? I shouldn't have been able to burn your skin. I'm not a fire witch—"

"You're still my witchling," he said, his face softening and the traces of his arrogant amusement fading. He watched me like I was two words away from a breakdown, and maybe I was.

Breakdowns usually meant I cried in the shower where no one could see me, but out here, surrounded by nature and the natural course of life . . .

I didn't know what would happen. Not now.

"You're my wife," he added, touching a single finger to the underside of my chin.

"Am I even still human? Am I still a witch?" I asked, glancing at the forest around me. I still felt the hum of the trees in my blood, louder than ever, so I didn't think that my connection to that part of me had been affected.

But something was distinctly different.

"You were never human," Gray answered, stating a fact I'd never reconciled. I might have had magic in my veins, but I bled the same as a human. I hurt and hungered, and all the parts of me that mattered felt human.

The little brother I loved felt human, remaining powerless until his sixteenth birthday. It was through his eyes that I saw the world, through the life I knew he would live without me that I saw what I wished I could have.

But I wasn't strong enough to be alone in my body without my magic to get there. I wasn't strong enough to face the empty void my life had created, the hollows where love should have resided and there was only hurt and pain and anger.

"Am I a witch?" I asked, watching as he reached out toward one of the trees nearest us. It responded to his call, swaying a single branch toward him so that he could take a leaf between his fingers and feel it. He stared at it as if it was a curiosity, as if he couldn't understand why I cared so much for something so . . . common.

"That's complicated," he said, his golden stare meeting mine finally. I swallowed, trying to fight back the tremble of my lower lip. I couldn't stand the thought of losing everything I knew.

"How?" I whispered, a tenseness to my voice that hinted at my fading patience. He'd brought me back to life when I hadn't asked for it; the least he could do was explain what he'd done to me in the process.

"In order to bring you back, I had to give you a lot of my blood. More than I would now that you have accepted the marital bond. I've only given one person that much of my blood in the past, and it was for a very different purpose, but some of the consequences appear to be similar."

"Charlotte?" I asked, scoffing. Of course my ancestor would be the only other person. I seemed to be doomed to repeat her life story. "Were you two . . ."

"No. Charlotte and I had a relationship of mutual respect, but there was never anything beyond tentative friendship. She didn't trust me, and I didn't trust her, but I respected her tenacity," Gray answered, pausing to glance toward the woods as his body tensed. "She is also not the one I gave my blood to, though it was at her request."

"Who?" I asked, my brow furrowing as the realization of the only other possibility struck me. "The Covenant?" I asked, the words feeling torn from my throat.

"Yes, my love. The gift of my blood was what resurrected Susannah and George from their graves. Even Charlotte's magic could not animate a person beyond the brief moments where she commanded them. Once she released her magic, they returned to their natural state," he said, making my blood run cold. I glanced toward the woods at the sound of crunching leaves, trying to quell my rising panic.

"Does that mean . . ."

"That means you are what you were always meant to be. Our people have the opportunity to live in true harmony with you to lead the witches back to the old ways and with me to guide the archdemons and Vessels to a new way of living," he said, and something hopeful lit his golden eyes. "We can build a home here."

I wondered if, even for a brief moment, Hell had ever felt like home. Or if it had been a reminder of his punishment, a place he couldn't escape any more than the souls trapped there. I shoved back that pity, determined not to allow myself to feel anything for the man who had used me and broken my heart without remorse.

"You killed twelve witches to bring me back. The Coven isn't going to forgive that," I snapped, shaking my head at his stupidity.

"I killed twelve witches who came from families outside Crystal Hollow," he said with a devious grin. "Ones who had no family or lasting relationships here. The Coven will be angry for a time, but humans are so fleeting. Even if their rage did persist, they'll be dead soon enough. The future is ours to write," he said, giving me one last smile before he spun suddenly.

One of the Cursed leapt from the trees surrounding us, throwing his entire weight at Gray. The devil caught him around the throat, his grip unrelenting as he held him aloft. The bones on my neck rattled, straining toward the creature with the call of magic that felt so familiar and so different all at once. Whereas the pulse of earth in my blood felt like a warm comfort, this was the cold plunge of icy depths.

My fingers tingled with it, pain filling the tips as I fought to keep my hands pressed to my sides. This magic—black magic—wasn't something I'd ever wanted for myself. The only consideration I'd ever given it was in unmaking the Vessels for revenge.

I'd never planned to use it for anything else.

Gray held him still, his attention shifting to me and the struggle he could undoubtedly sense. "Always follow the magic, Witchling," he murmured softly, spinning the creature in his hold. He wrapped his palm around the front of the creature's throat, holding him still with unimaginable strength. The wolfman's arms thrashed, his hands fully formed with fur on the backs of them and claws that were longer than a normal wolf's. "If it wants his life, feed that craving. A necromancer has to feed the balance just the same as you feed the earth."

But it wasn't death that called to my magic, only the sacrifice of blood and flesh and meat. I stepped toward the Cursed, swallowing as he snapped his jaw at me. Those clawed hands thrashed, swiping to catch a piece of me as I pinned him with a glare.

A wave of my hand called to the earth beneath its feet, roots extending from the forest floor to wrap around his hind canine legs, which supported his weight. They wound around him, encircling his torso and catching his hands to pin at his sides. Gray released him slowly, backing away when he was certain that I held him firm.

He stepped behind me, wrapping an arm around my waist and molding himself to my spine. I shouldn't have relished the support or the way he made me feel grounded in reality, giving my body an anchor as the magic threatened to consume me. "Give it what it wants," he murmured, nuzzling the side of my neck with his nose in something that brought me as much shame as it did comfort.

"It's too much," I said, shaking my head. My hands trembled at my sides, the pull of the magic too much to ignore. I didn't want anything that could force me, that could strip me of my will with the magic taking control.

"Let it go. You'll drain yourself fighting this. The Madizza line is only one line of Green witches. There are two, and that means that the Madizzas only control half of the earth magic I gave. The Hecate line is the only necromancer line. All of it exists within you. You'll need time to adjust to the strength of that power," he said, wrapping his hand around my forearm. He raised it in front of me, pausing only a breath from the Cursed's chest and leaving me to cross the final distance.

I felt the beating of his heart without touching him, felt the throbbing of it pulse with the flow of his blood. His life hovered just out of reach, but it didn't call to me.

Because necromancy wasn't about death, but about giving life to those that had already lost it.

I touched my palm to his chest finally, a rush of black tendrils swarming to absorb my hand. They surrounded me, pulsing from my flesh, and wrapped around his neck.

His eyes held my stare, something human lurking in that gaze as he yelped. That yelp, a plea, escalated into a howl, the sound echoing through the trees as he tossed his head back.

Fur fell to the forest floor, draping off his head and fluttering in the wind until it touched the leaves below. They enveloped it, taking his fur as an offering.

Watching in horror, I couldn't pull my hand away as his skin followed, melting almost as if it had been dipped in acid. His snout faded into shadow, blood dripping from his face as it shifted into that of a man. His form shrank, his legs and arms twisting and the bones cracking. Nails retreated into his fingers as a human head of hair grew to replace his fur.

The tree roots retreated into the earth, returning to the place they belonged and leaving the man who had taken the place of the Cursed to sway on his feet. His arms rose, gripping my wrist gently as he dropped to his knees in front of me.

He was entirely nude, and a pulse of disapproval came in the form of Gray's warning growl.

The Cursed turned his stare up to my face, shocking violet eyes meeting mine from a handsome human man.

"Consort," he said, his voice full of awe as he leaned forward and nuzzled his face against the hand he held. "I am yours."

9

GRAY

Willow froze, staring down at the man kneeling before her in horror. A growl rumbled in my throat, watching him nuzzle my wife's hand like she hung the moon in the sky.

"My consort," I clarified from my position behind her. The bastard didn't so much as glance away from Willow, unable to tear that eerie gaze away from her. When Charlotte had imprisoned the Cursed within the woods, I hadn't thought it possible to undo. It shouldn't have come as a surprise, because all magic had a price.

I just had to wonder what the cost would be to Willow, what she would do with the newfound knowledge that she could free those who remained in the woods.

I pressed myself tighter into her spine, making my presence known when she seemed inclined to forget me altogether.

She released a deep breath, sagging into my body as if it was suddenly too much for her to support herself. My arm tightened around her waist, claiming her for myself even as the Cursed vaulted to his feet.

Willow accepted the help, her uncertainty about the male in front of her driving her to lean on the only support she had in the moment. If I had it my way, I wouldn't need to wait for the day when I was all she had left. When everyone she knew and cared for was gone, that was the day I knew Willow would be mine and mine alone.

"Your name," Willow said. The words weren't a question but a breathy demand. The creature's eyes pulsed with light, the violet gleaming. He seemed wholly unbothered by his own nudity.

"Jonathan," he said, his gaze going confused, as if he had to focus to try to find the memory of who he had been all those centuries prior. "Jonathan Hatt."

Willow righted her legs beneath her, pushing to her feet until she stood tall beside the Cursed male. She reached up with a single hand as she shrugged off my touch, cupping Jonathan's cheek. I stepped to the side ever so slightly, just far enough to observe what she did. Even though it physically pained me to allow her to touch another, the look on her face had nothing to do with carnal desires and everything to do with her recognizing her own capabilities.

"Your debt is not yet paid, Jonathan Hatt," she said, the words spoken softly. Even though they were barely more than a whisper in her exhaustion, there was no mistaking the power that thrummed in each note. Her violet eye glowed as she said the words.

"A debt like mine can never be paid in full, Consort," Jonathan said, the reverence in his voice making me clench my fist at my side.

Inky dark tendrils spread from Willow's fingertips, sinking into Jonathan's cheek. He didn't flinch in spite of the way they bit into his skin, sinking deep. The hum of magic filled the clearing, making my blood echo the symphony of my wife.

Fur spread along his skin as she touched him, his back bowing and bones cracking as he dropped to all fours. He was far shorter than he had been in the form of his Cursed creature, a smoother texture as his very being shrank.

He grew smaller and smaller, his screams muffled as he fought to withhold them. They trailed off with time, the shrill sound fading into a distinctly feline yowl.

The small black cat twirled around Willow's feet, nuzzling her ankles and tilting his head to stare up at her with admiration. His eyes remained that violet shade, and his yowl turned into a purr when Willow bent to pick up the useless creature.

She scratched the back of his neck, causing him to arch to get closer to her. Her other hand lingered in front of his face, her thumb and forefinger spreading to give the cat access to the webbing between them.

He licked the surface of her skin before biting her, sinking his fangs into her skin and taking what did not belong to him. I stretched across the distance, grabbing him by the scruff of the neck and yanking his head back.

His face elongated into the ghost of a snout, a reminder of the Curse that still lingered within him despite the new form Willow had provided, as he growled at me.

"What were you thinking?" I asked, snarling at my wife when she released the cat. I tossed him to the ground, glaring as he landed on his feet in a way that seemed all too natural for someone who hadn't been feline only a moment before.

She'd taken a Cursed and created a fucking familiar out of him, but I would never forget what he really was beneath his fur.

A fucking man who was too close to my wife.

"Blood is power," Willow said, swaying on her feet as her knees buckled. Her skin hummed with energy when I caught her, vibrating against every spot that connected the two of us. The necromancy within her had gotten a taste of connection, of being set loose after lying dormant for decades. The bones around her neck rattled even as her body sagged beneath the weight of that power, needing time to build up to the kind of use she was capable of.

That the magic demanded from her.

"Then why give it to someone who doesn't deserve it?" I asked, lifting her into my arms. She didn't fight, nestling her head against my chest in her moment of exhaustion. Willow might have fought our connection with everything she had when she was strong, but in her moments of vulnerability she showed exactly who she was beneath all the bravado.

A young girl who was terrified of the fact that she was facing the world alone.

She didn't think anyone would see it if she could only pretend to be unbothered, focusing on the shallow friendships she'd formed without ever allowing those who could care about her to sink themselves deeper within her soul.

To love was to lose. To love was to hurt. Whether it was a father who put his own needs before ours or the siblings we would be forced to leave, love was pain for beings like us.

"Because I take care of what is mine," she said, her eyes drifting closed as a growl rumbled in my chest. I had no doubt she could feel it, that the rage simmering in my blood as I stepped past the fucking cat that walked beside me and refused to leave her side was potent in the air.

She didn't sleep—though she didn't open her eyes to look at my rage, choosing to hide away from it instead. I let it slide, understanding it was due to the fact that she didn't know what was going on any better than I did.

Taking a familiar was usually relegated to *actual* animals, but from the way Jonathan had stared up at her and insisted on remaining with her, I couldn't think of any alternative answer.

It was a complication I didn't need or want in our lives, a being that would constantly try to demand attention that she didn't have the time to give.

Because her time belonged to me.

"I suppose you would be angry with me if I got rid of him then?" I asked, injecting humor into my voice in spite of it being no joking matter.

"Furious," she mumbled, still not opening her eyes. Her exhaustion leaked into me, spreading through the bond that existed between us. I turned, pressing my lips to her forehead as we made our way back to the school that would become our home for a time.

Eventually, we would move into the village of Crystal Hollow, becoming a fully integrated part of the community. I'd meant it when I told her we could build a home there, a place where witches and Vessels could learn to coexist in peaceful harmony.

It was the way it had been once, before Susannah and George had enacted the Choice to prevent me from obtaining the woman who would open the seal to allow my physical form on Earth for the first time since I'd been banished to Hell. They'd driven a wedge between us in a desperate bid for power, and I'd suddenly had to bide my time to achieve what should have been mine centuries prior.

Staring down at Willow's face as she finally succumbed to sleep, her breathing evening out to a steady rhythm that felt like home, I wouldn't have changed it for anything.

No one else would have felt the way she did in my arms. No one else would have tempted me to go to the lengths I did to keep her alive.

No one else would have mattered to me at all, simply a means to an end to achieve what I wanted, but Willow didn't just matter.

She was fucking everything.

I stepped out of the woods, staring up at the school as I made my way to the front doors. Leviathan stood guard outside, but a single glance from me and he nodded before taking up step behind me. He followed us to the bedroom where I would allow Willow to sleep, then he left to keep an eye on her from my office while I attempted to deal with some of the chaos that had ensued after my hostile takeover of the Coven.

She wouldn't attempt to run from me again. She knew it was

futile. I would feel her anywhere now that our bond had been completed, linking us irrevocably.

I would find her no matter where she tried to hide, and I would slaughter any who tried to help her.

Her conscience wouldn't allow that.

10

WILLOW

I strained forward, reaching into the darkness before me and searching for something that I could not see. Nothing but the black of pure night existed, the light behind me like something from a faded memory.

I took a deep breath as that light flickered, drawing my eyes to the vines that slithered along the floor to reach me. So close and yet so far; I knew they wouldn't touch me before I could plunge myself into the darkness of death.

It was void of all life, a barren landscape of dry dirt and ash beneath my feet. The hairs rose on my arms as I took a single step forward, driven by the rattling of the bones around my neck. They sought out whatever waited in that darkness, letting it call them home.

The darkness whispered my name, the sounds so much clearer than they'd ever been before.

I took a step closer, as far as my elbows plunging into the ice of the dark. A thorough look through the darkness confirmed the hazy images of women standing in a line for me to see. Twelve women stood before me. The woman on the far left wore clothing that was old-fashioned enough I knew who she must have been.

Charlotte's daughter.

She looked so like her mother, and the absence of the first witch weighed heavy on my heart as I glanced along the line. My aunt stood *at the very end, her hand extended to welcome me home.* "Come, *Willow," she said, her expression solemn as I paused.*

"I'm not ready," I said, shaking my head. I wasn't ready for death to consume me, to become another one of the Hecate witches linked by bones.

Our line would die with me.

As much as I'd thought I wanted that when I'd awoken after a brief death, I remembered the chill of that darkness on my skin. I remembered the emptiness inside me that came with knowing I'd failed.

"You will never be ready," she said, smiling sadly. "Do not allow him to make you into something you are not." The faintest image of a darkened path flashed behind her, the blurry form of green hedges drawing me closer like a trap.

*I paused, considering her words and the strangeness that I felt in my body every time I moved. I was too quick, too strong, too every-*thing *to be the same as I once was.*

As much as it terrified me, I also knew the one thing that mattered more than anything.

I'd come here to find Gray's weakness. I'd come here to find the bones and use them to Unmake the Vessels and get justice for my aunt. I'd thought the Covenant was responsible for her death, but they weren't.

My mission to Unmake the Vessels and avenge her were one and the same, and Gray had made a fatal mistake.

He'd given me his weakness.

I would make him live to regret it.

I woke with a start, my arm straining toward the ceiling. I let it fall to my side. Goose bumps dotted my skin, the physical remnant of the vision lingering to tell me it was real. The Hecate line had always blurred the lines between life and death, between what was real and what was only *seen.*

I sat slowly, wrapping my arms around my stomach and finding a simple silk nightgown. Gray must have changed me when he returned me to his room, and I forced myself not to feel violated by the knowledge. It was nothing he hadn't seen and touched only an hour before anyway.

The disconnect from my flesh felt strange, as if I'd suddenly realized that my body was only that. Even if my soul had been separated from my body briefly, I'd still been *me* in the time I'd had without it. My body was just a Vessel, the same as Lucifer's.

Was Hell the opposite of that dark place filled with cold and nothingness? Was it heat that burned his skin for every moment of his existence, a void filled with Helfyre?

I shook off the thought, tossing back the covers and sliding my legs over the edge of the bed. I forced myself to move slowly, attempting to shift in the way I thought I had before. It seemed painfully slow, like it took everything in me to ignore how much time I had wasted.

I made my way to the bathroom, reaching into the shower and turning on the water. Tearing off the nightgown Gray had dressed me in, I watched it fall to the floor as I stepped into the shower. The water felt too warm on my skin in contrast to the cold of that hollow darkness. I let it wash over me, bringing me back from the brink of the place I didn't want to go just yet.

Once the Vessels were gone, once the Coven was righted to the traditions that never should have faded, then I would step into that darkness and accept my fate.

In doing so, I would free the ancestors who were trapped there, offering their power to the bones that powered me. They couldn't truly move on until our line had fulfilled its destiny, and I felt that in my soul as the bones seemed to cool against my collarbone.

I held them against me, felt the whisper of their desire for peace within me. I would give it to them when our work was done and Charlotte's wrongs had been righted.

Finishing with my shower, I stepped into the cool air of the bathroom and dried off before dressing. I couldn't bear to pick up the forest-green uniform that marked me as a Green, not when

I felt so disjointed from that girl. The green magic still pulsed within me, but I felt disloyal to it when I felt it warring with the black magic.

Rummaging through Gray's drawers for something to wear, I was shocked when I opened one to find my clothes from my room. Every piece that he'd arranged to be brought to me when I first came to Crystal Hollow sat in his drawers, as if I'd moved in with the man who considered himself my husband.

But I hadn't done it.

I donned my armor instead of fixating on the wrongness of the situation, slipping into what was familiar to me even before I'd become a Hecate witch in truth. My black jeans and combat boots made me feel more me, and I slipped a loose black sweater over my head to go with them, letting it hang off one of my shoulders before I went in search of the man who had taken everything from me.

Who knew what my life might have been if he'd never whispered plots of vengeance in my father's ear.

I pulled the door to the bedroom open, glancing down at my feet when Jonathan meowed and curled himself around my ankles. Bending low, I scooped him up and cuddled him to my chest, letting him nuzzle my chin as I stepped out into the living area. He nipped at my skin, drawing a tiny drop of blood with the sharpness of his teeth.

"Greedy familiar," I scolded, turning a quick, stern glance down to him as I headed into the living room.

One of the archdemons lingered in one of the chairs with his back to me, but I watched him raise a single hand to tap a long black talon against his cheek once.

Leviathan.

He rose slowly, towering as he filled the space with his height. I swallowed as he turned to face me, leveling me with a glare that made me feel insignificant. He was the tallest of the archdemons, making the room feel small. He wore no shirt, as if they hadn't been able to find one to fit the broad swell of muscles that strained his shoulders and biceps. His forearms were covered in faint pearlescent scales that half blended into his skin. They sparkled lightly as the sun touched them when he moved, reminding me of a sea serpent. His eyes were the vivid blue of the Caribbean, set into an impossibly square face and a defined jaw. He'd pulled his shoulder-length dark hair back from his face, showing off the lines of his harsh features without hindrance.

"Consort," he said, tilting his head to the side as I nodded and turned to make my way to the door. "He has requested that you stay in your rooms for the time being."

"Please," I said, stopping in my tracks and spinning with a scoff. "He wouldn't know how to make a *request* if his life depended on it."

His mouth spread into a smile, his straight teeth perfect and white. It was only the length of his fangs that made that smile look anything but human, longer even than those of the Vessels. "I am glad to see you know him well enough to read between the lines."

"I don't know him at all really, though, do I?" I asked, scratching the back of Jonathan's neck to bring myself comfort. It grounded me against the pain, against the turmoil inside me.

I hadn't wanted to know him before, even though it was the smart thing to do. I needed his weakness, but didn't want to discern the things that made him human.

Now I realized how little he'd shared with me. The bits and pieces of his humanity were shared strategically to endear him to me, to serve his purpose and get me exactly where he wanted me.

In truth, even if I didn't want to admit it, was it really so different from what human men did to the women they wanted to sleep with? Omitting the ugly truths in favor of sharing pretty lies felt like a standard part of the courting process from what I'd seen.

But most human men didn't stab their dates and summon archdemons.

"I suspect you know him better than you believe right now, Consort," Leviathan said, taking a step forward to get between me and the door.

I swallowed back my ire, forcing out a quiet protest. "I have a name."

"Consort . . ."

My next reply was louder, firm as I stood my ground and re-membered who I was. I did not cower in the face of pain, and it didn't matter that the worst harm that had been done to me was to my emotions and not my body. "I. Have. A. Name," I said, leaning forward. Jonathan jumped down from my hold, hissing at my feet when Leviathan was too close for his comfort. "I am more than just—"

"His wife?" Leviathan asked, finishing the sentence before I could. *Wife* would not have been the word I chose, but it hardly mattered. Even I couldn't deny it now, not with our marks upon one another and the pulsating knowledge of him somewhere deep within me.

His rage was potent, fueling my own, even when I could not see him.

"My name is Willow, and you will address me as such from this moment on," I ordered, feeling the bones press deeper into my skin. They agreed with my assertion, with my attempt to put distance between Gray and I, even if it was only an illusion that helped me sleep at night.

Leviathan smiled again, the expression softening the harsh lines of his face. "As you wish, Willow," he said pointedly, giving a mocking bow without taking his eyes off me.

I waited until he paused in the deepest part of that bow, spin-ning and racing for the door as quickly as I could. Suddenly grateful for the inhuman speed, I pushed my body to the limits as I wrapped my fingers around the doorknob and twisted, pulling the door open.

Leviathan was just as fast, following behind me with a speed I hadn't thought possible. His hand came down upon the wood above my head, the webbing between his fingers and those long talons consuming my vision as he shoved the door closed with a loud bang.

I fought to pull it open, groaning when I couldn't and releasing a snarl of frustration. Spinning to face him, I raised my hand to his face and cupped his cheek. Flowing that black magic into my touch, I watched the tendrils of darkness spread over his skin. They radiated out from my hand, from my fingers, moving within the surface of his flesh like veins of death.

The bones rattled as I poured their magic into him, willing him to return to nothing.

The bastard grinned at me as the black lines sank deeper into his skin, fading from view and leaving me reeling.

"I am not made from mud, Little Necromancer," he said, clearing his throat. He forced his smile to fade, adopting a serious expression as he corrected himself. "Willow."

I fell back against the door at my spine, my hand colliding with the wood. The magic within me refused to let go, surging through the room as those dark veins spread over the walls, searching for life. "You cannot just keep me locked up here forever!" I shouted.

My anger reverberated through the room, spreading out like a pulse. It slammed into the furniture like a shockwave, rocking it in its place. Something burst, the sound coming only a moment before the windows shattered where they overlooked the gardens, glass falling down to the ground below.

I winced, squeezing my eyes closed. "What's wrong with me?" I whispered, more to myself than to the archdemon in front of me. He wasn't the one who could and would provide answers.

"Nothing is wrong with you," Leviathan said as he reached out, touching a single bone where it hung around my neck. His touch was surprisingly gentle, his fingers working to avoid touching my skin as much as possible. The magic retreated into me once more, sealing itself away inside the bones and making it feel like I could breathe once again. "But believe it or not, He's doing this to protect you. Some of the Coven have declared war on Lucifer. They blame Him, but even more than that?" he asked, glaring down at me as if he dared me to try to escape again. "They blame his pretty wife for betraying her own kind."

"I didn't know what he was doing. I—"

"You know that, and I know that, but the Coven doesn't know that. They aren't exactly going to believe your side of the story, are they? They weren't there to see what He did to you," he said, his features softening as he took a step back. "Your safety is all that matters to Lucifer."

"If that were true, He never would have hurt me in the first place," I said, thinking of the burn of His blade when He'd shoved it into my stomach.

"You're alive, aren't you? He went to a great deal of trouble to keep you that way."

"It's not enough," I mumbled, pushing away from the door and making my way to the sofa. I dropped down onto it without finesse, my body feeling heavy with the realization that in spite of the stupid fucking bond between us, he intended to keep me prisoner, too.

"Then I suggest you decide exactly what *will* be enough. If you don't even know, how the Hell is He supposed to?"

11

WILLOW

The door to Gray's rooms opened later in the day. I shot to my feet, tossing the book I'd been reading down on the couch beside me in my anxiousness to get out of the room. Leviathan didn't bother to glance up from his book, but I saw his smirk from the corner of my eye.

"You're worse than a caged animal," he said, his voice light in spite of the mocking words.

Grabbing the book from the sofa hurriedly, I threw it at Leviathan's laughing face. He reached up, snatching the book out of the air and neatly straightening the pages.

I appreciated that, even if I would have rather it hit him first.

"Then maybe you shouldn't treat me like one," I said, tipping my head to the side with a mocking grin to match his.

Gray stepped into the room, leaning his shoulder against the doorframe with his hands tucked into his trouser pockets. He'd rolled up the sleeves of his white dress shirt, leaving the top button undone far enough to reveal a small piece of the maze I'd marked him with.

His lips tipped up into a smile as his golden eyes heated, drifting over me from my head to my feet. "Witchling," he said, his voice dropping low. I felt it in the deepest parts of my body, sinking into my stomach. My legs pressed together on instinct, blocking out that overwhelming need that he seemed to be able to create with nothing more than a word. It was worse now, as if consummating had only strengthened the bond that pulsed between us like a living entity.

I wanted to tear it from my soul.

His smirk spread into a grin as he sensed my reaction to him, and he pushed off the doorframe to make his way into the room. "I brought you a surprise," he said as he approached. I swallowed as he came up in front of me, lifting my chin with a finger so that I met his gaze. He leaned forward, stopping when his mouth brushed against mine ever so softly. "But maybe I should just take you to bed instead."

"I want answers," I said, shaking my head and pulling back from his touch. Just because he was able to convince my body that he was exactly what I needed didn't mean I had to be reduced to a mass of flesh and desire.

Desire did not equal love.

Attraction didn't mean we were allies.

I could want to fuck him and plan to slit his throat all in the same breath, and maybe that was the best way to do it. My breath hitched at the thought, and I brushed it away before he could sense the shift in my thinking.

Jonathan came between us, slinking between my legs to glare up at Gray. The devil glanced down at the tiny creature as he pounced, sinking his claws into Gray's pants. I grinned down at him, wincing when Gray grabbed him by the scruff of the neck and held him up. Jonathan bared his teeth, his tiny fangs ferocious. "Useless pest," Gray grumbled, dropping Jonathan to the couch with a twist of his lips.

"At least I *like* him," I said, reaching down to rub the top of Jonathan's head soothingly. My familiar settled, leaning into my touch with a look that I might have said was arrogant.

If he hadn't been a fucking cat.

"Keep it up, Witchling. I'll let your little pet watch so he can see just how much you like me when your clothes come off," Gray said, earning a startled gasp from me.

"Gray!" I scolded, glancing toward where Leviathan had pressed his lips together and taken to reading my book as if he couldn't hear the conversation.

His chest shook with silent laughter.

I needed another book to throw at him.

"Maybe next time you'll think twice before you insinuate you like another man more than me," Gray said, taking a step toward me and closing what remained of the distance between us. His torso pressed to mine, leaving me to bend backward if I wanted any space. Jonathan hissed again, but Gray didn't so much as glance his way as he pointed a finger in the black furball's face.

"He's a cat!" I protested, tossing an arm out to gesture toward my familiar.

"Is he, though? Is he really?" Gray asked, tilting his head to the side.

I looked down to the cat, which had taken to swatting at Gray's finger with extended claws, swiping them over his flesh and leaving shallow cuts that healed immediately. "Kind of looks it to me, yeah. Your jealousy is ridiculous. I don't need to fuck my familiar if I want to get laid. There are plenty of men I could choose from."

Gray growled, taking his finger from Jonathan. He buried his other hand in the hair at the back of my head, gripping it harshly and using it to yank back my neck. I bent, glaring up at him as he held me still and pressed his groin against me. "Let's get one thing clear, Witchling. I am not *jealous*. I am possessive over what is *mine*."

I ignored the way that growl hummed through me, resisting the urge to press into him. "I see no difference."

"The difference is that to be jealous implies I do not already *own* you. He exists because I allow it. Never mistake that his very presence in your life is my gift to you, and I can take it away as quickly as I granted it," he said, touching his mouth to the corner of mine as I twisted away from him. "Tell me you understand."

"I understand," I said, fighting through the words. His grip on my hair was too strong, the strands pulling only when I struggled.

He released me finally, straightening his shirt sleeves. "I didn't come here to fight," he said, and he sounded genuinely remorseful. He didn't offer any more information, either, instead turning to face the door. My eyes widened as I took in the sight of Della, Nova, and Margot standing there uncertainly, having seen our entire display.

I glanced back at Gray quickly, stepping around him to approach the witches hesitantly.

What if they hated me, too?

"Willow," Della said, her relief palpable as she took the first step into the office. I hurried to her, catching her hand with mine and reaching out with my free hand to take Margot's. The blond witch flinched but recovered as Nova stretched out to touch my arm with a smile, and I glanced at Juliet where she lingered in the background.

"Are you all right?" I asked, ignoring the Vessel's presence in favor of focusing on my roommates.

"Us?" Nova asked, her voice rising in concern. "What about you?" She waved a hand toward where Gray remained behind me, observing our interaction with something between malice and boredom.

I looked down, unable to find the words to answer the question. I couldn't answer it truthfully with Gray's watchful eyes, and I knew what would come the moment I opened my mouth.

I sank my teeth into my bottom lip when it trembled, pulling my hands back from the girls and turning to face Gray as he spoke. "I'll be back in an hour. Juliet will escort the girls back to their rooms if you need privacy before that," he said, stepping up in front of me. He touched my cheek with a gentleness that I shouldn't have found comfort in, his eyes so warm as he stared down at me that I wished he would revert to the hatred I knew I'd seen when he first met me.

Mutual hatred was easy. I knew how to cope with that.

"I'll be outside, Willow," Leviathan said, following him out the door as Juliet stepped into the room. She watched Della as she made her way to the office, taking a seat at Gray's desk as Della returned her gaze until the Vessel was out of sight.

"Della, she's a Vessel," I said, warning my friend from making the same mistake I had.

"And? You're fucking the devil. I hardly think you're in any place to judge me," she snapped. I winced, shrinking back physically as I made my way toward the sofa and dropped onto it. I buried my face in my hands, huffing out a bitter laugh.

"That was harsh, Del," Margot said, glaring at the other woman and taking up a seat beside me. She reached up, prying my hands away from my face even though I felt certain that the touch and show of care cost her.

"She's right," I said, shaking my head. "I fucked up, and I of all people have no right to tell you what to do or what not to do. I just wish I hadn't made my mistake in the first place."

"She's not a mistake," Della said, stepping toward us. Nova took a seat beside Margot, leaving the place next to me for Della.

"You care about her," I said, the observation hanging between us.

She glanced over her shoulder to the area where Juliet sat, knowing as well as I did that she would hear anything she said. "I love her. She's not like him. She would never hurt me," she explained as she wrung her hands in front of her.

I reached over, clasping them in mine and stilling the anxious energy as I smiled and spoke. "Okay."

She paused, freezing as she raised her stare to meet mine. "Okay?"

"If you say she wouldn't hurt you, then I believe you. As long as she makes you happy, that's all I can hope for in the end, isn't it? I think that our history isn't as black and white as we've been made to believe. It stands to reason that Vessels and witches wouldn't be, either. And if she ever does hurt you, she knows I'll make her regret it. Don't you, Juliet?" I asked, not bothering to raise my voice for the Vessel eavesdropping.

"It would be nothing less than I deserve, Consort," Juliet called back, and Della smiled as she leaned forward to rest her head on my shoulder.

Jonathan jumped down in all the shuffling, reaching beneath the couch with a stretching paw. He swatted around a single white feather, following it as it fluttered across the floor.

I watched him play, held captive by the iridescent mix of colors that gleamed on the feather in the light.

Nova stood from the couch and distracted me finally, moving to sit on the coffee table in front of me. She perched there, staring at me and waiting for me to crack in that silent, watchful way she had. It wasn't often that she was highly vocal, instead preferring to keep quiet like a calm summer breeze. "What happened?" she asked, reaching out a hand to touch the bones around my neck.

She flinched as she felt the magic in them, her brow furrowing as she took in the black clothes. She'd probably thought nothing of them since I'd always preferred black to the greens of my uniform, but I watched the information dance in her head.

"You're a Hecate," she said, her chest sagging with the realization.

Della went still at my side, and I felt her gaze probing the side of my face. I nodded, not daring to speak the words. I'd assumed everyone would know the truth by now, that what had happened in the Tribunal room would have been shared with the Coven in depth.

"Did you know?" Della asked. Her voice had hardened, a symptom of the secret I'd kept from them. We hadn't been close enough for me to disclose truths that would require them to go against the Covenant, but guilt still ate at me. I'd come here to strip away everything they knew and loved.

"I knew. I came here to find the bones," I said, watching as she leaned back on the couch. Her shock was palpable, ringing between us with the bitter taste of betrayal.

"I don't understand," Margot said, her voice uncertain. "You're a *Green*. We've all seen it."

"My mother was a Madizza. My father was a Hecate who never made the Choice," I answered, letting that confession hang between us.

Was.

Because Charlotte had killed him for what he'd done to me.

"Wow," Margot said, her breathy voice echoing everything I felt from the others.

"Did you know? What he intended to do? Is that why you were practically attached at the hip the moment you got here?" Nova asked. There was a tinge of anger in her voice, but more than that there was disbelief. They didn't want to think me capable of such a thing.

"I swear I didn't know. He used me, made me think he didn't know who I was to let me believe I was looking for the bones of my own accord, but he wanted me to find them. He wanted me to use them, because he needed me to open the seal. I had no idea he was killing the witches. Please believe me," I said.

If I didn't have these three and their friendship, I'd be completely, entirely alone, and in the wake of losing Ash all over again, I couldn't bear it.

"Okay," Della said, echoing the word I'd given her earlier.

I turned to her, watching as she processed the information and tried to connect the dots. "What?"

"If you say you didn't know, then I believe you," she said, sinking into my side. She felt the hitch in my breath, wrapping an arm around my back to rub soothing circles against the fabric of my shirt.

"I believe you," Margot said, mirroring Della's posture on my other side.

A strangled sob clawed its way up my throat, forcing me to swallow it back and shove down the emotion threatening to consume me. I couldn't give in, couldn't let the tears start.

I suspected once they did, I would never be able to stop.

Nova leaned forward, taking my hands in hers and rubbing the backs of them. "It's okay to break," she said, watching me fight.

"We'll be here to help put you back together," Margot said, cracking the wall open. I pinched my eyes closed as the tears came uninterrupted, making my entire head throb with the pain of them. My hands turned, gripping Nova's as my rage manifested in tears.

"I feel so fucking stupid," I mumbled, shaking my head from side to side. I couldn't believe I'd fallen for his lies, thinking I was so fucking smart.

"You're not stupid. You were manipulated by the master," Della said, her voice heavy at my side.

Nova caught my chin with a thumb, forcing me to meet her gray eyes. Her anger was tangible, even if it wasn't directed at me. No, it was all for *him*.

"Now, what are you going to do about it?"

The houses are fighting for power," Della admitted when I'd calmed my crying. My face felt puffy, my eyes swollen and dry, but I felt more grounded than I had since waking up after my death. I had a purpose again, a reason to keep going.

I was going to make him *hurt*.

I would make him feel every bit of pain he'd caused me.

"Let me guess, Headmaster Thorne is encouraging the infighting?" I asked, rolling my eyes. Sometimes, I wondered how he and the archdemons had survived this long if all they wanted to do was kill.

"No, actually," Nova explained, raising her brow at me. "He's trying to keep the witches from fighting themselves and the Vessels and demons. He claims that there is far more reason for our kinds to live together in harmony now than there has ever been. Do you know what he means?"

"He means that Lucifer has taken a witch for His bride," Juliet said, coming into the room and taking up residence in a chair on the other side of the coffee table. She lounged, propping her feet over one of the arms and draping her back over the other to stretch. Della tracked the movement for what it was.

A tease meant for her.

Juliet grinned, knowing she'd had the desired effect as she righted herself and leaned forward.

"But who would he have married? We both know he's been obsessing over Willow . . ." Della said, silencing when Juliet raised her brow in challenge.

"You?" Margot asked.

"It isn't like witch marriages. There's no ceremony. He marked me in a *dream*. I didn't even know what it meant at the time," I explained, trying to make them understand how the Hell I'd let this happen.

"That didn't stop you from marking him back," Juliet said, smiling at my discomfort.

"I didn't know what I was doing. My magic has a mind of its own now," I said, shame heating my cheeks. I peeked at each and every one of my friends' faces, expecting judgment but only finding sympathy.

They all remembered what it was like when we turned sixteen and suddenly came into our powers, that overwhelming feeling that we were no longer alone in our bodies. I'd had more magic than any of them even before the Hecate bones locked around my neck, but after it was like drowning in an endless well I could never climb out of.

"That's fair," Juliet said, nodding her head in agreement. I sighed a breath of relief, grateful that she'd decided to stop pressing me. "But when the magic wants something, the heart *will* follow."

"Enough, Juliet," Della said, giving her a stern look. Juliet raised her hands to say she was done, shocking me with the respect she gave to my friend.

"Then he wants you to rule at his side," Nova said, shrugging her shoulders. "You have to do it, Willow."

"What? The Coven barely knows me. There's no way they'll agree to follow me," I said.

"Some will, just from the power they will know you have once you reveal yourself wearing those bones. Witches are dying trying to kill the archdemons. You have the chance to bring peace between us all," she said, shaking her head. It was clear that she hated what had become of the Coven, the displays of violence just to gain power. Turning on our own had been a crime once in our history; maybe it was time to make it so again.

"Weren't you just asking me what I was going to do to get even?"

"I didn't say not to fight. I just said bring peace to our people while *you* work to take out the source of the issue. We need to get rid of the archdemons and we need to do it as efficiently as possible," she said, casting a glance at Margot at my side.

Juliet raised her brow at Nova, seeming to challenge her openness in admitting she wanted a coup. Nova raised hers back, a silent reminder that *everyone* expected us to fight. It shouldn't have come as a surprise.

Margot stiffened when I turned to look at her, watching as she shrank back inside herself. "Is one of them bothering you?"

"He's been as kind as he can be, I think. But he's made his

intentions clear," she said, crossing her arms over her chest. "If I were anyone else, he wouldn't have done anything wrong. Nova is just protective."

"As she should be," I said, pulling Margot's arms down to release her hold on herself. "You are in charge of who is allowed in your space. Not a fucking archdemon. Which one is it, anyway?"

"Beelzebub," Nova said, placing her hands on her hips. She seemed to be in the same camp as me as I shook my head at Margot.

"I think the fuck not," I said, earning a startled, uncomfortable chuckle.

"I'm fully aware they're all bad news, Willow," she said, her voice going quieter with the uncertainty that I hated for her. "He's respectful of my need for distance, even though I've never told him where it comes from."

"Two things, Margot," I said, taking her hands in mine. "First, Beelzebub? Snapped my fucking neck. He literally killed me, and the *only* reason I'm here is because Gray brought me back to life."

"Fucking Hell, Willow," Della said, but I silenced her with a look. This conversation wasn't about me beyond giving Margot the warning she needed about exactly what kind of man Beelzebub was.

"Second, I hope one day you get revenge for what was done to you by that man that makes you feel like Beelzebub not assaulting you is a green flag when it should be the bare minimum. I don't need to know what it was or how, but I hope you make that man fucking bleed," I said, hating the way she shifted her gaze down to where our hands touched.

"I don't think I have that kind of violence in me. I'm better than that," she said, but the cautious tremble to her voice said everything she wouldn't.

She was afraid of him, whoever he was.

I shrugged, pulling my hands back from her slowly. "Then I hope one day you trust me enough to tell me his name at least."

"Why?" she asked, looking sheepish as she raised her eyes to mine and saw the rage staring back at her.

"Because you might be above it, but I'm sure as fuck not," I said, standing and ignoring the approving nod from Juliet as I made my way to the windows I'd shattered. A cool breeze drifted in through them, lending a chill to the air that I imagined would only worsen until a crystal witch came up with a temporary solution.

"It was Itar Bray," Margot said, making everything in me still as I spun to look her.

I watched her face even though she wouldn't look at me, observed the way she picked at her nails. "How old were you?" I asked, watching her eyes drift closed in confirmation of everything I needed.

"I was fourteen," she said, her eyes wide as she looked at me finally.

I nodded simply, knowing I couldn't leave the room. No matter his faults, I knew if I told Gray he would take care of it for us. He might be evil, but even he had limits he would never cross. "Not a word," I said to Juliet, pointing a finger at her.

"You want him for yourself?" Juliet asked, rising to her feet. Something like respect flashed over her face as she approached me, placing a hand on top of my shoulder. Her fingers brushed against the mark Lucifer had put there, making ice fill my veins.

"I want the last face he sees to be a woman he thinks is beneath him," I said, gritting my teeth. "If it can't be the survivor of his abuse, then I want to make sure that he remembers her face when I cut off his cock and feed it to him."

Margot blanched, but Juliet grinned.

"As you wish, Consort."

12

GRAY

Willow had retired to bed after Juliet escorted her friends back to the sanctuary of their rooms. She'd barely been able to look at me, but it wasn't because of some sense of shame.

She was pissed, and I didn't want to think about what realization she'd had while with her friends.

I poured my scotch into a tumbler, standing before the crystallized window. The witch who had come to repair it hadn't been thrilled to be summoned, but she'd taken a single look at Willow's puffy face and the way she huddled into herself in the cold and taken mercy on her.

I couldn't feel it and would have remained unbothered by the cold temperatures. The heat of Helfyre had long since burned away any sensitivity to temperature for me, a consequence of my eternity of imprisonment.

"Gray," Juliet said, stepping through the open door to my office. I hadn't bothered to close it, knowing she would return after seeing the girls home. She knew me well enough to understand I would expect a report.

"Tell me," I said, my voice as melancholy as I felt as I took a sip. I let the scotch burn me from the inside, let it warm the cold hollow that had settled into me. It had been so many years—centuries—since I'd had feelings and emotions that could impact the decisions I made. Even when I knew Willow was mine, even when I felt that bond to her, it hadn't been *this*.

It hadn't been anything beyond obsession and the need to possess her. Now it was a twisted, gnarled thing that made me want to see her happy with me. I needed it more than I needed anything, but I didn't know how to get there. I didn't know how to be anything other than what I was, even with the all-consuming love I felt for her.

"She blames herself for what we did," Juliet said, her voice sad as she dropped into a chair dramatically. Out of all the Vessels, she was the one who seemed to be the most in touch with the feelings of humans and the witches. As if she remembered what it was like to have those things herself, even if the rest of us had so quickly forgotten how the shadow of their memory felt.

"That's ridiculous. She blames me, believe me," I scoffed. Willow's hatred was potent in the air when our eyes met, and I knew I should expect a difficult journey in getting her to understand.

"You weren't there, Gray," Juliet said gently when I approached and stood in front of her. She reached up, taking the tumbler from my hand, and tossed back a gulp of the liquid. "I watched her break. She thinks she should have known better."

I tried not to let my fury over Willow breaking down for someone else influence how I moved forward. I wanted to be the one to hold her when she cried, to comfort her in the shower when she thought about giving up.

I hated the thought of anyone else seeing through her tough exterior to the fleshy, vulnerable heart she kept locked away.

"She never stood a chance," I said, taking my scotch back and lowering myself onto the sofa. I knew damn near everything about her. I knew what buttons to push and how to get her to believe that maybe I was something more than her father had raised her to believe. "She's never been protected from harm. Her father evidently went out of his way to hurt her, and her mother allowed it because of her own ignorance."

"She's always been the protector," Juliet said, nodding as she thought of the little boy I'd had her remove from the situation. I could never harm him, not if I wanted to be able to come back from it. "So when you protected her from harm . . ."

"I used what I knew to manipulate her, but I would have done it either way. Her history simply worked in my favor," I explained, nodding my head. Willow would eventually recover from her self-loathing, turning all that ire onto me, if she hadn't already. It was only a matter of time.

"Did you know about her father?" Juliet asked, and I clenched my jaw as I thought of what Charlotte had done to him. She'd watched over Willow all her life, grown attached to the girl as she became a woman. She wouldn't have chosen such a brutal punishment for her father if it hadn't been warranted.

"I still don't know any of the details, but I trust Charlotte's judgment that he deserved that fate," I answered.

"Do you think it has to do with her fear of the dark?" Juliet asked, earning a raised brow from me. "Della told me."

"You're going to hurt her," I said, ignoring the breach of trust. Della believed Juliet to be an equal partner in their secret relationship that they'd hidden from the Covenant, but at the end of the day, Juliet was a Vessel.

She could not love her in truth.

"One day, Willow will be strong enough to open the seal on her own. Even if she only does it long enough to allow one of us to pass at a time, I'll have my body back. I'll be able to give to her what you can give to Willow now," Juliet said, clinging to the hope that we could convince Willow to do just that. She was a ticking time bomb, more likely to Unmake every Vessel she could get her hands on than she was to willingly open the seal.

"It could take years," I explained, remaining gentle as I gave her the reality check she needed. She felt the hollow place where love should have been, felt the connection as if it were a whisper of what it could have been.

It was the slowest form of torture I could imagine, *knowing* that I loved someone but unable to really feel that. I wouldn't have wished it on my worst enemy, let alone a friend who had been there for me in every way for centuries. She was one of the first demons I'd created after the archdemons, haunted by the memory of my father and the family that had cast me out simply for disagreeing with him about the future of the humans he'd created.

His new children.

He said that pride was a sin, and that mine would condemn me. He claimed it was my own selfish desire for attention that drove me to become obsessed with my own needs and no longer turn my mind to him when I discovered I could manipulate others into giving me what I needed.

I'd wanted the love of my father, but settled for the love of the children I'd created in the home he cursed me to.

Now, staring at the door to my bedroom and knowing Willow slept behind it, I wondered if they would feel similarly neglected when I inevitably started a new family with her. I would do anything I could to make them feel valued, but I couldn't deny the sense inside me. The feeling that spoke to what lengths I would go to to protect our children.

I would burn it all down rather than see them harmed.

"She's going to try to kill you," Juliet said, ignoring my statement about Della entirely. There was nothing left to say, not when we both understood it would be a long battle.

"I'd be disappointed if she didn't," I said, setting my tumbler on the coffee table and standing slowly. The knowledge that Willow waited beyond that door, warm and sleepy and feeling like home, was suddenly too tempting for me to ignore. I needed to lose myself in her after the chaos of my day.

"Leviathan said she doesn't think she knows you," Juliet inserted, interrupting me as I prepared to make my way to Willow.

"She knows me," I said, brushing off her commentary.

"Does she? What have you told her of yourself? If you want her to fall in love with you, then she has to at least *know* you. Yes, she feels the connection the two of you share because of the destiny that unites you. But that doesn't make it love, especially not with all the bad you've given her," she said, pushing to her feet. She approached, touching the buttons of my shirt and parting them to reveal more of Willow's mark. I flinched back from her touch, unable to stomach the feeling of her hands on me.

From the way her brow rose and the soft laughter in her throat, the volatile reaction was as surprising to her as it was to me.

"What would you have me do?" I asked, staring down into the face of one of the people who had been there to witness my suffering after my father's rejection. Loving Willow and accepting that I wanted her to love me back would mean putting myself at risk of rejection all over again.

"Get to know her," Juliet said with a laugh.

"I already know her," I said, pointing out the truth. I'd researched her in depth, had spies report her moves to me. I knew what grades she'd gotten in high school, for fuck's sake.

"Do you, though? What you know is what is documented on paper, not what exists within her. You don't know what her father did to her or how that has affected her as a person. You know better than anyone that the simplest of events can change us in ways nobody understands but us," she said, pausing to let those words sink in. "But regardless of whether or not you *think* you know her, she doesn't think that. No woman wants to be reduced to a list of facts on paper. She is a person, Gray, and you need to treat her like one."

"She won't answer me if I just start asking her the hard questions," I said, knowing the truth in those words. Willow would only push back if I started interrogating her about her father and the life she'd lived with her mother and Ash.

"You're courting her, not interrogating her. It's give and take. You will have to give her your truth to get hers. Let her know you, Gray, or so help me, you will lose her in a way you cannot recover from," Juliet said, clenching her jaw in frustration. Sometimes it was easy to forget that as a woman she understood the way Willow's brain worked. For so many centuries, I'd considered her a friend. We'd seen eye to eye, and I'd seen the ruthlessness with which she survived in a world dominated by men, so at times I forgot she wasn't like me entirely.

"Fine," I growled, unhappy with the turn of events.

I stepped around her, making my way toward the closed door to my bedroom. Pushing it open slowly, I took in the sight of Willow curled up in the center of the bed. She hadn't bothered to change or get under the covers, and if what Juliet said was true, I suspected it was because of the emotional exhaustion of her day.

Jonathan stretched on the foot of the bed, twisting his body to rub his cheek into the bedspread before turning to his back. He hissed when I picked him up without finesse, carrying him to the couch and dropping him onto the cushion. His violet eyes glared up at me, narrowed in annoyance as I pointed a finger in his face. "The bedroom is off-limits to you," I warned, watching as he tipped his head to the side.

He may not have been able to speak, but I knew exactly what the motion meant.

Is that so?

"You can pretend to be a cat all you want, but you and I both know all she has to do is snap her fingers and you're a human with a dick. Stay the Hell away from my wife," I said, ignoring Juliet's disbelieving laughter as she sat down on the sofa and patted her lap for Jonathan to cuddle up with her.

I left them to it, heading for the bedroom and closing the door behind me. Stripping off my clothes to the sound of Willow's relaxed, even breathing, I lifted her off the bed to pull back the bedspread and cover her up before climbing in beside her.

My boxer briefs rubbed against her jeans as I pressed myself against her back, wrapping an arm around her waist and enjoying her warmth.

She sighed happily, murmuring a sleepy "Gray."

"Go back to sleep, Witchling," I said, ignoring the desire to use the moments where she was soft and pliant, half asleep and willing, for my own pleasure.

The next time I got inside her, it would be her who begged me for it.

13

WILLOW

I woke with Gray's warmth wrapped around me, feeling far too hot in the clothes I'd never changed out of. There was something comforting in the fact that he hadn't stripped me down while I slept, but it made me wonder what had changed. He'd never hesitated to do it before, not recognizing the boundaries that should have existed.

I'd cried myself to sleep the night before, letting all the rage I felt out. The hot, angry tears had served their purpose, diminishing my anger until I felt like I could do what was necessary to survive in this place and this odd, complex relationship. Gray might be my husband, but that didn't mean that anything less than absolute hatred would motivate me going forward.

He just couldn't know it, not when my only chance at defeating him involved using his weakness against him. He was too powerful in his own right, but if I was the thing that made him vulnerable?

Then I would manipulate him the same way he did me, until he never saw the blade coming.

I stood from the bed, being careful not to disturb him, and made my way to the bathroom. I knew what I needed to do. I knew that Gray's love language was physical touch, and nothing would manipulate him quite like having access to me would. It felt like a betrayal to myself, like I wouldn't be able to survive the seduction.

I'd be forced to admit how much pleasure I found in his body and would need to find a way to keep that pleasure separate from my heart. He could have my body, as other men would when he was gone, as much as it might pain me to think.

But no one would ever have my heart again. He'd made sure of it.

I stood in front of the mirror, washing my face and brushing my teeth before I stripped off the clothes I'd worn to bed. My hands grasped the edge of the vanity, clenching it tightly as I let my eyes drift back toward the door.

I'd been here before. Known what I was doing when I allowed Gray to touch me for the first time and take my virginity, but that had been distinctly different. Every time before this, I'd fooled myself into thinking I was acting out of my need for revenge and the need for answers. In reality, I'd only been reacting to him.

He'd initiated it all; he'd laid claim to me, and I had simply not stopped him. It was fortunate it fell into the plan that had been set forth probably from the moment I was born, because I didn't know that I would have had it in me to control it.

But this? This time, I was in control. This time, I would knowingly step into that bedroom and do what I needed to make him lower his guard even a little. I didn't delude myself into thinking that it would tear down all the walls between us, that he would believe I'd suddenly welcomed him with open arms and forgiven him.

But I could use his body against him the way he had mine.

He didn't have a heart for me to sink inside when he was a Vessel.

But he did now.

I released the counter, staring at the depressions in the stone for a moment while I sighed. The fissures in the marble made me swallow, hating the reminder of all that he'd taken from me.

I left it behind me, pulling the door to the bedroom open slowly. Gray still slept peacefully, having turned onto his back in my absence. The bedspread was draped over his waist, leaving the expanse of his chest uncovered. The mark at the center of his skin stared at me as if it had a mind of its own, a symbol of the power that I didn't understand.

My body hummed as I padded over to the bed with soft steps, taking care not to wake him. The gold of his skin gleamed in the sunlight drifting through the window at the edge of the curtain. The dim light did something to him, showed me a whisper of what he must have been once before being cast out from Heaven.

It was as if he shone from within, but instead of pulsating with light, he just emanated power.

I swallowed as I knelt on the end of the bed between his legs, pulling the bedspread down farther. The deep cut of his muscles beneath his abs led way to the black boxer briefs that covered him, and I watched him stretch even though his eyes never opened and his breathing remained steady.

I trailed gentle fingers over the notch of his hips, pressing lightly with my thumbs as I moved closer and leaned over him. Touching my mouth to the mark at the center of his chest, I attempted to ignore the distinct power thrumming through that mark and sinking inside me.

It felt like me, like death and life, decay and fresh growth all in the same breath. The next breath I drew in was sharp as I forced myself to calm, trailing my lips down the ridge at the center of the muscles of his stomach. Gray groaned beneath me, the sound of his pleasure making me burn in an entirely different way as it chased away the chill in my blood.

I slid my hand into the fly of his boxer briefs, wrapping my fingers around him. He was already hard, and the moan that sounded the moment I touched him felt like an echo of the desire building within me. "Witchling," he groaned, and I glanced up at him from beneath my lashes as I pulled him free.

His eyes were still closed, and I wondered if he recognized me in sleep or if he was only pretending to let me take what I wanted.

I leaned forward, running my tongue up the base of his cock. He twitched in my grip when I circled the head with my tongue, kissing down his shaft. He buried his hand in my hair, gripping it harshly and tugging my head back to meet his eyes as he woke. They burned with a combination of fury and desire, the pull sharp and everything I needed.

I could claim I needed to take charge all I wanted, but there was something addictive about knowing I was only in control because he allowed it. There was something in the cruel punishment of his grip that made me want to please him, even aside from needing to do it so that I could hurt him the way he had me.

"What are you doing, Witchling?" he asked, his eyes dropping to where I stroked him with my hand.

"I would think that was obvious," I said with a chuckle. His hand loosened, maintaining its place on my head but relenting some of his control. I leaned forward, pressing a teasing kiss to the head of his cock.

"Fuck," he hissed, bucking his hips up as he watched me. "Why?"

"Because I want to," I answered, spreading my mouth wide and slowly drawing him in. At first it was just the head that I enveloped, swirling my tongue over it before I sank farther down and took him deeper. He groaned when I pulled back, shifting to get a better angle and taking him in once more.

He pressed up, thrusting his hips to give me more than he thought I could handle. I swallowed around him, taking him into my throat and watching as his eyes widened in surprise. His grip on my hair tightened, pulling me off his cock as I glared at him smugly.

I wanted him to know. I wanted it to bother him.

I wanted it to drive him to rage, because he'd been a part of what was done to me. He'd had a hand in what I'd had to learn to please him, even indirectly. "You've done this before," he said, his voice dropping low into a growl as he pulled me up. I had no choice but to release him, letting him draw me up onto my knees as he moved to sit in front of me.

I said nothing, but I couldn't resist my smirk in the face of his jealousy. "I had to save my first blood for you. That doesn't mean I never had to do other things to learn how to please you."

He stilled, releasing my hair as he dropped his hand to his side. "What did you just say?"

"Don't pretend you didn't know," I said with a scoff, unable to stop my anger as I reached down and wrapped my fingers around him all over again. He was still hard in spite of his anger, and he hissed between his teeth when I squeezed and worked him.

He covered his hand with mine, stilling me as he raised his other hand to cup my cheek. "Who?" he asked, clenching his teeth as he bit out the word.

"I got to choose who I wanted most of the time, unless I lost a fight," I said, shrugging. His intensity washed away my anger and desire for him to know, making me waver on whether he'd been a part of it or not. He was furious, and the fact was undeniable looking at him.

The room seemed to grow darker with his fury, that light I'd felt shining from within him dampening until only darkness remained. "Unless you lost a fight . . ." he said, his voice trailing off.

"By the time I was eighteen, I'd already learned not to fucking lose, and that was when my father started betting things other than money," I explained, making an excuse for the few times I'd lost. In my father's words, if I weren't going to be the best fighter, I could at least learn how to distract a Vessel properly so that I never had to fight in the first place.

"What Charlotte did to him will never be enough," Gray said, holding my gaze with his as he took my face in his hands and pressed his forehead to mine.

"You really didn't know?" I asked, shock consuming me. After he revealed that he'd known my father, that he'd guided him to this path of vengeance, I had to assume he'd known everything about the way I'd been prepared for him. That it had brought him sick satisfaction to know he was training me to please him long before I ever even knew his name.

"He was supposed to give you a good life. Raise you for revenge, yes, but I told him to treat you well and make sure you were happy," he said.

"And in doing so, that is probably how you guaranteed he would abuse me. You took everything from him. You killed his sister, and even if he didn't know it was you in particular, he blamed the Vessels for it. You took what he loved, so he hurt the one thing that seemed to matter to you, in some way," I answered, shaking my head. Gray had thought he understood my father well enough to anticipate how he would behave.

He didn't know shit.

"I may not have been able to love at the time, but I remembered what it was to love all the same. I couldn't imagine a man would ever do something like that to someone he loved—"

"And there was your first mistake," I said with a laugh, shaking my head from side to side. "My father never loved me. I was nothing but a tool to him, an idea *you* planted."

He swallowed, dropping one of his hands to grasp the bedding beneath him. He gripped it so hard he shredded it, making me gulp when those golden eyes held mine. "Why are you afraid of the dark?" he asked, and I knew without a second thought that he meant the blindfold during the Reaping.

It was my main concern when I found out it had been him that night, that he'd felt my fear. I thought maybe I'd hidden it well enough when he never spoke of it.

Exposing this part of myself felt like a betrayal, like giving him access to information he could use against me one day. I forced myself to offer it anyway.

If my past was what I needed to sacrifice to get my freedom in the end, then I would gladly give it.

"When I was younger, and I lost one of the cage fights . . ." I said, hesitating as I drew in a deep breath. It was a stupid secret to keep, foolish to hide the truth when he already knew the likely culprit. But it had always been *mine*. "My dad had this coffin that he buried in the yard beside the house. There was a steel door at the foot that opened into the basement. He used to put me in there and lock the door. There was no light to speak of, just the coffin walls pressing in on me," I answered, ignoring the way he flinched with every word.

"Why didn't you break out?" he asked, and I knew he meant that a coffin buried in the earth should have been easy work for a Green witch.

"My magic hadn't manifested yet," I said, giving away the answer as to how much younger I'd meant. A witch's magic manifested at sixteen, meaning that I had to have been younger when my father took to burying me alive.

He ground his teeth together, the sound of it making me shiver. I didn't offer any more details about how young I'd been when it started, or the nightmares that had plagued my sleep for years after.

"That's why Charlotte buried him alive of all things," he said, his voice trailing off as he considered it. "I'm sorry, Witchling. I had assumed you would be protected. That was my mistake, and it is not one that I will ever make again. You deserved to be loved. You deserved to be worshipped."

I huffed a laugh, the sound coming as bittersweet as it felt. "I was loved. My mom *loved* me. She made up for him."

"No. She loved you the way she should have, but that doesn't mean you didn't deserve more. You deserved everything," he said, touching my bottom lip with his thumb. He tugged it to the side as he leaned in, sealing his mouth over mine. The kiss was gentle, lacking the anger and heat that I'd wanted when I came into the bedroom.

I'd wanted to piss him off, not make him act sweet. One was

another battle in our war, but the gentleness he kissed me with was something else. It felt like I'd lost a battle, and I didn't even know why. Endearing myself to him was a good thing.

So why did I feel like it was my heart that had been cracked open all over again?

14

WILLOW

We showered together, his touch reverent but not sexual. It was caring and gentle, soothing and comforting.

His aim in that moment hadn't been to seduce me with his body, but with the heart he wanted me to believe in.

He'd left shortly after, leaving me to my thoughts for the day until he returned with a dress bag in hand. The promise of leaving the room had lightened something in me, drawing a smile from me that I hated the moment it appeared. I shouldn't have had to feel grateful for a semblance of freedom.

"I'm doing what I must to keep you safe. You know that, right?" he asked, forcing me to recognize just how much of my thought process he understood.

"I don't need to be protected," I snapped, crossing my arms over my chest. He dropped the dress bag, draping it over the bench at the foot of the bed and raising his hands to unbutton his suit jacket. He shrugged it off his shoulders in silence, laying it on the dress bag and moving on to the buttons of his shirt.

"You can say that all you want, but do you want to know what I think?" he asked, stepping closer as he shrugged off his shirt. He moved into my space, grasping my top by the hem and lifting it gently enough that I had to cooperate by raising my arms to help him. I hadn't bothered with a bra, not wanting to suffer through the discomfort just to hang out in a very limited space with one other occupant. He leaned in, putting his mouth by my ear as his chest pressed against mine.

"Not particularly, but I'm sure you're going to grace me with your opinion anyway," I mumbled, earning a deep chuckle of amusement from him.

"There's my cruel little witchling," he said, his voice warm as he settled his hand at the base of my spine. His fingers spread over me, pulling me tighter into his body. "I think you like knowing there's someone who cares about you enough to protect you from harm. I think you want to hate me for it, because you know there is nobody else who would do what I have for you."

I swallowed, hating the way those words tore through my wall. I'd said as much myself that night in the shower after the witches had attacked me. Who would care that I was gone aside from the brother I could never see again if I wanted to protect him?

As much as it pained me to admit, Gray would care. On some level, in some way, he would notice my absence.

It was more than I could say about anyone else.

"You're a bastard. You aren't supposed to take joy in reminding me I'm alone in the world," I said, pulling back as I fought the tightening in my chest.

He refused to release me, holding me firm as he raised a hand to my face and touched my cheek. "You've been alone, but you aren't anymore. When are you going to understand that?" he asked, holding my gaze. His golden eyes were so intense as he watched me that it felt like he was looking through my eyes and seeing every thought in my brain—feeling every emotion in my heart.

When the urge to run spread through my limbs, I ignored it. Pressing up onto my toes, I touched my mouth to his gently. His lips moved against mine slowly, guiding me through the careful kiss. He held me like I might shatter, as if I were made of glass, until I lowered my hands to his belt, tearing it open and yanking it out of his slacks.

He smiled against me, deepening the kiss as I made quick

work of his button and fly, shoving his pants down his thighs with quick, economical movements as he did the same to mine. He kicked off his shoes and the pants, stripping off his socks before making his way to the bed.

He settled against the pillows, crooking a finger at me to summon me to his side. I knelt on the end, crawling up his body the same way I had earlier that morning. Straddling his waist, I let the length of him brush against my center and groaned when I found him hard and ready for me. "For the record, Witchling," he said as I leaned over him, reaching up to tuck a stray hair behind my ear. "You cannot fuck me every time you don't want to confront your feelings for me."

"Can't I?" I asked, tilting my head to the side as I reached between us to grasp him. He laughed, his lips spreading with a blinding smile when I didn't bother to deny his insinuation.

There was no point. Even if it hadn't served my purpose, we both would have known it for the lie it was.

He reached down, putting his arms parallel to his body and pulling me farther up to where I was straddling his chest. He adjusted his hold, doing it all over again until I straddled his face.

"What are you doing?"

"Grab the headboard and hold on tight, my love," he ordered, wrapping an arm around each of my thighs. His fingers pressed into the skin, causing dimples to appear where he touched the soft flesh. He used his hold to force me to lower myself, holding tighter when I tried to resist. "Now sit," he growled, jerking me lower. His mouth touched my pussy, his tongue immediately moving against me as I gasped.

I threw my head back, my hands grabbing onto the headboard to steady myself as ordered. He devoured, drawing out a steady stream of moans from me I couldn't have held in if I'd tried. Curving my body forward with deep breaths, I glanced down at his face between my thighs. Golden eyes shone from beneath me, looking up at me and taking in the entirety of my body. From the swell of my thighs where they wrapped around his head to the curve of my stomach and the valley between my breasts, there was nothing he couldn't see.

There was nothing he didn't like.

I'd always been comfortable in my skin and in my body, but something about having a man who appreciated every inch made me love it even more. I felt beautiful with his eyes on me, raking in every part of me he could see. My hips moved of their own accord as he circled my clit with his tongue, applying just enough pressure to drive me closer to my orgasm without ever shoving me over that edge.

"Gray," I begged, my hips moving shamelessly and grinding against his face. He didn't speak as he let me take what I needed, using his mouth for my own pleasure. I leaned forward, pressing the top of my head against the headboard and dropping a hand between my legs to bury it in his hair. I held him still, pinning him where I wanted him as my need coiled tighter.

His fingers tightened on my thighs, yanking me back so suddenly that I felt airborne for a moment until my back bounced off the bed. He was on top of me in the next moment, placing a hand behind my knee and lifting it high as he drove inside me.

"Oh fuck," I groaned, spasming around him as he laid his weight over mine fully and plundered my mouth with his. I tasted myself on his lips, on his tongue as he ground deep between my thighs.

"Want to feel it when you come," he murmured, his mouth moving against mine as he pulled back and thrust forward with slow, hard strokes. My orgasm came on the third, forcing me to scream against his mouth as he swallowed the sound.

He fucked me through it, touching his mouth to mine when my breathing steadied. His thrusts slowed, something shifting as he shared my breath. I opened my eyes to find him staring down at me intently, his arms leaning into the bed beside my head until there was nothing but him and the warmth of his golden stare.

"Gray . . ." I trailed off, closing my eyes when it became too much.

"Let me love you," he said, his words softly spoken against my mouth. He took my hand in his, guiding it to the mark on the center of his chest and splaying my fingers over the place where his heart beat in tune with mine.

"I can't," I said, a sob breaking free.

"Oh, Witchling," he said, smiling sadly as he stared down at me. "You already are."

He hiked my leg higher, burrowing closer to my body as he kissed me. He didn't speak another word as he sought his own release slowly, building me up to another orgasm before he finally went over the edge. He lingered after he'd finished, his weight on me giving me comfort instead of claustrophobia.

I was so fucked.

15

GRAY

Willow sat on the edge of the bed, her hands on her knees as she stared toward the window at the edge of the room. She wanted to be out with nature, with the part of her that felt familiar in the chaos of what she was becoming. I unzipped the garment bag, watching as Willow rolled her eyes and stood to look at the dress I'd brought her. She wasn't normally overly concerned with dressing for anyone but herself and her own taste, and I could guess from the state of her mother's home and the reality of what her father had done to her life that she hadn't had much cause for formal celebrations.

But as the garment bag parted and allowed for the black fabrics to appear, she rose to her feet and came to get a closer look. The tulle skirt had sporadic vines and flowers falling from the waistline where it would drape over her legs—except for the slit that went high up the thigh and would let her move freely if needed. The torso was corseted and covered in silk and lace that reminded me of the lattice ironwork of the Tribunal doors. The delicate fabric vines looped over one of her shoulders, accentuating the sweetheart neckline.

She touched a gentle finger to the vines, her matte black polish a perfect complement to the gown that had been made for her.

"Where exactly are we going?" she asked, crossing her arms over her chest.

"The Tribunal room," I said, going to the dresser where I'd had some of the staff move her clothing. I grabbed a black lace thong, taking a knee in front of her.

She was still nude, not having bothered to dress after I'd had my way with her. I'd tugged on a pair of boxer briefs when I stood to get her dress, but I loved that Willow owned her sexuality. Her body was perfect as it was, everything I could have wanted in my wife, and it pleased me that she was comfortable in it.

"You do realize most men take a knee when they propose, not after they've manipulated a woman into marriage, yes?" she asked as I smirked up at her. I wrapped a hand around the back of her calf, lifting it toward me so that she had to balance. Where others might have stumbled from the change in stability, Willow didn't so much as shift as her other leg took over. Slipping her foot into the thong, I repeated the process with the other leg and then rose in front of her as I glided the fabric up her strong thighs and settled it into place.

Cupping her face in both hands, I ran my thumbs over the apples of her cheekbones and watched her eyes flare to life. More than just filling with *her* and with the challenge that always came from my physical ownership of her, the magic within her recognized its previous owner and brightened for me.

Her naturally unique eyes lit with the glow of magic, the gold in one of hers so similar to mine that it took my breath away. A symbol of the way our fates had been linked since the moment Charlotte and I struck our bargain, I'd never expected to find so much comfort in the fact that I'd never really had a choice.

I didn't like not being in control of every aspect of my life and my home, except for Willow Morningstar. She was the exception to every rule I'd ever made for myself and my kind.

"And what are we doing in the Tribunal room that requires a gown like that?" she asked, swallowing through the touch and the discomfort she felt because of it. She thought I didn't see every nervous tic—even though she seemed determined to convince me she was on her way to forgiving me.

Whatever purpose that served for Willow, I'd allow it. If she faked it for long enough, eventually she wouldn't be able to see through her own lies and they would become her new reality.

"We are settling the disputes among the witches by announcing the Covenant's replacement," I said, stepping away from her and pointedly ignoring her sigh. She would have merely argued it was of relief, but we both knew it was because she regretted the lack of touch as much as I did.

"Who?" she asked, stepping to the bench and lifting the dress from the bag. She unzipped the corset, stepping into the dress and turning to give me her back. She was many things, but she would never forgo her responsibility to her Coven. No matter what she might have convinced herself she was here to do, she felt the urge to repair what she had played a role in breaking.

I raised my brow at her, smirking as she fought to find the zipper. Guiding her to the mirror in the corner, I brushed her hair over one shoulder. Wrapping that hand around her and pressing it to her stomach, I used my free hand to zip the corset for her. It glided up like butter, fitting her perfectly and hugging every one of her curves in the way I'd known it would. "There's only one witch fit for the job."

"The Tribunal will never accept me as Covenant," she argued, shaking her head as if I were ridiculous. "If you're hoping to quiet the fights, this isn't the way to do it."

I stepped away from her, moving to the top drawer of the dresser and the jewelry boxes I'd stashed there. Willow reached into the intricate vine details crossing her chest, pulling her mother's amulet and her bone necklace free so that they draped over the fabric, looking menacing compared to the delicate nature of the dress.

Her mother's amulet hung low, and I knew that even though it no longer served a purpose and did nothing to protect her, she would wear it for the rest of her life. The bones protected her from compulsion by nature now that she'd claimed them as hers.

She touched the bones with a grimace, and I knew she was desperately wishing there was a way for her to wear them the same way all her ancestors had, in a pouch at her waist rather than draped at her throat. I reached a hand toward her, drawing my finger over the bones in a gentle path that curved over her collarbone. I liked seeing the macabre reminder of just how gruesome her power could be if she accepted it, but I also liked the sight of her chest bare without anything obstructing my view.

The bones clattered, releasing from around her throat with my touch. Guiding them to her waist, I watched as they settled across her hips like a low-slung chain, draping over her gently and accentuating the curve of her body.

Willow touched her chest and neck, splaying her fingers over her skin. Her relief hung between us as she shifted her weight, the bones clanging against one another. "And who from the Tribunal would you be willing to have take your place?" I asked, setting the jewelry boxes on the bed. I opened the first one while she gawked at it, watching me warily as I settled the gold choker around the back of her neck. It was structured, draping over the front of her throat without ever connecting and lingering between the sides of her mother's wire chain. I accompanied it with the matching gold earrings I'd bought her, threading them through her ears while she stared up at me with a glare.

She didn't appreciate my gifts, in spite of my intention to court her.

"That's not fair," she said finally, unable to come up with an adequate solution to the question I posed.

"That's because they were all aware of the previous Covenant's intentions for this Coven, and you know as well as I do that you would never give one of them your support," I said, dropping the earring box to the bed. I grasped the final box, ignoring Willow's gasp. The rings in the box were the perfect culmination of everything that made her the witchling she'd become, a gold band carved into the details of vines and leaves. The center stone was moss agate in place of a traditional diamond, but the meaning of that and the simple matching band of golden vines beneath it far outweighed tradition.

"Gray," she said, shaking her head as I reached for her left hand.

I smiled as I took it, holding her still as I slid the rings onto her ring finger. "You said you weren't a demon, and our marriage traditions aren't yours," I said, admitting to the truth and using her own words against her. "I intend to marry you in every tradition, Witchling. You'll wear my rings, and as soon as we are able, you will summon the Goddess and we will seek her approval for our union."

"Why would she ever agree to this marriage? The Goddess claims the witches you abandoned," she claimed.

I scoffed, tucking a stray hair behind her ear. She looked up at me, finally tearing her eyes away from the rings I'd placed on her finger. Another mark of my ownership of her. Reaching into my pocket, I removed the single golden band and slid it onto my own, marking myself the same as her. "Where does the Coven teach you their Goddess came from?" I asked, watching as everything in Willow stilled.

"She is the personification of nature itself. She represents the balance," Willow argued, the ignorance of what I allowed as teachings showing in every word. Even if she hadn't been in the Coven to learn, her mother had relayed the message.

"She represents *me*," I said, pausing to see if she had any response. Her mouth tensed into a line, revealing her frustration that I'd been playing the chess game before the Coven even realized one existed. "Because your Goddess is my sister." I grinned at her shock, straightening her necklace as she stared up at me.

16

WILLOW

Gray laced up the boots he'd bought me as a compromise on the combat boots he knew I would have demanded to wear. I sat processing his words, silent as I tried to understand just how far back all of this went. How was I supposed to function on the path to revenge when there were centuries of history I didn't even *know*?

"Your sister?" I asked, pressing my lips together.

He nodded, glancing up at me with bright golden eyes through dark lashes. "Another angel cast down from Heaven," he answered, standing smoothly as he caught my hand and guided me to my feet before him. He fluffed out the length of my hair, the bright red ends standing out sharply against the black fabric. "I am not the only one who has earned my father's wrath over the centuries since our creation. I was merely the first."

"What did she do?" I asked, avoiding asking him about his own banishment. I knew what we believed. I knew what the humans believed. I had no doubt both versions of the story were biased in the opposite way of what his would be.

Gray grinned as he guided me to the mirror in the corner of his bedroom, taking his place behind me as he left me with no choice but to stare at my own reflection. Even with the wedges on my knee-high boots, he was far taller than me. "The same thing as me," he said, giving me a vague response. The fact that he didn't trust me enough to provide a sliver of the truth shouldn't have surprised me given my own nefarious reasons for even asking the question in the first place.

If I weren't trustworthy, I couldn't exactly be angry that he didn't trust me. He shouldn't, but I needed him to anyway.

"And what was that exactly?" I asked, swallowing as I asked the question I didn't really want to know the answer to. I wanted everything to remain black and white, not muddled with personal bias and middle ground.

"I'm sure you've heard the story," Gray said dismissively.

"I want to hear it from you, not an ancient text that has passed through so many hands and translations nothing is certain anymore," I said, holding his stare.

"You're hoping it won't be true," he said as I turned to face him slowly. It suddenly seemed so important that I felt his gaze on me for this conversation, not saw it reflected in the mirror.

Mirrors were gateways, and I didn't want to risk someone sharing the intimacy of this moment centuries from now when my great-granddaughter wandered into my memories.

"I'm not hoping for anything. I just want to understand my husband," I said, hating the truth in the words. He knew my deepest shames, my darkest secrets, yet I knew so little of his history from him directly.

"I loved my father," he said, the somber expression on his face reminding me so much of the portrait of Lucifer falling from grace that he kept in his office. *His reminder.* "I loved him so much that I never wanted to risk anyone turning away from him. The fact that they might not make it to Heaven and feel the warmth of his embrace was unfathomable to me. I wanted to make it so that humans could not choose to sin at all, rather than risk them being condemned."

I sighed, hating the sympathy I felt. Was it any different from when a parent placed restrictions on their children until they proved they could make good choices?

I didn't know, and I hated that lack of clarity.

"You wanted to strip them of their free will," I said instead, seeking for him to own up to the actions he knew I wouldn't agree with. I wanted his honesty more than anything, even if it couldn't change anything about my opinion of the creature he'd become.

"I wanted to do whatever it took to make sure that they never made the *wrong* choice," he corrected, his conviction of those words striking something deep inside me. His eyes flared as if he understood it, too, the parallels we could draw between what he'd wanted for humans all those years ago and the situation he'd forced me into now. "It's different," he said, shaking his head in frustration.

"Is it? Am I free to make a choice you don't agree with then?" I asked, wincing when he took a step back from me. I grabbed on to his forearm, holding him still and forcing him to stay with me for this conversation.

If he could trap me in this relationship, then he could damn fucking well listen to what I had to say about it.

"You can choose anything else you want, *anything,* as long as you choose *me,*" he said, covering my hand on his forearm with his own. His fingers curled around me, gripping more fully than I'd expected since I'd thought he meant to be gentle.

"That's not how it works and you know it," I said, my voice stern but soft.

"Why not?!" he yelled, pulling back from me. He paced in a circle, his breathing erratic in his anger. The display was so out of character for him that it made me flinch, but the pain on his face when he turned to look at me finally had my shoulders dropping, the fight draining out of me. "I have given enough. I have *lost* enough. I am not going to lose you, too."

In spite of my best intentions, the back of my throat burned. His pain was so palpable, so like mine, that it struck me just how similar we were in so many ways.

I stepped toward him cautiously, closing the distance until I stopped just in front of him. Reaching up to cup his face in my hands, I gave him the truth even if I knew it would hurt him. An eternity of *this* would hurt more. "Because until you're willing to let me go, you're never really going to have me at all. You're always going to wonder if I would stay—if I would *choose* you if given the chance, and not knowing is going to haunt you for the rest of your days."

His brow furrowed, his face twisting as he considered my warning. That sounded like an eternity of absolute misery to me, never being able to trust in anything the man I loved said.

Always waiting for him to leave.

I released his face, turning to walk away. He still needed to dress for the evening, and I'd done enough to put him on edge for the night. "I'll let you get dressed," I said, the gentleness in my voice surprising even me. If he was truly like me, he needed a moment to gather his thoughts in privacy.

I headed for the door, pausing when Gray caught my arm gently. I turned my head to look at him over my shoulder, finding his back still mostly to me. "Would you?" he asked. "Stay? Would you choose me?" he asked, and the vulnerability in that question reminded me of someone so much younger than Lucifer Morningstar.

"I don't know. I can't choose you until you give me the choice," I said, pushing through my hesitance to answer. I'd wanted to hurt him, wanted to get revenge for what he'd done to me. But this somehow felt like kicking an injured puppy when he was down. "And you never will."

I walked out of the room, leaving him to his thoughts. I'd thought hurting him would make me feel better, would help me feel like I'd taken a little bit more of my power back.

But I just felt like shit.

I waited for Gray to emerge, keeping the notion of winning his trust in the back of my mind as I approached him and straightened his tie. He'd donned his careful mask all over again, the vulnerability of a few moments ago a thing of the past.

But I saw it in the way he studied me, in the way he considered if there were any truth to my words. Maybe he was without a conscience and what I wanted didn't matter to him at all as long as he had what he wanted.

Or maybe I'd struck a nerve.

"What exactly are you expecting from me tonight?" I asked, peering up at him from beneath my lashes in a peace offering. His gaze was intense on mine, as if he saw right through my actions, so I turned my stare to the window to hide them. The lights surrounding the school illuminated the gardens just outside the building, casting eerie shadows over the cemetery in the distance. The bones pressed into my waist, reminding me of their presence as I stared at the witches who'd been buried unceremoniously. The call of that magic was so overwhelming I barely managed to tear my gaze away, looking toward Gray's knowing stare.

"It's okay to answer the call," he said, turning my face to his again. He touched my cheek, cupping it with a gentleness that grounded me against the violence in that magic. It was life and death, the swirl of a storm of two clashing forces.

One could not exist without the other, and yet it felt as if the two would tear me to shreds long before they ever managed to successfully coexist.

"Why did you tell my father to seduce my mother in particular? Why did it have to be a Green?" I asked, unable to stop the question from escaping me. The more pressing question was what he expected of me, but in the moments where I felt like I was only an inch from breaking, I couldn't be bothered to care.

Gray sighed, moving to the arm of the sofa. He sat down, perching gently as he spread his legs and guided me between them. Even sitting, he was so tall he came to my throat. Taking my hands in his, he worried them with the anxiety of answering things he thought better left in the past.

I could read it on his face, that bond between us pulling taut. I didn't need to read his mind to know his thoughts, and I hated what it did to my emotions regarding him.

"Charlotte was the most powerful witch I'd ever known," he said, his voice sad—as if he missed the woman he'd admired in his own way. "Until you."

"So you wanted me to be powerful?" I asked.

"No, if anything you being stronger than her would put me at a disadvantage, but I watched countless Hecate witches, Charlotte included, be corrupted by the call of death and the overwhelming power it gave them. I wanted to take the opportunity to give you a chance to still feel alive, even if you were surrounded by the bones of the dead," he said.

"But you'd never planned for me to survive," I said, because his words didn't make any sense.

"I didn't plan for you to survive until I saw your dream self lurking when I killed Loralei. I claimed you that night," he said, reaching up to brush his fingers over the mark I'd woken with fifty years after he gave it to me. "I never intended for that claim to be anything less than permanent, and I knew adding some life to the necromancy would be your best chance."

"My best chance for what?"

"Surviving me," he said, pushing to his feet. He guided me to the door as I stumbled after him, faltering as I considered his words. Did that mean he thought I would outlive him? Or simply that I would be able to survive the things he put me through?

Jonathan meowed as we headed for the door, jumping down from his perch on the back of the sofa and stretching.

"I don't understand," I said, letting Gray guide me into the hallway. He held out his arm, and I took it even though I wanted to snub him. I didn't think I had many allies outside him and my friends, and I wasn't dumb enough to think the Coven would welcome me with open arms. They'd tear me apart with their bare hands if I let them.

"I'm not an easy man to love, Witchling, but if anyone stands a chance of doing it and coming out the other side, it's you," he said, leaving me reeling. Knowing what he said was true was different than hearing him admit that he knew it, too. "You asked what I expect of you tonight," he said, shocking me when he paused in the middle of the hall and changed the conversation. I understood the urgency with where we were about to go, but my brain struggled to keep up nonetheless. "I don't *expect* anything of you, but I would appreciate it if you could set aside your animosity toward me long enough to present a united front."

"Are you asking me?" I asked with a scoff. Gray didn't ask for anything.

"Juliet reminded me that if I'd wanted an obedient plaything, I could have had a dozen choices who would be willing to do just that," he said, smirking at the fury that overcame my face.

My cheeks went hot as I yanked back my arm. "Thank you for that explicit reminder."

"But I don't want that, and I never have. I want a partner. I want a woman who loves me enough to be willing to challenge me to see the world a different way. I want you, Willow, and I understand that I cannot have you if I tell you to do what you're told," he said. "I may not be ready to allow you to choose everything, but I can give you this right now."

"Who are you and what have you done with Headmaster Thorne?" I asked, quirking a brow at him as I crossed my arms over my chest.

"I'm not saying I won't piss you off or do shit you despise nearly every day, but I'm saying that in this, I can stand at your side and let you choose to do the same for me," he said, grasping my arm and tucking it back into his so we could resume walking.

"Why didn't you just let me make my choice when I tried to leave? I didn't *want* to abandon them," I said, referring to the Coven I'd condemned to infighting.

"Because I'm not ready to say goodbye, and you were reacting on impulse out of fear. The Willow I know would never back down from a fight, and do you remember what I told you when you asked what happens when you're tired of fighting?" he asked, making my heart skip in my chest at the reminder of that night. Of the beating I'd suffered and how broken it had made me feel that I had confided in a man who was supposed to be my enemy.

"This is different," I argued.

"I told you that you would let me fight for you. You gave up on us, but I never stopped fighting, Witchling," he said as we reached the top of the stairs. He released me long enough to let me gather one side of my dress in my hand and lift it so that I could descend them smoothly. The stones at my feet seemed to recognize me, rising up to meet me with every step and offering what comfort the cold surface could provide.

"So you want me to play the role of the woman in love with the devil who decimated the entire Coven?" I whispered.

"No. I want you to tell the truth. I manipulated you just as much as any of them, and I don't care if they know that truth. I'm the devil, not a saint," he explained with a smirk. "I want you to take the Coven that belongs to you regardless of your mistakes, and recognize the need for stability in this chaos. You and I will lead our peoples the same way the Covenant was always designed to do."

We continued down the stairs in silence, Gray seeming to understand that I needed time to process how this would play out and what I wanted to do to make it happen. I didn't want my Coven to be at war with the Vessels and archdemons and understood that would bring nothing but death, but what did I know about leading them?

I glanced out the windows as we passed, my eyes immediately drawn to that cemetery once more.

I'd give them something they hadn't had in a long time.

I'd give them the truth.

17

WILLOW

The Tribunal doors were cast wide open, the locking mechanism useless. Never before had the entire Coven been allowed within these walls, only the select few permitted to be in the private space of the Covenant previously.

But there was no Covenant left to respect, and I knew what would happen to the Coven after centuries of strict leadership. They'd descend into chaos; they'd turn on those who had once been friends in an effort to fill the vacuum of power.

Gray guided me within the doors, the murmur of voices immediately an assault compared to the normally quiet place of somber respect. I drew in a deep breath as we passed through the bubble to enter the center circle, which was far too crowded, that same popping sensation pulsing within me as I felt like I'd plunged underwater.

Even without the Covenant, this place was holy to our magic. Sacred to us.

I would not see it desecrated.

The boundary seemed to hum in agreement with me as Gray attempted to tug me through to the other side, the tiny pinprick of magic piercing the skin of my arms. The boundary held me steadfast, consuming me as blood welled from the minor injuries it had caused. I watched single beads rising from needlelike wounds float through the magic of the boundary as Gray watched in smug satisfaction. They collected into a large tear-shaped droplet, hovering in front of me until I raised a hand to rest beneath it.

The boundary released me finally, allowing me to step through to the other side. Sound returned immediately, the frenzied murmur of voices drowned out by one man's furious scolding as he launched a tirade toward Gray.

"What is the meaning of this? You decorate your whore in the bones of the legacy we *lost* now?" Itan asked, waving a hand toward me and the bones lingering at my waist.

Hearing Gray growl at Itan's foul name-calling, I took a step toward him, the bone clacking together, and moved directly past him to approach the abandoned Hecate throne where it had been left to rot. The blood moved with me, and I glanced back toward the boundary, which had somehow known I would need it and found myself without a knife.

Stupid.

"What is lost can always be found, Itan," I said, raising my chin and glaring at him. It was safe to say that most of the Coven hadn't heard the truth of my lineage, as they stared back at me in confusion.

Itan recoiled physically, looking as if he'd been struck, before he recovered with a shake of his head. "Bullshit," he said, tilting his face up. He left me with no choice, forcing me to do the one thing that I would never be able to come back from.

When I thought of the wrongs I could right, I wasn't sure I would ever want to.

The Hecate throne called to me as I stepped up in front of it and stared down at the aging seat that was crafted from the bones of those who had come before me. The ones settled at my waist were finger and hand bones, the smallest parts of my ancestors, but the throne had been remade from the remains of the first generations of Hecate witches.

Turning to look over my shoulder at Itan, I smirked as I cast my glance toward Gray. He crossed his arms over his chest, watching in amusement as I dropped my hand to my side. The blood that had levitated in front of me fell, splashing all over the yellowing bones.

"Congratulations. You can make a mess as well as any child attempting to play with the grown-ups. What was that supposed to prove?" Itan asked, resulting in the chime of laughter from his supporters who hid behind him.

My smirk shifted into a smile as I turned to face him fully. Lips pulling back over my teeth, I refused to look at Iban as I prepared for his uncle's shame. "Are you completely unfamiliar with foreplay?" His brow furrowed as I raised my hand, waving it in a lazy motion toward the bones that were now covered in my blood.

Covered in my magic.

The chair groaned, creaking as the bones began to shift, collapsing to the tile floor until the throne was gone.

"I don't understand," someone whispered, lacking patience.

I waited for that somehow familiar sound of bones clacking together, feeling every touch resonate in my soul. I didn't bother to look as I felt the bones assemble themselves into the body of a man, standing on top of one another and moving until his figure shifted forward to stand at my side.

Somewhere in the room, Gray barked a laugh of pure joy, the warmth of it coating my skin as Itan stared at the skeleton beside me in horror. "You." He paused, looking back and forth between me and the creature I'd summoned from the dead with merely a wave of my hand and the release of blood. "But you're a Madizza! I've seen it with my own eyes."

I turned my attention toward the Madizza throne, lifting my dress slightly and stomping a single foot upon the floor. The vines of the Madizza throne squirmed instantly, sliding out of the places they'd been trapped for centuries. The throne slid along the ground, shifting into nothing but a tangle of roses and vines and thorns as it made its way across the center of the Madizza circle. It climbed the steps of the dais, centering itself where the two thrones of the Covenant had once been.

I had no idea what Gray had done with them, but the knowledge that he'd paved the way for me to do exactly what I'd chosen to do sank deep into the pit of my stomach. I didn't like being predictable.

I nodded to the skeleton, earning a wordless nod back before he proceeded to the dais along with the vines. He crumpled to the floor on top of them, and I watched in satisfaction as the vines wound around the remnants of my ancestors.

Uniting them as one.

They twisted and turned, maneuvering their way into a throne anew. A throne of bones and blood and life.

I took the steps slowly, one at a time, as I exhaled a single sigh with my back to the Coven.

Turning to face them, I took the throne that could belong to no one but me in the place where the Covenant had once sat. "Anything else, Itan, or are you done questioning me now?"

18

WILLOW

I tan glared at me, taking the first step toward the dais. He paused only when Gray moved to join me, stepping up the two stairs to stand beside the throne I'd claimed. Gray faced the windows at my back, pausing and reaching to capture my chin. Tilting my face up to his, he smiled down at me with something that felt far too much like pride. Considering the Coven couldn't see his face, my heart throbbed, knowing it was just for me and not part of the spectacle.

When was the last time anyone but him had looked at me like that?

He leaned down, touching his lips to mine gently for the Coven to see. I sighed into his mouth, both loving and hating the public display that would leave absolutely no question about Itan's accusation. For those who believed in demeaning the place of women by reducing us to whether or not we enjoyed sex, Gray had added fuel to the fire.

Except by those standards, I wasn't Lucifer's *whore*. I was His fucking *wife*, and I would not let my sex life determine my value.

"Never stop surprising me, Witchling," Gray said, turning to stand beside my newly crafted throne. He looked far too comfortable there, absolutely willing to allow me to have a moment to shine if we wanted to achieve what we'd set out to do. True power wasn't about bluster and bravado. It didn't lie in the moments where I put on a show to make the weaker minds of men like Itan understand.

It was in the quiet peace of the night, where men like Lucifer could be comfortable in their own skin and the knowledge that nothing and no one could stop them from taking what they wanted.

"You don't deny it then? You've reduced yourself to being a plaything for this asshole?" Itan asked, turning to glare at Iban where he watched with a face that had paled with shock.

"I deny nothing," I said, getting more comfortable in my chair. I leaned back, letting my hands rest on the arms and crossing my legs carefully. "Though I think we can agree, I seem to be far more than a plaything. Perhaps the real reason you find him to be such a threat is because he actually respects women enough to allow me to sit at his side."

"Willow is my wife, and soon we will make it official before your Goddess. At that time, I expect you will all fall in line and accept this union for what it is: the chance for us to start anew. We have the opportunity to come together in truth, our peoples united by marriage," Gray said as I leaned forward in my seat.

"I must confess though, Itan, you will not be around to witness what becomes of this Coven," I said, tapping my finger on the vines of my throne. They moved forward slowly, and Itan panicked and fought for control of the plant life that should have belonged to him just as much as me.

But he hadn't nourished his relationship with the earth, had in fact acted against it for his own self-interest. I'd only taken what I'd given in equal measure, maintaining the balance to the best of my ability and offering as much love as I received.

The vines ignored his call.

"Willow, stop this!" Iban called, his voice penetrating the silence of those observing. The vines wrapped around Itan's ankles, holding him in place when he turned to flee.

He struck out with his magic, catching a single vine from the

Bray throne. It struck me across the chest, tearing the delicate organza at the top of my dress and ripping into my skin. I stared down at it, looking at the parting of my flesh for a moment. The pain was bearable when it should not have been, a dull throb when it should have been nothing but blinding heat. Gold spread over the wound as if it were molten, the same exact color as Gray's eyes as he stared down at me and clenched his teeth.

His nostrils flared as I held up a hand, watching with a horrifying realization as the gold receded and the wound healed over for all to see.

"That's impossible. Only the Covenant is eternal," Itan said, struggling against the bonds of the vines as they spread up his chest and over his shoulders. They pulled him to his knees, the thump of him striking the stone echoing through the room.

"Were they really, though?" I asked, scrunching my nose as I remembered the way they had burst into chunks of flesh and blood.

"You backstabbing bitch! She was your grandmother," Itan said, spitting at my feet.

"She was an abomination to this Coven," I said, rising to my feet. I descended the steps, stopping directly before Itan as I looked around the room. "And you are going to tell them exactly what she conspired with the Tribunal members to do."

Itan blanched, staring up at me as his brow furrowed. There was a question there, a sincere lack of understanding as to how I might have come to know the truth.

"How—"

"That's right, Itan. I know what you did to this Coven, and I know what you did to their daughters," I said, gesturing to the Coven members staring at me. "And you are going to confess to it all."

The vines squeezed tighter around him, making him groan as the creak sounded through the room. "Go to Hell."

"Tell them why the witches are buried in boxes when they should be with their elements. Tell them why you have deprived the Source of our magic when we return it to the balance. Tell them how you starved it and weakened them, all with the intent for each and every one of them to be a sacrifice so that you could live free of the Vessels when they were all dead."

I raised a hand, touching a single finger to the front of his throat. One of the vines followed, wrapping around his neck and squeezing there as he glared up at me. He gasped for breath, struggling against the binds that held him tightly secured.

"Willow!" Iban protested, coming to stand beside me. Gray blocked his path, forcing him to keep his distance as his uncle sputtered for breath. I leaned in close enough for my face to fill Itan's vision, making sure it was all he could see as everything went fuzzy and he fought for breath.

"Tell your nephew what you did to *her*," I said with a sneer. I didn't give her name, but the shocked gasp drew my eyes to the center of the crowd. Margot's deep mahogany eyes met mine, gaping at me in surprise as she covered her mouth with her hands. Iban followed my stare, his brow furrowing as he glanced between us and his uncle.

I raised my hand, motioning as the vines wound between Itan's legs and put pressure on the part of him that he'd used for violence against a girl who hadn't wanted it. "Uncle," Iban said, but the caution in his voice broke something inside me. Iban was all about family and the bonds of it, having given up everything for the potential to create a new one of his own. Knowing that someone he loved and valued with a bond like that could be capable of such horrible things would ruin him.

Margot shocked me, stepping forward to make her way through the crowd. She came up beside me without a word, slipping her hand into mine. Her grip trembled as she took her place and stared down at her abuser as his face turned purple.

"Enough," she muttered. I released the vine around his throat immediately, watching him collapse to his chest on the tile. I allowed him to fall, smacking his face against the floor as his lip split beneath the force.

"Margot, thank you," he wheezed, the hoarse sound of his voice barely reaching us, though we stood in front of him.

Margot took a step forward, pressing the toe of her heel to the top of Itan's hand. She ground it down, drawing a scream from his throat as those mahogany eyes of hers heated to liquid fire. "I did not stop her for your sake," she said, squatting down in front of him carefully. There was such grace in the movement, a fluidity that I would never hope to possess as she tucked her dress neatly behind her knees. "I want to hear you say it."

"Say what?"

"Tell them what you did to me," she said, her voice holding steady even as her nostrils flared. The wetness of tears filled her eyes, but she never allowed them to fall. From the corner of my eye, I watched Gray shake his head at Beelzebub as he stepped forward. There was fury written on his face, his body tense and a barely controlled killing machine. He froze in place, staring at Lucifer as if he might rip His head off. Margot pressed her foot down harder, shifting to put the stiletto of her heel in the center of his hand.

He groaned as I twisted my hand, allowing my vines to wind their way beneath the hem of his shirt and touch the waistband of his pants. The threat alone was enough to make him startle, jumping in place as if he could stop it. "I snuck into your room at night," he said, keeping his words vague.

"And did what?" Margot asked, shocking me as she stood and took a step back from him. I used the vines to force him up from the floor, putting him back on his knees so that Margot could have a shot at the most intimate part of him if she chose.

"Touched you."

"No," she spat, leaning into his face. "You didn't *touch* me. You raped me. Say the word."

"You little bitch—"

"Say the fucking word. Admit what you did to her and what you and the rest of the Tribunal conspired to do to this Coven, and I will give you a swift death. But make no mistake, Itan, you will die either way. I will make sure you suffer for every day you made her have to look at your disgusting face, fearing that it would be the day you came back," I said, waiting as he considered.

He glanced toward the other Tribunal members, the horror on their faces bringing me sick satisfaction. It would only take one confession for the victims of their plan to rally. For them to realize what their own family had intended to do to them to gain more power.

"*I raped you,*" he said, making the only correct choice. Margot slumped in relief, her breathing turning ragged at the words finally being spoken. Beelzebub was there immediately, tucking her into his chest so that she could hide the emotions. I glared at him but didn't say a word, knowing that she didn't need me to draw attention to her any longer.

"And the rest?" I asked, feeling Gray take his place behind me.

"The Covenant and the Tribunal conspired to rid Crystal Hollow of the Vessels once and for all," he said, and I smiled at his attempt to word it as if they were the heroes.

"Tell them how you planned to do that."

He groaned, clenching his teeth. "Don't say another word!" the Petra Tribunal member shouted.

"We were going to starve them. To do that, we were starving the Source. When the magic dies, so do the family lines. Breeding becomes more difficult, witches fall sick. Their blood becomes less potent until . . ."

"Finish it, Itan," I said, watching him carefully.

"Until only the Tribunal remained. The Vessels cannot feed on us without breaking the bargain, and the Vessels would then be weak enough to fade away. The Tribunal members would carry the magic within us then, and we would return the power to the Source. We'd fix it," he said, as if it changed anything.

"You mean after everyone in the Coven was dead, you'd fix it for yourselves," I said, waiting for him to put the final nail in his coffin.

"Yes. That's exactly what I mean," he agreed.

Granting him the swift death he didn't deserve, I wrapped my vine around his throat once again and twisted, snapping his neck quickly and efficiently.

It was more than I could say for the Coven members, who turned on the elders of their lines, eradicating the current Tribunal from existence.

I spun from the bloodshed, making my way to the doors that would take me outside. "Where are you going?" Iban asked, staring at me as if he'd never seen me before.

"I'm going to right another wrong."

19

WILLOW

Gray shouted my name from the carnage of Coven members turning on their Tribunal behind me, and I could practically sense him making his way through the crowd to follow after me. I waved a hand, slamming the doors of the Tribunal room closed behind me. Vines threaded through the gilded iron of the gates, entwining around the locking mechanisms and sealing it like a tomb. Gray would be able to escape but I had to hope I'd bought myself some time.

His golden eyes met mine as the vines consumed the gate, slowly filling the gaps. His face was set in stone, but it wasn't only rage that filled his expression.

It was fear.

This was something I had to do alone, in the quiet of the night, without the bluster an audience would need. They deserved to be put to rest in peace, brought to the very places where they always should have lain. It didn't matter that the silence would haunt me, that it would make every whispered word of the dead sink inside me and strike deep.

I made my way through the hall, going straight for the doors. Leviathan waited in front of them, leaning his back against the doorway lazily and fiddling with a dagger. I snatched it from his hands as I approached, ignoring the way he snapped to attention and stared down at me. "Consort?" he asked.

The doors were open, the quiet murmur drifting through the night air as I stared out. Leviathan stepped into my path when I didn't halt, blocking my way. "I have a name," I reminded him quietly, not daring to speak too loudly. The restless spirits were too close, the joint force of their whispers rising as even the quiet ones began to speak.

They knew I was here. They knew what I'd come to do.

"Willow," Leviathan said, drawing my attention off that horrifying cemetery to meet his stare finally. "What are you doing?"

"I can hear their cries," I admitted, steering my attention back to the cemetery in the distance. Leviathan turned to look over his shoulder, following the path of my gaze. His body seemed to deflate when he finally made the connection. I took the opportunity, slipping past him easily and stepping into the night air.

He grabbed my arm in a gentle hold, his fingers wrapping fully around. "Where's Lucifer?" he asked finally, holding me still as he looked back toward the Tribunal.

"He's otherwise occupied," I said evasively, pulling my arm out of his grip. My time was limited before Gray broke free from the Tribunal doors. They were meant to answer to witch blood, and I had to hope that he did not possess what was needed to open them himself.

Leviathan released me rather than risk hurting me, allowing me to hike up my skirt and continue on my way. Each step took me closer, the murmur of those voices growing louder until it felt like I was surrounded by the screams.

"Fuck," Leviathan grunted, hurrying forward and abandoning his post. He stepped in front of me again. "Just wait—"

"I have to do this," I said, keeping my eyes on that cemetery. I couldn't look away, could barely even hear myself speak over the pain of those witches, who had been separated from everything they held sacred.

Leviathan stared down at me, carefully studying the desolate determination on my face before he finally nodded and stepped aside.

He took up his stride with me, following along. "What are you do-ing?" I asked, faltering when he refused to leave me.

"You may have to do this, but that doesn't mean I'm going to let you do it alone," Leviathan said, his voice soft beneath the thrum of the dead. My veins pumped with the magic in my blood, the call of it singing through me.

I couldn't have turned back if I'd wanted to, not as my feet moved forward without my permission.

I glanced over at Leviathan sadly. "I'm *always* alone," I admit-ted, smiling as his face fell in response to my words. He stopped in place, and I turned away from him as I continued on. I didn't sense his footfalls behind me as I moved on, making my way toward the cemetery. Glancing back briefly, I found the space he'd stood before empty.

I ignored the pang of loneliness in my chest, letting it sink deep into that hole at the center of my very being. I was no stranger to going into terrifying situations alone, and in fact, it was where I found comfort. I could rely on myself, always.

It was everyone else who constantly disappointed me. Every moment of every day, I stood alone when things got tough.

I strode forward, only stopping when I reached the edge of the cemetery. The dirt beneath my feet changed, the rot and decay of those buried within making it more fertile. I felt the shift with one side of my magic, the way that life could thrive here as op-posed to the other sacred burial sites throughout Crystal Hollow.

Life went on, even when other kinds of magic had been starved.

I lifted my dress, carefully stepping into the inner ring of the cemetery. The chill of death washed over my skin immediately, the bubble of life outside bursting. A familiar woman waited for me in the center of the tombstones, her hair far too similar to mine and her purple eyes staring back at me.

"Hello, Willow," Loralei said, a small smile on her face. She raised a hand, and the voices of the other spirits lingering here faded to background noise. My relief was immediate, having not realized just how piercing the sounds had become and the way they'd battered at my skull.

In the quiet of the night, a piercing yowl finally penetrated the haze. Jonathan paced at the edge of the cemetery, hissing at it furiously but entirely unwilling to cross the boundary himself.

Loralei took my hand, her touch as cold as ice. I couldn't help the anger I felt looking at her, the knowledge that my father's love for her had been what had derailed my life entirely. He'd loved her in a way he'd never even thought to care for me, willing to sacrifice me for her even in death. "You must leave this place. You're not ready for this kind of magic yet."

"I can't leave them," I said, shaking my head. I raised my hand that held Leviathan's dagger, pressing it into the other palm, which Loralei released, and dragging it over the surface. Blood welled immediately, slipping onto the ground.

"It won't be enough," she said sadly, staring at the wound as it healed over. Whatever Gray had done to bring me back, it made me heal far too quickly for the shallow cuts I was used to giving offerings with.

"Willow," Gray said, stepping through the mist of Loralei. She vanished from sight, dispersing through the air as he appeared in front of me and took the dagger from my hands. I sighed, my frustration rising at the loss of her. I knew it had been a dream to think I could hold Gray for long enough, but I'd dared to have it anyway. "What were you thinking?"

"It has to be done," I said, closing my mouth as I looked around for the spirit of my aunt.

Gray shoved the dagger into the pocket of his suit, cupping my face in his hands and holding me still as he looked down at me. "What do I have to do to get through to you? You are *never* alone, and you didn't need to do *this* alone, either."

I clenched my teeth to fight back the burn of acid rising up my throat, the emotions surfacing as he used my own words against me. There was no doubt as to where Leviathan had gone, fetching the one man he thought could get through to me. "I can *hear* them, Gray. I'll never be able to sleep now that I've felt this pain, but I'm not strong enough. Loralei says I don't have enough control for something like this."

If it surprised him to know that my aunt had visited me, he didn't show it. "She's right. You aren't strong enough for this," he said, running his hands down over my arms. He took my hand in his, turning my palm to face the sky and staring at my forearm. "But we are together."

"I didn't think you would care about them," I admitted, swallowing as he withdrew the dagger once again and placed the tip to the inside of my wrist. "I thought you'd try to stop me."

"I don't, but I care about you. If this keeps you from being happy? Then I care about it." He pressed the tip into my skin, and I winced back and stared at him in horror.

"I'll lose too much blood."

He smiled at me, slowly pulling me back into his space. "I won't let anything happen to you. Do you trust me?"

"Absolutely fucking not," I said, my brow pinching when he laughed.

"Good girl," he said, tipping his head to the side. "But do you trust me to keep you *alive*?"

I paused, studying him and the blade pressed to my wrist that could end it all. He'd given me pieces of himself to bring me back once, and I'd felt his fear in the moments before I lost all sense of my surroundings when Beelzebub snapped my neck.

I couldn't trust him in the slightest, but I could trust him with that.

"Yes," I said, nodding as he pushed the knife deep. White-hot pain spread through my arm as it sank deep enough to cut through muscle and sinew. My arm trembled as he held me still, slicing his way up to my elbow efficiently before he moved to the other arm and did the same.

My arms fell to my sides, blood dripping down over my hands

and fingers to fall onto the earth. My vision swayed from the pain, my eyes drifting closed for a moment until Gray's grunt of pain echoed my own.

He cut through his own flesh, carving his arms in the same way he'd done to mine. He lent his blood to my resurrection, the taste of life and death coating the air around us. It was the same as the decay of leaves in autumn, as the first budding of leaves on the trees in spring.

Tossing the dagger to the side, he took my hands in his and turned my arms to face the ground as he gently pulled me to kneel upon the earth. Threading our fingers together, he guided them into the ground, which seemed to part, allowing us to slip into the grave dirt easily. It surrounded me, sinking beneath my fingernails and sticking to the blood coating my skin until my hands were buried like the corpses beneath me.

I swayed as I bled, my eyes landing on Gray's ethereal stare. "I don't know what to do," I admitted. This was so different from raising one skeleton from the throne, so different from the magic of the life that normally called to me. I didn't know how to call to so many different things at once.

"Just feel," he said, letting his eyes fall closed. His fingers entwined with mine reassured me he hadn't abandoned me, and I followed suit. My entire world narrowed to my fingers in the earth, to my blood flowing through the grains of fertile dirt. I followed the flow, followed the path the earth took to spread our blood through the cemetery like a river, delivering it to each and every witch who needed it.

A single drop was all they needed to become mine.

"Now *breathe*," Gray whispered, his voice warm and comfortable. He was the hearth on a winter day, his word a reminder of everything living. I followed the dirt in the other direction, to the blades of grass and the tree roots spread through the cemetery grounds. The green of my magic reached me, the familiar feeling of life spreading through me. I let it build within me, feeling it fill me with warmth.

I breathed, sucking in a deep, ragged breath that filled my lungs with spring.

I released it, breathing life into the death of the cemetery. The ground shook beneath me, forcing my eyes to open as Gray guided me to my feet hastily. He lifted me, carrying me to the edge of the boundary as the ground split open where we'd been only a moment before. I swayed in his hold, watching as skeletal hands burst from the dirt.

The witches clawed their way to the surface, a mix of bones and rotting flesh emerging from the earth. The ground beneath them settled, fresh grass and flowers sprouting where the empty graves sat. The dead got to their feet in varying stages, some staggering on bones alone and others with flesh falling from them as they moved.

I held back my gag, watching as the group of them formed a circle. There had been around fifty witches buried in that cemetery since the Covenant had turned its back on the balance.

Gray pressed his arm to my mouth, letting the blood from his skin touch my lips. I opened, drinking from him for the first time since he'd brought me back. I only managed a few drops before his wound healed over entirely, and a moment after that, mine followed suit with a flash of gold.

Gray released me when he knew I'd steadied myself enough, taking a step toward the cemetery. "What have you done?" he asked, turning to look at me in shock.

I looked past him to the rotting figures of the witches who had come before me, watching with dawning horror as flesh knitted back together. As fresh muscle and sinew covered bone anew.

They turned to me as one, but it was the youthful face of my aunt who snagged my gaze, raising her hand to turn it over as she studied it in fascination.

"I didn't mean to—" I said, but the gears were already turning in my head. The implications of what I'd done, of what I *could* do. I'd taken in life.

And then I'd breathed it out.

Gray spoke, his voice quiet with his surprise. "Willow, you didn't raise the dead. You fucking resurrected them."

20

GRAY

Willow's gaze darted over the fifty people who had been dead and gone only moments before, taking in the bodies of each and every one of them. Those I'd killed to open the seal stared back at her, having been freshly buried while she slept off the effects of her own resurrection.

I hadn't stopped to think about what her green magic would do to the necromancy in her veins. About the complications it might cause if she was inexperienced with shutting out one of the forces swimming inside her. They could be two separate entities if she trained them to be, but until then . . . *clearly* her natural instinct was to combine them and use them seamlessly.

I should have seen it coming after the way the thrones had melded together, creating something new.

Willow herself was something *new*. She wasn't a Madizza or a Hecate, not a Green or a Black. She was part of me, and that was before she'd even discovered the faint impressions of the other magics on her soul. To bring her back, I'd given her enough of my blood that she'd gained access to magics that weren't hers.

Just like the Covenant before her had.

They were the ghost of what I had, and that was why the Covenant was never strong enough to challenge me in truth. But Willow already had the gifts that were hers by birthright, and then I'd gone and added to them like a fucking moron.

She was a ticking time bomb, and it was a miracle she hadn't done something far worse than this.

"Gray," she said, and the smile that transformed her face made my heart hurt. I almost wished I didn't have it again, so that I wouldn't feel the echo of her pain when she accepted the reality of what she'd done.

And what she would have to do to make it right.

"They're alive?" she asked, as if she couldn't quite believe it for herself. She knew enough of her lineage to understand that they should have been mindless zombies, an army of the undead that existed only to serve her. Instead, they made their way around the cemetery, greeting anyone they knew with hugs and signs of affection.

The Coven had emerged from the Tribunal room shortly after me, but Willow had been too lost to the magic and the call of the dead to notice. She spun as I looked over her shoulder, finding her people staring back at her. Everything in her went still, and I reached out to take her hand in comfort.

Della was the first to step toward us and reach into the fabric of her skirt. Bunching it into her fists so that she could lower herself to her knees gracefully, she knelt before Willow and turned her stare up to her. *Mihi donum tuum est,* Covenant," she said, touching her hands to the ground at Willow's feet and lowering to press her forehead to the earth in a bow.

Water gathered on the blades of grass, winding into a single rope that curved its way up Willow's legs. Winding over her dress, it circled her like a serpent as it approached her chest. My wife shivered when the cold of it touched the bare skin of her arms and chest, sinking into her body and becoming one with her. Della was too young to make such an offering of allegiance, but her loyalty moved others to step forward and take a knee.

"Why?" Willow asked when one of the eldest witches struggled to get up from her bow. She reached out an arm to help the old woman, the yellow of her clothing bright against the black of Willow's gown.

"We have no Covenant. We have no Tribunal. There is no one to lead us through this chaos after centuries of rules and order," the old woman said, glaring at me over her shoulder. "We may not like your proximity to the Morningstar, but our ancestors trusted Charlotte. She saved us from certain death and gave us this place. She gave us something to believe in."

"I'm not Charlotte," Willow said, holding her chin high. She wouldn't accept the mantle of power if they gave it because they expected her to be something she wasn't. She would either rule with fire in her blood, or she would watch the Coven burn, but either way she would do it with honesty.

"No, you're not. But I think you're *our* something to believe in," Della said, stepping back so that the others could take her place and continue the procession of allegiance. The only people who might have opposed her were those who had once sat on the Tribunal and had a closer proximity to power than Willow.

But Willow had already taken care of them when she turned the Coven against them, leaving them to die in the Tribunal room they'd ruled in.

When the last of the witches watched Willow and gave her the promise to listen, Willow turned to me and looked at those she'd resurrected. That hope in her eyes made me want to die, knowing that I would have to be the one to tear it away from her. "I know things are a mess right now, but I have to go to Vermont," she said.

Loralei stepped forward as if she might approach Willow, but I took my wife's hands in mine. "Willow," I said, pausing as I fought to find the words to explain.

"She's all alone," Willow said, a smile so beautiful transforming her face. Tears stung her eyes as she thought through what she could give to her mother without the threat of the Covenant who had chased her from her home in their efforts to make her obedient. "But I can bring her back."

"Witchling, they can't stay," I said, watching as her smile froze in place. It fell the next moment, confusion flittering with a furrow of her brow. She took a step back, tugging at her hands when I didn't release her.

"What are you talking about?" she asked, staring at me as if I'd ruined her world.

"You of all people know how delicate the balance is. You *took* something from death," I said, tipping my head to the side. My face hurt from fighting back the surge of emotion I felt pulsing off of Willow. It struck me like a bolt to the chest, shoving deep into my heart with the sharp pain of a thousand blades. "You have to give it back."

"You saved me!" she yelled, tearing her hands out of my grip and stumbling back. "You didn't put me back!"

"I was willing to pay the price to keep you here! I was willing to murder *anyone* the balance demanded of me if it meant I had you, and I won't spend a single moment regretting that choice. Who would you offer in their place?" I asked, stepping forward as she shook her head. She glanced at the group of witches behind her, the implications of the number of deaths she would need to satisfy making her chest heave.

As much as my witchling wanted to pretend she could be ruthless, she cared. She cared far too fucking much to condemn innocent people to death to save those who had already had their chance and lost it.

"I can't just leave her," Willow said, her bottom lip trembling. "I don't care who it is, I'll—"

"Never forgive yourself," I said, stepping forward to cup her face and stare down at her. "What if the balance demanded Ash take your mother's place?"

She blanched, shaking her head furiously as her nostrils flared. "What is the point in having this power if I can't *fucking use it*?!"

she screamed. She buried her face in her hands, sliding them into her hair in her frustration.

"The point in having it," I said, shoving my hands into my pockets to keep from reaching out to touch her, "is that you care enough not to abuse it." I smiled sadly. She would need my comfort in the quiet of our room later, when she could break without other eyes to watch her.

For now, she needed my strength.

Anyone else, and I never would have believed that they would go through life without ever disrupting the balance for selfish gain. But Willow would never want to play God with people's lives.

"It's okay," Loralei said, stepping up beside Willow finally. She didn't show any signs of her hatred for me, revealing nothing of remembering I'd been the one to take her life. She just stared at her niece, willing her to understand. She took her hand in hers, guiding her to the tree line. I knew what waited in those woods, the crypt that many remained unaware of. "Lay us to rest. Give us peace, finally."

Loralei was the only one to go with Willow into those woods, respecting the sanctity of the Hecate crypt. It may not have held the bones that acted as the conduit of power, but it housed the bones that couldn't be contained in the pouch most Hecate witches carried at their sides.

I watched her disappear with her aunt, knowing that this was something she needed to discover on her own. I could feel the emotion surging off her even if I couldn't see it, knowing what Loralei asked of her. What she guided her through when I couldn't.

The Coven watched, looking at one another with somber expressions as Willow did the work that they could not. She laid the last of the Hecate bones to rest properly, taking what had been denied to Loralei. She was the first witch to be denied her burial rights, done in a quiet way when the Coven still remained ignorant to what was happening.

It was only fair that she was the first to find peace.

Willow stumbled out of the woods with a tense expression on her face, her lips pressed tight. She cradled the bone of a finger in her hand, wrapping her own fingers around it before she slipped it to the chain of bones dangling around her waist. Her aunt's bone had found the place it belonged, settling against her hip as her wet gaze met mine.

"Witchling," I said from across the cemetery, taking a step toward her. She turned away from me, moving to the center and calling out to the Whites. Those who belonged to those houses stepped forward, allowing Willow to guide them to the crystal cliffs beside the ocean. She made her way toward the rocky path down the hillside, the line of White witches following behind her. Their flowing white dresses made them look like ghosts, and even if they were corporeal, they might as well have been as they followed wordlessly. Willow stood on the edge of the cliff, watching with the wind in her hair as those witches robed in white draped themselves over the crystals.

The moon played off the reflective light, casting a dazzling array of colors through the night and off their white gowns. When the youngest of the witches draped her body over a purple crystal, laying her back upon it with her dress falling toward the ground, Willow raised her hands toward them.

Her eyes caught mine where I watched from the top of the cliff, a single tear accompanying the tremble of her lips as she let her eyes drift closed.

Her lips parted.

Willow drew in a deep breath, trapping it in her lungs as she pulled life back into herself. Her skin glowed as she drank it in, shimmering with golden light. On the crystals, the witches returned to their natural state without the magic she'd given.

Flesh melted from bones, the scent of decay filling the air. It slipped over the crystals, spreading the blood and essence of magic back to the very Source they drew from.

Willow swallowed, her features twisting in concentration before she finally dared to release her magic completely.

Her eyes opened slowly, looking at the carnage of the dead she'd dared to hope she could save. She turned her back on them, her face a blank mask of strength as she ascended the cliff.

She'd gone with a group of four at her side, but as I was coming to realize was standard for Willow, she always returned alone.

21

GRAY

Willow didn't break.

She didn't bend.

She didn't show any sign of emotion as she set to work, laying the witches to rest as she had intended to do in the first place.

She laid the Purples beneath the stars, watching as their magic left their bodies and returned to the Source in the sky.

She laid the Greens within the cemetery, buried in holes without a casket to keep them from the very earth that they would return to.

She let the wind wash over the Grays, turning them to dust and scattering them through the air.

She watched the Blues walk into the tide, returning to death so the water could speed the process of decay.

She brought the Reds to the garden, watching them hold one another close in affection beneath the old willow tree as they all went to their deaths together.

She took the life from the Yellows, watching as one of those who lived on set them aflame and let the fire claim what remained.

She did what was necessary, going through the motions as if each and every life did not weigh on her soul. As Willow sagged beneath the heaviness of what she'd had to do, the people of her Coven grew stronger. Magic returned, part of the balance restored because of her actions.

She gave what the old Covenant had stolen from them.

When it was done, Willow merely turned away from her people and strode back toward the school. They remained, overjoyed at the return of what they'd lost so slowly they hadn't even been able to see it.

Willow had given them a gift, and no matter what it cost her, they would never forget it.

I followed behind her in silence, keeping my distance as she moved slowly. She walked as if she herself were merely a ghost, making her way to the room she shared with me. She didn't stop to think about returning to her dorm where she knew Della, Margot, and Nova would return.

She sought out the comfort of privacy, where no celebration would infiltrate her mourning.

I followed her, stalking after her in silence. I couldn't even say if she were entirely aware of my presence until the moment she let the door slam in my face. I smiled as I pushed it open, finding Willow where she had moved to the window overlooking the party that raged around the fire down below. The witches danced in ways I hadn't seen since the Coven first formed, the restoration of balance and the lack of strict rules setting them free.

She slid to the floor beside the window the Whites had repaired, uncaring for how uncomfortable she must have been in her corset. Leaning her face against the crystallized glass, she didn't bother to look over at me. "Leave me alone," she mumbled, the broken sound of that quiet voice driving me to take another step toward her.

I sat beside her, close enough that our hips touched. I didn't dare interrupt her further, merely offering her my presence so she would know I was there. "I told you already, Witchling. You aren't alone anymore."

Willow's face contorted, her brow furrowing as Jonathan emerged from the bedroom and curled up on top of her feet. She stared down at the witches and the celebration she couldn't bring herself to join, separate from the Coven she'd fought so hard to save.

She didn't belong there any more than I belonged partying with my Vessels.

She pressed her lips together, her nostrils flaring as Jonathan started to purr. I hated that fucking cat more than anything, but I stretched out a hand to scratch his neck regardless.

A thank-you for the company he offered to Willow in her time of need.

A broken sob cut through the room, Willow's chest heaving with the force of it. She turned her face away from the window, finding my chest and burying herself in the fabric of my suit.

"I must look like shit if you're being nice to the fucking cat," she mumbled, rubbing her cheek against me and using it to brush away the moisture she didn't want me to see.

I wrapped my arms around her, tucking her head beneath my chin and holding her close. I did not understand her capacity for love, for caring about people she'd never even known so much that their deaths could affect her so strongly.

There was only one person in my heart.

"You're as beautiful as you were the day I met you," I said, even knowing that her eyes would be swollen and her face red.

"And you are full of shit," she said, a tiny chuckle in her voice.

She looked up at me, the gold and purple of her eyes glossy and rimmed with red from rubbing them. I cupped her cheek, willing her to finally believe me. "I love every side of you, Witchling. Even the parts that make you human."

Her eyes softened, something warm lingering in the back of that gaze as she watched me. She shuttered it just as quickly, ducking her head down so that I couldn't see her break. "Gray . . ."

"I've got you, love. It's okay," I said, murmuring the words against the top of her head. Willow nodded against my chest, falling silent except for the sounds of her ragged breathing.

We waited out the celebration together, separate from those who depended on us.

But never alone.

22

WILLOW

I grabbed Della and Nova from the courtyard the next day after Gray left me to tend to the archdemons and inform them of what had happened in full. I couldn't help the insidious, relieved sigh when I discovered that Margot wasn't with them. I didn't want to consider where she was instead, the sinking feeling in my gut all but confirmation of those suspicions.

All the more reason to keep this from her, as much as it pained me to have any secrets. The need for them had become apparent when I watched her turn into Beelzebub's embrace as if she were well familiar with it.

For a witch who didn't like to be touched at all, but by men in particular, she'd found solace in him.

Iban stood before them, turning to find me approaching. I slowed my steps, unsure what would wait for me. I'd killed his uncle in cold blood the night before, and even if the man had deserved it, I more than anyone could understand that it wasn't always simple to untangle emotions from logic.

Sometimes, you could love someone and still admit that they were an absolutely terrible person.

Jonathan poked his head out of the messenger bag I'd slung over my shoulder before leaving the privacy of the room I shared with Gray. I didn't have the heart to ask to return to my dorm, knowing that doing so would only drive a wedge between us.

A week ago, I'd have insisted and said damn the consequences. Getting close to him should have been my aim even then, but I hadn't had any personal stake in the end goal.

Now . . .

Now I wanted nothing more than to deceive Gray the way he'd deceived me. I wanted him to believe that I'd settled into our lives.

Because I needed to send him back to the pit he'd come from sooner rather than later. Even if the very idea of removing him from my life, of hurting him, made a shock of agony streak through me, the night before had proven why it was necessary.

I wasn't strong enough to resist him. I wasn't strong enough not to fall prey to his sweet whispered words. I'd thought sex would be my undoing, but it was the way he seemed determined to sink inside my heart and make his new home there.

Margot wasn't the only one who'd been compromised by the enemy, and I knew that it was only a matter of time before I was lost completely.

Iban shoved his hands into the pockets of his jeans, not reaching out to hug me in the way he might have before. The distance was necessary, and it was to be expected, but that didn't stop the jolt of sadness that I felt anyway.

"Where did you get a cat?" he asked, glancing down at Jonathan.

"It's a long story," I said, turning to the girls. "I need your help."

"What are we doing?" Nova asked, shoving the last bite of her lunch into her mouth and standing. She tossed the trash into the garbage can, brushing her hands together to rid herself of any crumbs.

"I want to find a way to send them all back. The Vessels, the archdemons, Lucifer," I whispered, looking between the three of them. I'd hoped I could trust Iban with this, and he nodded in approval and alleviated my fears for the moment.

"I think I know where to look," Iban said as Della got to her feet. "There's a section in the library. It was forbidden by the Covenant, but I can take you there."

"How?" I asked, studying him.

"While all of you spend your time playing with magic, I read. That library is my courtyard, Willow," he said, gesturing at the plant life around him. "I may not have magic in the real world anymore . . ."

"But you do in books," I said, nodding my head in agreement. There'd been a time when I was younger when all I wanted to do was bury myself in books that told of quests and magic, because I couldn't spend every waking moment watching my mother practice.

He smiled, the mannerism a ghost of what it had once been when he looked at me. Turning to lead the way to the library, he guided us through the halls. I kept my head down, trying not to draw attention to myself or where we were going. If any of the archdemons caught on to my plan, I'd never be able to stop them from leveling this school and everyone in it.

I still felt the memory of Beelzebub's hands on my head when he snapped my neck, and the possibility of him doing that to Margot was exactly what motivated me to keep going in spite of the risks. She deserved so much better than a male who was capable of hurting an innocent woman he didn't know like that.

I scoffed, imagining Beelzebub's reaction to my imagining myself to be innocent. He would claim something very different if and when he found out about my plan to rid this world of the demons who had been banished long ago.

It was the only way to put things right after I'd torn them apart. Gray might claim that he wanted to build a home in Crystal Hollow, but how many years would it take for him to want to expand his territory?

Now that he was not bound by his need for witch blood to survive, he would soon realize that there were other points of power within this realm. There were other witches, other clans, others who connected with the earth in spite of him not opening the doorway.

If he could get them on his side, if we could make them a part of the Coven, then there was no telling what boundaries he would cross in his quest for power. Lucifer had been cast down from Heaven because of his disregard for human life and the free will his father valued.

What would it take for him to remember that?

"Tell me about this forbidden section of the library," I said, distracting myself from my turn of thoughts. If I could only send them back, I would never once more have to wonder.

I'd just be alone again.

I shut out the insidious thought, focusing on the life I could have without any of the complications Gray brought. I hadn't chosen him for myself. I could have the chance to *choose* for myself rather than having my fate determined centuries before I was born.

"The Covenant used to forbid anyone from entering. She said it was full of magic that only they were capable of using," Iban said, shaking his head. "But I've never seen either of them go into that room."

"Then how did you gain access?" Della asked, her brow furrowing in that way that said she thought he was full of shit.

"Susannah asked me to catalog everything for her over the summer. She gave me the key and swore me to secrecy. I wasn't physically able to speak of the room with anyone but the Covenant until . . ."

"Until I became the Covenant last night," I said, huffing a breath of disbelief.

Nova stepped closer to him, blocking our way through the empty halls of the school. Most of the students had made their way to their next class, because as much as our entire world had been disrupted, Hollow's Grove wanted to pretend that it was business as usual.

I couldn't very well attend classes as a student when I was meant to be leading the Coven. I'd just have to learn another way, but I still felt guilty that my friends were missing an important part of their education.

"What was in it for you?" Nova asked, crossing her arms over her chest. Her face was stern, solemn as she studied him, as if she already knew.

"I was able to read about the strongest magics in the world," he said, but the uncomfortable smile on his face made my body freeze. He'd made a deal with the Covenant, agreed to do this for her in exchange for something he wanted.

"Iban, what did you do?" I asked as he stepped around Nova. I grasped his arm, pulling him to a stop. "What did she give you?" The possibilities were endless, and none of the gifts the Covenant could have offered could be trusted. Any of them could have ulterior motives.

"*You*," he said finally, staring at the floor in shame. I blanched, a gasp leaving me. I'd known the Covenant had preferred Iban as my mate, but I hadn't realized that Iban was an active part in that plan. "She told me there was another Madizza witch, and that she would be attending Hollow's Grove in the fall. She promised to make it clear to the other Bray males that I had earned the right to first courting."

Della groaned, rubbing her temples in frustration as she turned and strode up the stairs. Gripping Nova's arm, she dragged her friend with her to give us privacy, muttering a soft "fucking idiot" as she went.

I considered his words, going over the timeline. In the *days* after my mother's death, before the Covenant had sent Gray to come for me, Iban had been negotiating to marry a woman he hadn't even met. I expected that behavior from Gray, from the literal devil in the flesh, but I'd somehow expected better of the man who claimed to be my friend. "You didn't even know me," I said, trying to ignore the hurt.

I wasn't naive enough to believe my last name hadn't played a role in the way Iban had approached me. I knew I was the only Green witch he could pair with. I'd just thought he was above such politics, and I'd bought all his lies about finding someone he loved. "Didn't you ever wonder why none of the other Brays approached you? You're our only hope if we wanted our children to have the same magic as our families," he asked.

"I didn't think anything of it at all. Your uncle hated me, so I just thought you were different from your family," I said, turning away from him. I continued on my path to the library, determined to make something of the news that someone I'd considered a friend had acted so selfishly. If what he said were true, the other Brays still hadn't approached me for a reason.

He'd laid his claim over me when he had no right.

"Willow, listen to me," he said, reaching out to grab my hand. I shook him off, spinning on him with a glare. He raised his hands placatingly, a silent apology for touching me. Nova and Della continued on toward the library, leaving us to our spat. "I didn't think anything of it at the time. I figured you'd come, I would have a chance to get to know you before the others, and if there wasn't any connection, then I would tell your grandmother that I wasn't interested in being chosen as your mate."

"Then why didn't you tell her that? Why was I never approached by the other Brays?" I asked, my anger fueling my words. I was too hurt to realize I shouldn't have asked the question when I wasn't ready for the answer.

I was too angry to realize I'd opened Pandora's box, and I'd never be able to put the truth back in.

"Because then I met you. You came here and you were . . ." He trailed off, looking toward the window that looked down on the gardens. Life had returned to them since I came to Crystal Hollow, my blood the sole reason for the return of vibrancy to everything that surrounded us. "Full of life," he said, letting me know that his thoughts had gone to the same place mine had. He looked toward me, taking a step closer, though he didn't dare to touch me.

"Iban," I murmured, closing my eyes as I tried to think of a way to undo this.

"You're beautiful and intelligent. You *care* about the people here more than most who have spent their lives in the petty fights for power. Most witches would have looked at me only to evaluate me as a mate. I have no power, and that means that I have nothing to offer to anyone outside of being a husband and a father. I *chose* that life, but I didn't stop to consider what I was giving up outside of my magic. People stopped *seeing* me," he said, slowly taking my hand in his. "My own family stopped treating me like I mattered to them, but you were different."

"Stop."

"You looked at me and you saw a person. You looked at me and you saw me. You made me realize everything I'd given up, because the magic I abandoned was nothing like yours! But it could have been if I'd had someone like you to teach me. You gave me hope, Willow. You made me hope that one day I would have a little girl who *felt* the plants around her the way you do. I'm not saying I'm in love with you. I'm not saying that you'll be the woman I marry one day, but I'm saying that I wasn't ready to let go of the hope for that future just because you were distracted by a Vessel who I thought wouldn't last," he admitted.

"You should have told me about your deal with the Covenant," I said, my voice sad. The unfortunate reality that Iban hadn't faced yet was that neither of us knew what my magic would do to my children when it passed on.

I might have been the last Madizza, but I was also the last Hecate. I was the first witch with more than one type of magic in my veins, and I didn't know what that meant for my children. Would they inherit both? Would they inherit one?

Iban could have just as easily ended up with a child who summoned the dead as the life he so desperately wanted.

"I should have told you," he agreed with a subtle nod of his head. "But I thought, if nothing else, I could keep the rest of the Brays at bay for a while."

I smiled with a little laugh. "There is that. I was never interested in marriage at all."

He brushed his finger over the ring on my hand. "All the more reason to get rid of your husband then," he said, releasing me to make his way up the stairs that led to the library. I followed behind him, not daring to say another word.

If getting rid of my husband was exactly what I wanted, then why did the thought of it make my stomach hurt?

23

WILLOW

I ban and I walked into the library, meeting up with Della and
Nova where they lurked by the windows. Iban pulled a skeleton key from his pocket as he moved to one of the back rooms,
leading the way as we approached. He looked over his shoulder as
he pulled one of the unmarked books from the shelf, revealing a
hidden lock in the wall.

Making sure there were no Vessels to uncover the secret trove.

I stared in fascination as he inserted the key, turning the lock
slowly. The clink of metal gears moving against one another came
from behind the bookshelf as he pulled the key free and returned
the book.

Della moved as the shelf slid forward, revealing a narrow passage between it and the wall. Iban cut her off, stepping inside and
pulling a cord. Light filled the space as the three of us followed after
him, and I winced when the shelf slid back into place and locked
us inside.

Iban wasted no time going to the shelves, searching the spines
of books as Della and Nova explored. I ran a finger over the leather,
the whisper of magic within those books brushing against me.

"You can feel it, can't you?" Iban asked, pulling a book from
the shelf when he found the one he wanted. He set it on the
table carefully, flipping through the pages as I found one that
called to me and did the same opposite him. Della and Nova

took longer to explore, pulling books out before they inevitably returned them.

"These are all in Latin," I said, opening a book about Charlotte's bargain and skimming the first page. It told the details of her life prior to making the bargain, and listed the names of the men who'd accused her of witchcraft.

Jonathan's name stood out in bold, and it horrified me to think of what he'd done to earn a place among the Cursed. He'd accused a dozen women before Charlotte, forcing them to prove their innocence by dunking them in the river.

When they survived, he'd condemned them to hang in the gallows.

It seemed a far cry from the cat sleeping peacefully in my messenger bag, purring away happily as he dreamt. I let the bag drop to the floor slowly, settling him even though he probably didn't deserve such kindness from me.

If he'd never named Charlotte, none of this would have ever happened.

The next page told the story of how she'd gone into the woods, and I touched a finger to the neatly scrawled cursive upon the page. How many years after had she gone back and told her story, laying it out here for any who came after her?

"This is Charlotte's journal," I said, looking over at Iban as Della and Nova took their seats.

He nodded, glancing over at it. He'd clearly already read or at least skimmed the contents enough to recognize it. "You should take it with you. She would want you to have it."

I nodded, setting the journal aside as I stood. If I was going to take it with me, then I wanted to find something that might contain the answer to Gray within the texts that would stay behind. If Iban had already read the journal, I assumed it would not provide us with the answers we needed.

"Here it is," Iban said, turning another page and getting to his feet. I moved to stand behind him, looking over his shoulder as he pointed down at the drawing on the page. The weapon on the page was crude, a handle carved from bone set into steel. I read the words on the page, skimming over them and swallowing back the immediate protest.

Diabolus Interfectorem.

Devil Killer.

"That kills them. I thought we were looking for a way to send them back to Hell," I said, attempting to keep my calm. I walked back toward the shelves, thumbing over the spines as I ignored the pointed silence of the others behind me. My pulse rang in my head, drowning out all sound as I touched the books. The words blurred, dizziness settling over me at the thought of what they might ask me to do.

"Willow, are you all right?" Della asked, being the first to cross the gap and approach me. She touched my arm, pulling it down from the shelves and forcing me to look over at her.

"I'm fine," I said, turning my attention back to the shelves.

"Then maybe we should at least see what Iban has found and what it would require," she said, her voice far too gentle.

"Juliet will never forgive you if we kill them," I whispered, unsure if Iban were aware of her relationship.

Her face softened. "You let me worry about that." She guided me back to the table, forcing me to look down at the dagger that made a hollow pit in my gut.

Lucifer could be killed.

"We would infuse it with the magic of every house," Iban said, moving toward one of the shelves. He grabbed a chest from the top shelf, pulling it down and setting it on the table. He opened it slowly, turning it so we could see the dagger resting within the case. All creations had a distinct feeling of the Source within them, and the handle being carved in bone should have meant that I felt the magic of it within me. But this dagger was different.

Where there should have been *something*, there was only an empty void waiting to be filled.

"It's too risky. He'll kill anyone involved in this," I said, shaking my head as I crossed my arms over my chest.

"It's not going to be risky at all, Willow," Iban said, his face softening. "Because you're going to be the one to do it, and you'll just have to make sure you follow through."

I swallowed, staring at the knife in horror. "Sending him back is one thing; killing him is another entirely. I'm not . . ." I trailed off. I couldn't admit that I wasn't strong enough to watch the breath fade from his lungs and the light dim from his eyes. Doing it would break something in me, even if I didn't want to admit it.

"My fucking God," Iban said, taking a step back as if I'd slapped him. "You have fucking feelings for that monster?"

"I didn't say that," I said, shaking my head as Della's eyes grew wide.

"He stabbed you! He has lied to you the entire time you've known him! He killed twelve of our witches!" he yelled.

I raised my hands, gesturing with them as I searched for the words to deny the accusation in his glare. "You think I don't know that?!" I shouted back, ready to tear my hair out. "I know what he's done!"

"Then how can you have feelings for him?" Iban asked, and the unspoken question hung between us. *Why him? Why not me?*

"He sees me," I answered, trying to ignore the hurt look on Iban's face. "He sees all of me, and he accepts me as I am. Not just who he wants me to be."

"I see you," Iban said softly, his voice sad as his hands dropped to his sides.

I smiled, the sadness in my chest easing as I raised my chin. "You don't even know me."

Iban squared his shoulders, nodding as his nostrils flared. "You're right. If you're capable of loving him, then I don't know you at all. If you want to get rid of him, this is the only way."

"Find somebody else," I said, glancing at the dagger on the table and ignoring the judgment in Iban's stare.

"Sweetheart," he said, reaching out to touch my cheek. The gentleness hurt more than his anger would have, as if he could see just how close this would take me to the breaking point. "You're the only one who can get close enough. You think others haven't tried to seduce him to find a vulnerability? It's only you."

I fought back the rising growl in my throat, the twist of my lips that showed I cared too much. Jonathan climbed out of the messenger bag on the floor, jumping onto my chair and prancing across the table to sniff the blade.

He hissed at it, leaping back with an arched spine.

"We can send them back then. I'll open the seal again," I said.

"And die in the process? Absolutely not," Nova argued from her seat.

"There has to be another way!" I screamed, wincing when Jonathan spun and approached the edge of the table, rubbing his cheek against my side.

"There's not," Iban said.

"Willow, if you can't do it, it's all right. We will find a way to coexist for now, and we can always do this after you've had time to think about it," Della said, her voice hopeful. As much as she'd tried to pretend that the conflict it caused with Juliet wouldn't tear her in two, I knew it would.

"He can't stay here, Del. Every day I spend with him is . . ."

"Another day he spends getting under your skin," she said, understanding on her face as she grasped the dagger from the case. She twirled it in her hand, standing and approaching from the other side of the table. She stopped beside me, holding the blade on her outstretched palms. "Then you have to make a choice."

I swallowed, drawing in a deep breath as her cool gaze held mine. My bottom lip trembled with the rage I held in, but I did the only thing I could if I wanted to do what was right.

I took the knife.

24

WILLOW

Della and Nova left the library first, leaving Iban to put the books back in their places. The knife rested in an exterior pocket of my messenger bag, carefully angled to avoid Jonathan as I hefted it onto my shoulder. He curled up on the opposite side of the bag, growling at it as I shifted the bag.

I didn't bother to say goodbye to Iban as I made my way out the tiny crack between the shelf and the wall where Nova had pushed it open, needing time to process all that had happened.

And what I'd agreed to do, but couldn't.

Even knowing it was the right thing to do, I didn't think I'd be able to follow through with killing Gray myself. I shook my head as I walked down the hall toward the stairwell, frantically racking my brain for an alternative. There had to be someone else.

Anyone else.

"Willow, wait!" Iban called, hurrying out of the library behind me. I paused even though I wanted nothing more than to get to the gardens below, to bury my hands in the dirt and feel the earth. I needed the reminder that there was something more to me, that I was allowed to have feelings and thoughts of my own in spite of what the world seemed to think.

"What do you want?" I asked, spinning to pin him with a look that conveyed all the desperation I felt.

He adjusted his own bag on his shoulder, smiling sadly at

whatever he saw on my face. He didn't stop pushing, continuing to invade my space as he took another step closer. In any other situation, the proximity might have been a comfort, but instead it just felt suffocating. "You're doing the right thing," he said, his voice quiet. I felt it like a snapping twig between us, the crack in my heart echoing through the space until I couldn't hold back my indignant huff.

"Am I, though?" I asked, watching as horror made that gentle smile fall from his face in confusion. A few students passed us by, making their way into the library with downturned eyes and pointedly avoiding looking at me. I'd gone from the outcast to being in charge, but nothing would change the judgment and fear that came from the witches because of my connection to Gray.

"What are you talking about?" Iban asked, taking another step closer. I backed away, shaking my head and raising a hand to show him that I needed him to maintain his distance.

"What exactly am I fighting to protect here? People who will never accept me?" I asked, waving my hand out as the library door slammed behind the witches. Iban and I were alone again, the silence of the stone walls pressing down on me and my feet far too distant from the earth below.

It felt like a storm surging in my blood, like I was two minutes away from a catastrophe that would swallow Hollow's Grove in my rage.

"Just give them time. If you do this, they'll worship you," Iban said with a laugh. He thought it was humorous, but we both knew it was true. An act of service to earn the affection of people who might have been my family in another life.

Another test to prove my worthiness to people who were meant to love me.

My lips pressed together tightly, the grinding of my teeth making my head hurt.

"Willow . . ." Iban said, seeming to realize that he'd said something wrong.

"Did it ever fucking occur to you that maybe, just maybe, I deserve to be accepted for who I am and not what I have to offer you?" I asked, taking another step back from him. At least Gray owned his actions and didn't pretend to be innocent. I needed the distance so I didn't do something I'd regret, so I didn't lash out with the magic that coated my skin in anger. Even Jonathan yowled, poking his head out of my bag to look up at me in warning. "For *once,* I would like to be allowed to do something for myself, and not because the fucking Coven depends on me to fix its shit."

"I know you. You don't want *him.* You're confused, and I understand that. He's a master manipulator, sweetheart. He knows exactly what to say to get you to turn your back on everything that matters to you. That's all the more reason that you have to fight to free yourself from him, because we both know he will never let you go so long as he's here," Iban said, leaning his shoulder against the stone wall.

I glanced at the tiny window at the top of the stairs, looking out at the woods with the reminder of the bargain we'd struck. As long as he stayed, I would never be free of this place.

"You don't know that," I said instead, shrugging my shoulders. "He could get bored."

"He won't," Iban said sadly as my shoulders dropped into place. Dejection replaced the rage, knowing that no matter what I did, I would have to choose between the Coven and Gray. I couldn't have both, not if I wanted the Coven to value me the way it did its own.

Maybe Gray and I weren't all that different in the end, because the sorrow that clung to my chest wasn't because I couldn't ever leave Crystal Hollow.

It was because I just wanted a place to call home—a place to belong.

Iban stepped closer, tucking a stray hair behind my ear. His fingers brushed against my skin, the warmth of them making me far too aware of the chill that had taken over me. "I wouldn't," he said, his voice sad.

I swatted his touch away, glaring up at him in warning. His words were a quiet manipulation, toying with me when he knew I was vulnerable. My opinion of him sank even lower, and I swallowed as I tried not to think about that loss on top of the potential grief already staring me in the face if I murdered my husband in cold blood.

"It's not fair," I admitted, shaking my head and crossing my arms over my chest. "Why does it have to be me? Why is it *always* me?"

"I know it's not fair. I'd take it from you if I could, but . . ." He trailed off.

"I know," I said, pursing my lips. I had no doubt that Iban would be more than willing to be the one to drive the blade into Gray's heart, ending his life and freeing me. I may not have been particularly familiar with the thoughts of men, but it didn't take a genius to assume he saw the benefit in ridding the world of Gray for more than one reason.

One was selfish. The other was not.

"I think I should take the blade for now," Iban said, reaching into the messenger bag at my side. I placed my hand over his, my natural instinct telling me to keep the powerful object within my grasp. "It wouldn't end well if Gray were to discover it before we've had a chance to spell it against him." Even if his words made sense, I couldn't take my hand off the bag where he'd slid his hand into the pocket. "It's useless without you, Willow. We *need* you to spell it with your magic in order for it to work," Iban said, his words reassuring and shoving away the guilt that was nagging at me.

I shook off the sinking suspicions, realizing the truth to that statement and letting out a sigh. Nodding, I pulled my hand back and allowed him to slip the blade into his own bag discreetly. The exchange put us too close, his face tilted over mine as he leaned into the wall.

The breath hitched in my lungs as he lowered his head slowly, his eyes darkening as I merely stared up at him. He moved at a leisurely pace, his eyes full of questions and waiting for the rejection that I couldn't bring myself to give.

I needed to know if Gray's compulsion still held me captive, if it was *any* part of the reason I reacted to him the way I did. If I felt something with Iban, I'd know it was genuine attraction.

His mouth touched mine gently, the softest brush of skin and barely a whisper of a kiss. I held perfectly still, not daring to move for fear of what my instincts told me.

I needed to know.

The tip of his nose rubbed against mine as he angled himself, an affectionate caress that felt wrong. He pressed his lips to mine more firmly, his hand sliding beneath the curtain of my dark hair to cup my jaw and hold me still. I let my eyes drift closed, shutting out the vision of the face of the man the world would have me choose. I couldn't bear to look at him, squeezing out the truth staring me in the face.

But when I closed my eyes, all I saw was the image of Gray's arrogant smirk looking down at me. All I felt was the smooth caress of his mouth on mine, the way he'd pry me open and force me to give everything.

Iban's mouth was too gentle, too coaxing as he tried to draw me to the surface. There was no battle or war in his touch, only sweetness where I wanted passion.

I drew back, cracking my head against the wall behind me as I tore my mouth from his. I covered my mouth with my hand, flinging my eyes open to watch Iban's open far more slowly. "Willow," he said, his voice low and husky. He seemed completely unaware of my disinterest, as if he'd experienced a different kiss entirely.

"This was a mistake," I said, quickly shaking off my stress as I frantically wiped my lips on the back of my hand. Sliding out from between Iban and the wall, I hurried toward the stairs and my escape to the gardens.

"He doesn't deserve your loyalty!" Iban called, but there was no ire in the words. Only the dejected sting of rejection.

Still, my hackles rose at the judgment of the statement alone. "You're right, but if we're being completely honest?" I asked, nodding in agreement. "Neither do you."

25

GRAY

Willow retreated down the stairs in a hurry, fleeing the scene of her indiscretion. It shouldn't have bothered me that she'd allowed him to touch her for such a limited time, not when the end result had been exactly what I wanted.

She hadn't been able to stomach his kiss, knowing that the only one who should be placing their lips on her was me.

I couldn't even find it in me to be angry with *her*, because I understood her better than anyone. She wanted to find something for herself, wanted to fight the destiny that had determined her life long before she was ever born. She didn't have enough experience to know that it was futile, that there was no fighting the kind of connection we shared.

I stepped out from around the corner where I'd watched the end of their exchange, having gone in search of my wandering wife to check on her. I'd found her having a quiet discussion with Iban, and the posture of his body and his head hanging over hers had left very little to the imagination.

The furious part of me had wanted to intercede immediately, but the other part had needed to see it. I needed to know how Willow behaved when she thought I wasn't watching her, to make sure that I wasn't imagining the warming she'd shown toward me in the last two days.

I slipped my hands into my pockets as Iban spun to look at

me, his nostrils flaring as he realized I'd seen his humiliation. "I take it that didn't go as planned?" I asked. He ground his teeth together, undoubtedly fighting his urge to punch me in the face. It wouldn't end well for the human male, and he had to know when he was outmatched.

"You're a fucking bastard for doing this to her," he said, turning his glare to the side. Willow hurried down the spiral staircase, oblivious to the altercation that took place above her, the sound of her rushing footsteps echoing up the atrium.

"For doing what to her, exactly? Being there for her when she cries?" I asked, taking a step closer to him. I didn't make any move to touch him, letting his own shame hang him out to dry. Nothing I could do to him would hurt as much as what Willow had already accomplished, choosing a bastard like me over the man who would have her believe he was morally superior. "Or was it the part where she screams my name every night but can't even tolerate a pathetic kiss from you?"

"That right there is why you don't deserve her," he spat, his mouth turning down with disgust. "I would never speak about her that way."

I leaned forward, lowering myself a little closer to his level. Iban wasn't short, but he was shorter than me, his human form frail and weak. "That's cute, but it has far more to do with you not having the ability to please her than it does any moral integrity."

"I guess we'll find out when she finally kicks you aside," he said. I tilted my head to the side, staring down at him as I stood straight.

I couldn't help the soft laughter that rumbled in my chest, my amusement at his completely oblivious response rising. "What exactly do you think happened here?"

"You saw what happened. Do you need me to spell it out for you?" he asked, crossing his arms and standing taller. "She let me kiss her, and then she ran away from me because of what that made her feel. It's only a matter of time before she wants more than you can give her," he said. If I hadn't already had a terrible opinion of him, the fact that he showed no concern for what I might do to Willow in retribution if I actually believed his words solidified it.

I nodded my agreement, because in theory he was right. With the way he saw me, I was sure he thought Willow would someday want a real life. A family of her own and a place where she could bring Ash and raise him safely.

Iban had no way of knowing that there was *nothing* I wouldn't give Willow, including a legacy that would span across history.

"Maybe you're right, but you're an idiot if you think she'll ever turn to you," I said, giving him my back and going to follow after my witchling.

She'd nearly reached the bottom of the stairs as I took my first step down from the library floor, but I knew exactly where she would go after something like this. She wouldn't feel comfortable seeking me out when she thought she'd wronged me, so she'd turn to the only other thing she could rely on.

Her gardens.

I'd fuck her in them to remind her exactly where she belonged, trapped between me and the earth.

"You're going to get her fucking killed if you don't let her go," Iban said, his words making me freeze in place. I wasn't an idiot, and I didn't doubt that the Coven still hoped to remove me from the situation entirely, but Willow should have earned their loyalty with the truth she'd given them the night before.

"What did you just say to me?" I asked, taking that single step up to the library floor.

"You care about her. On whatever fucking level you're capable of. I've seen it," Iban said, swallowing as he stared at me.

I pursed my lips, staring down over the railing in thought. "She's my wife," I said simply, not really answering his unasked question. He didn't need to know the lengths I would go to to keep her safe, because it didn't matter.

The one thing I'd never do was let her go.

"I care about Willow, and even I know using her is the best way to hurt you. One day, you're going to piss someone off enough that they use her, and it will be all your fault when they kill her to make you bleed," Iban said, not understanding just how true his words were.

Willow and I were connected in more ways than one.

"How many others suspect I love her?" I asked, watching as disgust and confusion flittered over his face in equal measure.

"Love?" he scoffed, a smile transforming his face. "You aren't capable of love. I'm the only one who knows she's more than a trophy to you."

I nodded, clapping my hand down on Iban's shoulder. He flinched, but I held him firm as I smiled at him. The arrogance fled his face, realizing he'd walked into some kind of trap.

"Good," I said simply, taking a single moment to revel in the fear on his face.

It was entirely too short-lived.

With a single firm shove, I pushed Iban over the railing.

And then I watched him fall.

26

WILLOW

I paused at the bottom of the stairs, glancing toward the doorway in confusion as someone screamed.

The sound seemed to surround me, and I couldn't place where it came from as I turned in a circle and looked around me. There was no one to be found, all the students locked away in their classes for the day.

"What the fuck?" I whispered to myself, wondering if I'd somehow found myself trapped in another vision. I glanced back up toward the library where I'd come from, wondering if I'd imagined the entire moment with Iban.

Lucifer's golden eyes stared down at me from the top of the railing, penetrating the darkness as something plummeted toward me.

Fuck.

I moved, racing into the center of the atrium. I recognized the clothing fluttering in the wind, even with Iban's back facing me. He raced toward the stone floor, setting frantic energy in my veins.

Raising a foot, I stomped it down onto the stone in the same way Charlotte had when she buried my father alive. It cracked beneath my feet, allowing me to thrust my hands into the dirt underneath. Moss grew, spreading up from the earth in a frenzy as I pushed everything I had into that dirt.

It answered the call, creating a soft bed that Iban crashed into. He bounced off the surface, landing again with a thump and then bouncing off the side. His face smacked against the stone, the sound making me wince as I rounded the moss. It returned to the earth much more slowly, creeping back to the place I'd summoned it from. I knelt at Iban's side, turning him on his back slowly and staring down at the blood seeping from his nose.

He pushed my hands away with a groan, sitting slowly as he stared at me. I glanced back up to see Gray glaring down at us, and there was no doubt in my mind that he hadn't expected me to still be at the bottom of those stairs. I couldn't explain what had made me pause, why I hadn't immediately gone into the gardens.

Something had driven me to find Gray, and I'd assumed it was my own guilt over what I'd allowed to happen. I might not have chosen whatever lurked between Gray and I, but the thought of him kissing another woman made me murderous.

I could only imagine how he felt about what had transpired, and as he knocked on the railing twice and turned away, moving for the stairs, I had absolutely no doubt that he knew precisely what did happen.

Fuck.

"Are you all right?" I asked Iban finally, turning my attention back to him.

He pushed to stand, cradling his broken nose. "I'll be fine," he said slowly, moving his fingers around on his face.

"Let me," I said, reaching for the moss on the ground. I grasped a handful of it, raising it toward his face.

"You've done enough," Iban snapped, making me flinch as I dropped the moss to the ground. As soon as it retreated back beneath the stone, I drew a circle with my shoe and watched as the stone righted itself once again.

"You knew what you were risking when you kissed me," I said, raising my brow. Only a fool wouldn't have believed that he'd incur the wrath of my husband when he touched me, and Iban was many things, but he wasn't a complete idiot. He'd just thought he wouldn't get caught.

Iban scoffed, dropping his hand. A new drop of blood slid down over his lip as it curved into a cruel grimace. "Yeah, I just thought it would be worth it."

He turned away, hefting his bag onto his shoulder. Thrusting a hand into it and rummaging around, his shoulders sagged in relief, confirming he still had the knife. Heading for the family he knew would heal him without any of the complications that came with me, he retreated from the situation. I brushed off the hurt at his words, as dickish as they might have been, understanding that they came from a place of fear and anger.

I'd said and done worse in my own pain and refusal to acknowledge it, but I would have been lying to myself if I didn't admit the pettiest part of me hated the lack of appreciation for the fact that I'd *saved his life*.

That would come later when the adrenaline faded, when he realized just how close to death he'd been.

I turned on my heel, forgoing my journey to the gardens in favor of the confrontation that waited for me in the rooms Gray and I shared. As much as I might be trying to worm my way beneath his skin, *this* couldn't go unanswered.

Students left their classes for the day as I made my way toward Gray's office and our bedroom, passing them by and going in the opposite direction. He should have been teaching a class of his own until he agreed to a replacement, but his last period of the day was once occupied by the new witches who'd been brought in this year.

Before he fucking slaughtered them.

My anger rose as I pushed open the door, finding him standing by the window with whiskey in his hand. He'd stripped off his suit jacket, tossing it over the back of the sofa while he waited for me. Iban's words had affected me more than I wanted to admit, the hurt combining with the way that Gray had betrayed me.

Attempting to kill someone I considered a friend was unaccept-
able regardless of the trigger event.

I slammed the door closed behind me, stepping fully into the
room and crossing my arms over my chest. Gray turned his body to
face me, quirking a brow in impatience. "Well? Let's hear it then,"
he said, the complete lack of remorse hitting me far worse than any
argument he could have offered.

He didn't care.

He hadn't done it in anger or rage, but made a cold, calculated
decision. My arms dropped to my sides as I laughed in disbelief,
shaking my head and turning for the bedroom.

I'd have understood his actions coming from betrayal. I'd have
understood the rage and anger when he looked at me after what
I'd done, but this was different. This was just another step in some
master plan I wasn't privy to.

And I wanted no fucking part in it.

I went to the dresser, gathering up an armful of clothes and
tossing them onto the bed. I then went to the closet, searching for
a bag to shove them into as Gray blocked the doorway. "What are
you doing, Witchling?"

"What does it look like? I'm not staying here anymore," I called
from the closet, returning to drop the bag on the bed. The clothes
came unfolded as I grabbed them again, tossing them into the
duffel bag as quickly as I could.

"Like Hell you're not," Gray argued, puffing up his chest as if
to prove the point that he blocked the only door out. Jonathan
scurried out of my messenger bag as I set it on the bed, hurrying
into the living room like the coward he was.

"You tried to kill my friend," I said, spinning to face him. "I
knew you were a murderer, but I thought you'd at least spare the
people I cared about after what you said in the woods that day."

He tensed his jaw, squaring it even further as he took a step
toward me. "Do you kiss all your friends like that?"

"Maybe I do," I said, leaning into his face. "What difference would it make if I did? Your compulsion means I can't even fucking enjoy it, you asshole."

Gray stilled for a moment, searching my face before he smiled broadly. His laughter was mocking as he closed the distance between us, stopping only when he filled my vision and obliterated everything but him. "You died, love. I brought you back using my own blood and magic. There is no more compulsion."

I stared up at him, my brow furrowing as I considered the unthinkable. "You're lying."

"My magic cannot work against you now because you have the same magic in your veins. They cancel each other out. You may not have enjoyed that boy's kiss, but it wasn't because I compelled you not to. It was because you're just not interested in him," Gray said, taking another step toward me. The length of his body pressed against mine, leaving me with no choice but to look up at him when he cupped my cheek. The gentleness he touched me with was in such direct opposition to the way he must have touched Iban that it made me wince. "You cannot be interested in him when I already have your heart."

"You don't," I snapped, taking a step back and putting distance between us. "Only a monster would throw a man over the railing because he dared to kiss me. I'm not like you, and I will not *waste* my love on a man like that."

"You're my wife," Gray said, twisting his head with frustration as he ran his tongue over his bottom teeth. "I will do whatever I please with anyone who touches you. Maybe it would be wise for you to take this as the warning it is, and make sure it never happens again. But I will have you know I didn't approach him with the intent to kill him. It was clear to me you didn't enjoy it, and I was content to let your rejection be punishment enough."

"Really?" I asked, leaning toward him as I crossed my arms over my chest. "Because I find that very hard to believe."

"I also knew you would likely find it difficult to forgive me for killing him on the spot, and I didn't particularly care to deal with you pretending you didn't want to be with me until you did," he explained, and I turned to sit on the edge of the bed, looking up at him in confusion.

"But you threw him over the railing," I said, stating the obvious. It didn't match up with his story.

"He might have mentioned that if he knew I cared for you, others would, too. He said anyone with half a brain would put it together and use you as my weakness to get to me. He said I'd get you killed," Gray explained, leaning against the dresser opposite the bed.

"Was he wrong?" I asked, staring up at the man who had somehow survived for centuries but had the emotional intelligence of a newborn who threw a fit anytime he didn't get his way.

"I didn't say that."

"So you threw him over the railing because he said something you didn't like? Even though it was true?" I asked, pulling open the drawer of the nightstand and shoving my phone charger into the duffel bag.

Gray shrugged, his smirk indicating he didn't see anything wrong with what he'd done. "I've killed for less . . ." The humor in his voice shouldn't have made me laugh, but the twisted humor got to me. I covered my mouth with my hand to hide my smile, ignoring the butterflies in my stomach when I glanced over at Gray and saw the heartbreakingly beautiful smile that warmed his face.

Absolutely not. I will not fuck the murderer.

He stood, making his way toward me with a grin as I fought to sink back into my anger. I was still furious that he'd thought it was appropriate to kill anyone, let alone a friend of mine. The thought that it might be Della, Margot, or Nova next was what finally made the smile drift from my face, my anger returning as he stopped in front of me.

He slid his fingers beneath my chin, angling my face to stare up at him. "I think you like the idea of me being so consumed with jealousy that I would kill anyone for you, so let me make something very clear to you. I was willing to look past this once, but the next time? It won't matter if he's your friend or not; the next person you let touch you will die by my hand, and I will make sure he suffers."

"Sometimes I think you want me to hate you," I said, my voice holding my warning as I pushed to my feet. I brushed past him, ignoring the way my body slid against his as I moved to get more clothing from the dresser.

"That's because sometimes you need me to distract you from the emotions you aren't ready to process yet, Witchling. You have to hate me right now, because we both know if you can forgive me for this, you can forgive me for anything," he said.

I scoffed, shaking my head at his arrogance. "I don't forgive you. I don't forgive you for any of this," I snapped, grabbing my duffel and messenger bag. I turned for the door, striding away from him with sure steps.

The worst part was that it was true, and he and I both knew it. *This* was unforgivable.

And I'd laughed.

Gray grabbed me by the arm, spinning me back to face him as the bags slid down to our feet. A burst of air erupted through the room as he moved me, slamming the door to our bedroom shut as his mouth slammed down on mine.

It was a brutal conquest, a possession, as he grabbed my cheeks in his hands and pried me open for his assault. I groaned, releasing the straps of my bags to shove at his chest. The distinct magic of air brushed over my skin, a strong breeze sending him back a step as he tilted his head to the side and stared at me.

I looked down at my hands in horror, the realization dawning on me as Gray grinned in pure male satisfaction. He'd given me part of him. His blood, his magic.

The same as he'd given to the Covenant.

No matter that Susannah had been a Madizza; she'd possessed the magic of all the legacies so that she would be impartial to any one element.

"There's my wicked little witch," Gray said, taking a single step toward me. This time when he reached for me, I met him halfway. My mouth crashed against his as I clawed at the fabric of his shirt, feeding buttons through the holes and eventually tearing through it with my nails.

Gray groaned when I scraped his skin, leaving red welts in my wake until I finally stripped his shirt off him. He tore my shirt over my head, tossing it to the side as I unhooked my bra and let it fall to the floor. His mouth was on mine all over again, his hand buried in my hair as I fought with his belt buckle and unzipped his fly, not even caring enough to take his pants off him before I turned my attention to my own. I pushed them down, kicking off my boots and fighting to never let him take his mouth from mine.

He turned, gripping me by the hips and tossing me to the bed. I bounced once before settling on the pillows. Gray's eyes on me warmed my body as he pulled my pants from my ankles, taking my underwear with them before he straddled my waist and pinned my hands beside my head. The roses I kept on my night-stand flourished, growing as a thorny vine spread from them.

There was just one problem. For once, I wasn't the one in control.

"Gray," I whispered, turning my attention up to him as he held me still. The vine wrapped around the posts of the bed, pulling tight before it extended toward me and wrapped around my wrists. It positioned itself carefully, nestling the threat of the thorns against my skin. I only felt the pinch of them when I shifted as Gray released his hold on me, leaning back to stare down at me.

He stood, stripping off his pants and letting that warm gaze trail over my body. I felt it like a caress, the sweet brush of air ghosting over my skin coming directly from him. My nipples hardened against the cool breeze, the brush of it between my legs forcing me to pull them closed.

Gray chuckled as he slapped the tops of my thighs, the sting making me jolt so that the thorns pierced my flesh. He smiled as he leaned over me, licking the blood from my skin with a groan.

I wondered if he had missed it, or if he enjoyed not having the need for it. A man like Gray didn't like to be dependent on anything or anyone. I knew it because I didn't, either.

He grinned down at me wickedly, formulating his plan.

I was so fucked.

27

GRAY

The taste of her blood on my tongue made me want to go feral. I wanted more of it, wanted to taste it always. I might not have had the fangs or the physical cravings anymore, but that didn't mean I did not desire the intimacy it brought with my witchling.

I straddled her chest, gripping my cock as I guided it to her lips. She pressed them tightly together, defiance shining in that challenging stare. She was still so angry with me, but she couldn't deny the need she felt, either. The violence of the dance between us meant we could simultaneously want to bleed one another and want to fuck, two opposing storms crashing together.

We just had to hope we would remain after the rain.

"Open your fucking mouth, Witchling. It isn't my blood you're going to drink this time," I said, smirking as her eyes flew wide. She opened her mouth to curse me out, and I used the opportunity to push inside. Willow grumbled around the head of my cock as I pushed toward her throat, slipping a hand beneath her head and angling her neck on the pillow so that I could get deeper.

She mumbled, fighting to get the words out. I didn't allow it, never fully withdrawing from the haven of her warmth as I fucked her face. I didn't need to hear the words to know what she said, the glare in her eyes only serving to make my cock harder.

You fucking asshole.

It was written all over her face.

I shoved deeper into her throat, not giving her the opportunity to swallow around me. She gagged, her eyes watering as that glare deepened. "Don't pretend your cunt won't be soaked by the time I give you my mouth, my love," I said, my voice scolding as Willow swallowed and let me in. I moved in slow thrusts, being gentler because of the angle than I might have if I'd gotten her on her knees in front of me.

She was at my mercy because she wanted to be, no matter what she might have tried to argue. The devious thing sucked as I pulled back out of her throat, allowing her to breathe.

"Fuck," I groaned, the feeling of her taking what she wanted enough to torment me. I wished I could feel her nails digging into my ass, feel her pulling me closer and farther into her. Instead I settled for shallow pumps, letting her work her magic with her tongue until I spiraled over the edge.

Willow kept her eyes on mine as she swallowed around me. I slapped my palm against the wall, leaning forward as Willow sucked until I came.

She was still glaring at me when I pulled out of her mouth, staring down at the swollen red flesh and sliding my way down her body. I settled between her hips, my softening cock pressing against her wet heat.

"See? You're soaked," I said, pressing a lingering kiss to her mouth before trailing a finger down between the valley of her breasts. With my immediate needs satiated, I took my time drawing circles around her breasts and nipples, watching as goose bumps rose along her skin.

"Don't be an asshole," she hissed, squirming beneath my touch.

"I would never," I said, feigning insult as I leaned forward, drawing her nipple into my mouth and biting it lightly. She arched her back beneath me as I gripped her other breast in my hand, the ample flesh spilling over as I squeezed.

I enjoyed every second of it as I kissed every inch of her chest and stomach, exploring every dip and valley and committing them to memory. I spent more time on her ribs, focusing on the spot where I'd stabbed her to pull Charlotte's rib free. Her breath hitched as if she knew exactly what I was doing, and I didn't miss the shift in her breathing or her anger.

This wasn't the anger of righteousness, but the anger that came from deep, festering wounds that wouldn't heal until she allowed me to soothe them. I might have done what I had to do to make sure she came out the other side alive, but Willow would never forget that I could have merely chosen not to do it at all.

In time, she'd come to understand that it had been necessary for us to have a future, that I wouldn't have been able to survive a lifetime *knowing* I loved her but unable to feel it. Left with only the faint memory of what love was after it had been lost, I knew Willow was important to me.

I just couldn't feel the imprint of her on my soul until my soul and my heart were united in one body.

Trailing my lips down over her stomach, I pressed my thumbs into the little valley next to her hip bones, reveling in the way she squirmed. The spot was sensitive for Willow, like an easy button I could press to get her to spread her legs wider. She did just that, spreading for me as I settled more comfortably between her thighs and trailed my mouth over her.

I inhaled her scent, the unique combination of flora and woman that only Willow could achieve. Slipping a finger inside her, I chuckled when she clenched around it. "You're being cruel," she said, staring down at me as I leaned forward and touched my tongue to where my finger pumped inside her slowly. Dragging it over the length of her pussy, I made a slow, leisurely path to her clit.

Carefully avoiding the spot where I knew she wanted my touch more than anything, I explored every ridge and part of her. Dipping my tongue into it, kissing her flesh, I enjoyed the way she squirmed beneath me in an effort to angle me where she wanted. The scent of her blood grew stronger as she struggled, the shallow cuts at her wrists reopening with her movement.

"Gray, please," she begged, finally giving me what I wanted. Willow could go rounds with me and fight me all she wanted during the day, but there was only one person in charge once our clothes came off.

"You let him touch you," I said, the words coming out in more of a growl than anything. He'd had his hands on her neck, his mouth on hers.

And no matter what I knew about his temporary nature and waiting him out, I needed to erase the image of them from my mind. I could think of no better way to do it than to force Willow to admit she was mine.

"It was just a kiss," she said, the quiet of those words betraying the emotion that still lingered beneath the surface of her skin. Sex was a distraction for her, a way to separate herself from the things she wasn't yet ready to admit to feeling. I wished I could say that she was only keeping them secret from me, but I knew better than that.

Willow hadn't even admitted them to herself yet.

"So is this," I said, pressing my mouth to the flesh of her pussy gently. I didn't give her what she wanted, earning a growl of frustration from her. "Would you want me to kiss another woman?"

"I'm going to fucking kill you for this," she seethed, her anger forcing her magic to respond. It pulsed along her skin, a tantalizing electricity that I knew few could feel. The vines responded to her call when she put that much into it, her blood satisfying them as they retreated back from her arms. She buried her hands in my hair, gripping me tightly as she glared down at me. "You ever touch another woman, and I'll—"

"What? Throw her down the stairs?" I asked, smirking at my wife and the fury on her face.

"No," she said, surprising me with a ruthless smile. "I'll throw *you* down them, and then bury you alive." She pressed me toward her center, angling me where she wanted me. With her admission of jealousy hanging between us, I gave her a brief reprieve of what she wanted. Wrapping my lips around her swollen clit, I sucked lightly as she bucked beneath me.

"Careful, love. Jealousy like that would be hard to believe if you didn't love me," I said, murmuring it against her before I circled her with my tongue. Her cheeks pinked with her anger at being caught and what it implied, leaving me to chuckle as I brought her close to her orgasm. She trembled beneath me, her legs shaking at the sides of my head as she came closer.

Then I stopped, staring up at her.

"What are you doing?" she asked, her eyes flying wide with panic. She was so wet and swollen and greedy, so desperate as I crawled up to cover her body with mine. I didn't give her my cock, staring down at her and pinning her still. There was no escape from my gaze, no retreating from the knowledge that I would see her.

"If you want to come, you're going to have to admit you're mine. Your vicious little mouth is mine," I said, leaning forward to kiss her. She sank her teeth into my lower lip, drawing blood in a way that only made me harder. "Your perfect little cunt is mine. All of you, and the next time you let someone touch you, I will find a way to make sure you can never do it again. Is that understood, Witchling?"

Willow smiled, arching her back and dragging her hips up the bed. She rubbed her pussy along my length, attempting to tease me into giving her what she wanted. When I didn't give in, her brow tensed. "Gray."

"Say the words, Willow," I ordered, giving her no choice but to choose.

She could keep her pride and choose to come on her own, or she could just admit the truth, and I'd fuck her until she couldn't breathe.

She cast her eyes down, staring at the maze she'd imprinted on my chest. I grabbed her chin, turning her stare up to mine in a way that communicated exactly what I wanted. She was mistaken if she thought I would accept her refusal and leave her alone.

I had every intention of tormenting her until she gave in.

I slipped my hand between her legs, grinding the heel of my palm against her clit and driving two fingers inside her. She whimpered, the defiance in her stare growing as she realized exactly what would happen if she didn't give me what I wanted. I wasn't above using her body against her, playing her like my favorite instrument until she crooned my favorite song.

"My body is yours," she said, her lips peeling back from her teeth in something between a smile and a snarl.

"Oh no, Witchling. *That* is not what I asked for," I said, continuing to play with her pussy. I leaned forward, burying my face in her neck and tormenting her with soft kisses and the brush of my tongue against her skin. She shivered, gasping when I sank my teeth into her skin. I wished I could break through, longed for the intimacy of her blood flowing down my throat.

Her body sagged beneath me, obedience winning out in her desperation to come. Her devotion when she was like this pleased me, even if it was a hesitant admission.

The things that came easy in life were never worth as much as the victories that came through blood, sweat, and tears.

"I'm yours," she said, her voice quiet even as she glared at me. She pressed at my shoulders, shoving me back with a burst of air that I knew she wasn't fully in control of. It helped pave the way as she twisted me to my back, coming down on top of me as she reached between us and guided me to her entrance. She slid her pussy down the length of my cock, enveloping me in her heat. She was so wet and ready from my torment that she sank as deep as she could on the first drop, settling herself against my groin as I stretched up and grabbed her by the back of the neck.

Yanking her toward me, I captured her mouth with mine as

my witchling started to move. She took what she wanted, dancing her hips over me so that her clit ground against me with every thrust. She tightened around me within a few thrusts, her eyes fluttering as she whimpered into my mouth. I flipped her to her back, continuing to fuck her even when her thighs trembled and she shoved a hand between us to try to stop me.

She was too sensitive when she came, needing a reprieve that I didn't give her. I took everything she had to give, fucking her through her orgasm and taking her hands in mine. I gathered them in the grip of one hand, pinning them above her head as my other hand slid behind her knee and shoved her leg high so that I could get deeper.

Her breasts bounced as I pounded into her, fucking her harder than I had before. Her body was more resilient, less fragile and more able to meet me as she took it. Her nails dug into my hands, clawing at me when she came back from the torment of her orgasm. I released her finally, moving my hand to her throat and gripping her there. Her eyes widened for a moment as I restricted her breathing, but she didn't fight off the possessive touch.

I leaned toward her, touching my forehead to hers as she reached around me and dug her nails into the flesh of my ass. Pulling me into her body harder, she encouraged the fury in my thrusts.

The determination to make sure that she felt me moving inside her for days drove me forward, slamming into her fast and hard. "Mine," I growled, watching as her mismatched eyes flared.

She surged up, taking my lip between her teeth and nipping at it sharply enough to draw blood. The sound that came from her throat was more animal than human, drawing from the deepest instincts of our bond. "*Mine,*" she practically purred.

I thrust my free hand between our bodies, rubbing her clit as I fucked her. She moaned, her face going slack as she tossed back her head and arched her back. "I can't," she said, grasping my arm with one hand to attempt to stop me.

"Give me another, Witchling," I said, ignoring her protest. I tightened my hand around her throat, cutting off her air as she sputtered beneath me.

Unrelenting, I fucked her and ruthlessly assaulted her clit, bringing her to the brink while she struggled to breathe. Her mouth opened, no sound coming out as she stared at me. Fear crossed into her vision, the moment where she wondered if she'd made a mistake.

Only when her eyes went lazy did I release her throat, watching as her lungs expanded with air. She screamed, clawing her orgasm into my back as I shoved deep into her and came, filling her with me.

She lay limp beneath me, her body lax and eyes closing as I pulled free from her. Her legs fell to the bed, spread wide for me to look down at her swollen pink pussy. I touched my fingers to her, gathering the moisture that had followed my retreat and shoving it back inside her.

She flinched away from the touch, her body too sensitive as I widened her legs and slipped my fingers back into her. She closed her legs around my head, attempting to slide up the bed to avoid me as I carefully kissed her clit and fingered her.

My release surrounded my fingers, easing the passage even as her body tried to expel me. "Gray, I can't—"

"What's wrong, Witchling? I thought you wanted to come?" I asked, my voice mocking as she stared down at me in shock.

"It's too much," she said, shaking her head.

"We'll be done when I say we're done, and not a moment before." I smirked, lowering my head to her pussy all over again.

Willow wouldn't sleep that night.

28

WILLOW

I strode through the hallway to the room where I knew the legacies were suffering through their channeling class. It should have been the most entertaining of classes, an opportunity to embrace the magic in our veins, but the professor who taught it had lost his way.

It was hard to channel when your magic didn't answer your call because of your neglect.

I waited outside for the bell to ring, leaning against the wall. My body ached with each step, but I was determined not to let it deter me from what needed to be done. All last night had done was prove that I needed to do whatever it took to rid this world of Lucifer.

I needed to do whatever it took to get Him out of my life and my body as soon as possible.

Iban walked out of the class with a group of male friends at his side, and I looked over his shoulder to find Della's stare. I nodded to her without a word, watching as she tightened her mouth and dipped her head. I hated what my actions would do to her relationship, but the alternative was unthinkable.

If Gray had already affected me so deeply in such a limited time, what would he do if he had years to manipulate me? How long until he had me so deeply entrenched in him that I believed he loved me? Even worse, that I loved him enough to forgive his faults?

"Willow," Iban said, his voice hesitant. His friends looked at him in question, but he waved them on and took me by the hand, guiding me toward a secluded alcove. "What are you doing here?"

"I'll do it," I said, my voice firmer than it had been yesterday. "Can you gather the people we'll need for the spell?"

He tilted his head to the side, releasing my arm and keeping his distance. His proximity to death seemed to work wonders for making him respect my personal space. "What made you change your mind? I know you weren't fully on board yesterday. Did he do something to you?"

I flushed, my cheeks heating at the reminder of all the things he'd done to me the night before. It had felt like both a punishment and a reward, as if he couldn't decide if he was furious with me or relieved that I had been honest about not feeling anything from Iban's kiss.

"He tried to kill you," I said, the lie sitting heavy in my throat. What kind of person had I become that *that* wasn't the driving force behind my decision to get rid of Gray?

Iban looked as if he didn't believe me, his wariness overshadowing his boyishly handsome features, but he didn't call me out on the lie, nodding and glancing over my shoulder. "I'll have them meet us in the library in an hour. Can you make that work?"

I glanced toward the hall that would lead to Gray's classroom, indecision warring in me. The cage around my heart had cracked for him, leaving me feeling restless and on edge. I couldn't shake the feeling that this would be the greatest mistake of my life, but I'd only be able to rebuild that shelter if he were gone.

I may not have been born without a heart the way his Vessel had, but that didn't mean I didn't prefer the numbness that came from a thousand jagged cuts against my soul.

Life had broken me. My father had broken me.

But Gray had *shattered* me.

I wouldn't give him the time and opportunity to do it again, even if it meant condemning myself back to that place where nothing really mattered. The irony wasn't lost on me.

Gray hadn't had a heart to love me with, but he'd been willing to do anything to get it back.

Only for me to be willing to throw mine away.

"I'll be there," I said, smiling softly at Iban's back as he turned from me without a word. I left it to him to gather those we needed, knowing that Della and Nova at least would stand at my side and be a quiet support until I had to leave to do the one thing I wanted to avoid more than anything.

"Are you all right?" Nova asked, coming up beside me. Della avoided my gaze, hurrying to find Juliet. I could only hope she wouldn't confess anything to her, but I wouldn't have been able to fault her even if she did. Just because I was willing to sacrifice my heart didn't mean I would have expected that from her.

Not everyone had to choose between love and duty, between doing what they wanted and what was right. Some loves just made sense. They fell into what was realistic and expected of a relationship, feeling more like the slow growth of roots beneath the surface than lightning striking the branches. Gray and I would burn the world to the ground if I allowed our love to grow, accepting it as part of me when it was unnatural.

"No," I admitted, staring into my friend's gray eyes.

Nova smiled sadly, dipping her head as though she understood. But she didn't. None of them did.

"You know, it's okay to not be okay. You don't always have to be strong for us," she said, leaning her head on top of mine.

I fought back the sting of tears, nodding. "I might need you to be strong for a while, but for now I have to keep fighting," I stated, refusing to look at her. "Because that's who I am."

The echo of Gray's words struck deep in my chest, and it wasn't lost on me that those were the ones I turned to for comfort.

It wasn't the memory of my mother's hug or her encouragement, but the words of the very man I planned to kill that night.

I stepped away from Nova slowly, making my way toward Gray's classroom. He stood at the front, looking unbothered by his lack of sleep the night before. I felt damn near dead on my feet as I approached him, forcing myself to ignore those who watched us through the open door.

He turned, raising his brow when he found me standing there. "Witchling?" he asked, setting his chalk on the metal tray at the bottom of the board and brushing his hands together.

"I hate you," I said, the words quiet. He tensed, preparing for the argument I knew he had expected. We'd done this song and dance far too many times for him to expect anything else, and I wrung my hands together, picking at my nails as I searched for the words to give him.

If I was going to strip him from my life, if I was going to say goodbye, then I at least wanted to admit my truth just once.

"Willow . . ." His frustration leaked into his voice, forcing me to take another step toward him. He met me at the side of the desk, his face softening as he read the uneasiness. He knew what I was trying to say. He knew that I wasn't *really* telling him I hated him. "I know," he added softly.

"Do you?" I asked, tilting my head to the side. "Do you know what it's like to want nothing more than to carve you out of my fucking heart? Do you know how much I hate that the person who has shown me the most kindness is the *one* person I'm supposed to despise?"

"I knew you were mine the moment I saw you, and then I spent the next fifty years waiting for you. I hated you for a long time, Witchling. You threatened everything I'd been planning and building for centuries. So yes, I understand," he said, running the back of his knuckles over my cheek. "The difference between you and I is that I do not care about what is morally right. I take what I want without shame. You would rather make a martyr of yourself to feel better about your feelings for me."

"That's not fair," I said, flinching back from the frustration in his voice.

"Isn't it? What do you owe to these people who you would fight so hard to defend? A few weeks ago, you would have laughed if I'd said you were one of them," Gray said, and I hated that I couldn't deny the truth to that statement.

I'd wanted nothing more than to go and live out my life with Ash, leaving the Coven to their own problems.

"They're my kind. Without the Covenant in the way—"

"You can only use them as a shield for so long, Witchling," he said, picking up a book from his desk. "I need to prepare for my next class, so if you've just come to argue, then I suggest you see yourself out."

I sighed, touching my fingers to the top of his book and pushing it down. He glared at me over the surface of the page, forcing me to swallow back my frustration with him. "I'm not using them as a shield."

"Aren't you?" he asked, flicking my fingers off his book.

"Why do you have to be so difficult?" I asked, turning my back on him. I made my way to the door, determined to give him the privacy he'd so desperately wanted only a moment before.

"Me?" he asked, snorting with laughter. "You came here just to pick a fight, and then have the nerve to get angry with me when I ask you the questions you aren't ready to ask yourself."

I sighed, letting my arms drop to my sides as the fight left me. "I didn't come here to pick a fight," I admitted.

"I'm not sure you know how to *not* pick a fight," he said, but there was a smile spreading on his face. "What do you need, my love?"

"I wanted to say I was sorry. I was wrong yesterday, when I let Iban kiss me. It won't happen again," I said, observing Gray. He set his book back down carefully, closing the distance between us. When he tipped his head to the side, there were only two thoughts on my mind.

Either he was about to be cruel, or he thought I was about to break.

I didn't know which reaction from him would hurt worse in that moment, knowing what I was about to do. His cruelty would hurt now but make it easier later; his kindness would be the opposite.

His steps were slow as he approached me, pausing just in front of me to lift my mother's necklace from where it hung around my neck. He toyed with it, holding my gaze. "I know it won't, and I appreciate your apology," he said, letting the necklace drop against my neck again. "But that's not what you came here to tell me, and it's certainly not what I want to fucking hear."

I swallowed, regretting the choice I'd made in coming to him. I couldn't find the words that had seemed so easy when I didn't have his golden stare looking down at me.

A golden stare that I would probably only see one more time, when the life faded from him completely.

"This was a mistake," I said, shaking my head and turning to retreat.

Gray caught me by the back of the neck, using his grip to turn me back to face him. His mouth came down on mine roughly, his tongue forcing me to open. He pulled away just as suddenly, leaving me following after him. "Say it."

"I hate that you made me love you," I said, the desperate words coming out as the barest whisper. I couldn't deny the need that pulsed in my heart, the way that every sweet and thoughtful act of his had wormed his way beneath my skin. He might have been the devil and capable of great evil, but he also took care of me in ways I'd never had.

He showed me what I meant to him anytime he had the chance, and that more than anything wore away at me until only that truth remained.

"I know you do, Witchling," he said, his mouth spreading into a dazzling smile. His eyes lit as if I'd given him more magic than he knew how to contain, the sun reflecting off him and making him seem like the angel he had once been.

"I'm pretty sure that's the part where you're supposed to say it back," I said, pouting up at him.

His grin widened as he leaned down, touching his mouth to mine far more gently. He lingered there, sharing breath with me and holding my stare. "I love you, Witchling. For everything you are and everything you are not."

I sighed in relief, smiling through the bittersweet pain.

A single moment of happiness to call my own before the memory became agonizing.

I pressed onto my toes, kissing him as I wrapped my arms around his neck. Lucifer wrapped His arms around my waist, lifting me from my feet and holding me tight.

I hoped he wouldn't see the knife coming later.

I hoped he would feel no pain.

29

WILLOW

I made my way into the library, knocking on the secret door softly. I hoped no one in the main library rooms had heard me, waiting impatiently to be let in.

Iban finally pushed open the door, hurrying to pull me inside before I could be spotted. The small space was far too crowded with a representative from each legacy house huddled inside, but it was the blade in the center of the table that stole the breath from my lungs.

I'd come here knowing what I planned to do, but that didn't make the sight of it any easier.

I strode into the room, never taking my eyes off the blade. Sound filtered out, my head filling with static. I felt as if I'd plunged underwater, as if the only way to survive this was to go entirely numb. I was drowning, suffocating beneath the surface.

I plastered the mask on my face, standing at the head of the table beside Iban. Nova caught my eyes, her lips moving with sounds I couldn't hear. I shook my head, trying to shake off the feeling of not being able to breathe. It was worse than when Gray had choked me the night before.

The numbness was always worse than the fear.

The figure of a man appeared against the back wall, his form hazy as he cast a leisurely glance up and down my body. He studied me, assessing me, and found me severely lacking if the way he chuckled and turned his back to me were any indication. The faint shadow of white wings hid his eyes, but I found myself straining toward him regardless.

Iban touched my arm, jolting me out of the trance that had consumed me. Breath returned to my lungs, forcing me to slap a palm down on the table to catch myself as I sucked back greedy gulps of air.

"Are you okay?" Nova asked, stepping around the group of people who had gathered to watch me crumble.

I nodded my head, clearing my throat, which felt hoarse. "I'm fine. Just a vision," I said, shaking it off as if it was inconsequential.

"Loralei used to have them, too," an older witch said, her blue eyes shining as she studied me. I turned to stare at her, finding comfort in the fact that my aunt had been unable to hide the more mysterious side of the Hecate powers. Everyone assumed that we merely raised the dead, brought back zombies that had no memory of who they had once been.

Few knew the truth. We had to commune with the dead and know we were unable to give them the one thing that they wanted more than anything.

Life.

Loralei had often spoken about guiding those with unfinished business on their journey to peace. According to my father, she'd considered that her true calling and the real magic she had to offer.

"I'm glad to know I'm not alone," I said simply, trying to push aside my embarrassment at having been witnessed in the throes of a vision. Especially because I knew that vision had been prompted by my agony over what I was about to do. "Iban told you all why you're here?"

Iban cleared his throat, nodding as he reached out to wrap his palm around the bone handle of the blade. I swallowed, hating the sight of him being the one to hold it. It felt like another layer to my betrayal, like working with Iban somehow made Gray's murder worse.

"Do you really think you can do this?" one of the men at the table asked. I didn't know him, but he was dressed in yellow, the color accentuating his warm brown skin.

"You've made yourself vulnerable by sleeping with that monster. What makes you think he doesn't know exactly what you have planned?" the woman at his side asked. She wore the white of the crystal witches, her silver hair hanging loose over her dress. Her eyes were purple, too, darker than those of most of the Hecate witches.

"Is there a time a man is more vulnerable than when his dick is out?" I asked, watching the way the older woman reeled back from my vulgarity. I wouldn't beat around the bush, and I certainly wouldn't tolerate the insinuation that I was the only one who was put at risk by our relationship.

I'd come here to find his weakness and exploit it.

I just hadn't known it would be me all along.

"I suppose not," the witch said, shaking her head as she laid out the crystals on the table. She made a circle around the center, placing a single stone at each point of the pentagram. Iban returned the blade to the center as everyone's eyes came to me.

A spell like this required three things.

Stone.

Blood.

Bone.

I waved my hand at the bones circling my hip, watching as they moved how I commanded. I hadn't understood at first, thinking Gray was the only one capable of determining where the bones rested against me.

I understood now.

They were a part of me, and all I needed to do was acknowledge that and they were mine to command. Loralei's resurrection and death had shown me the truth, enabling me to accept the darkest parts of my reality.

The bones swept out from my hip, moving in an arc to scatter around the table. They surrounded the center pentagram, spilling haphazardly wherever they landed. I alone reached into the pentagram, bending over the table to hold out my hand.

Dragging the blade over my palm, I winced at the drops of blood that dripped onto the surface. It felt like a waste, to let something that could bring so much life be used to bring death instead.

"*Sanguis terrae et os,*" I said, watching as the bones rattled on the table in recognition of my offering. The pentagram formed by the crystals lined itself with the vines that had burst free from the wood, drawing the symbol on top of the table.

I handed the knife to Nova next, ignoring the pointed way she stared at me. She followed suit, leaning forward and cutting her hand. She didn't hesitate to offer her blood to the spell even though such magic had been forbidden under the last Covenant's reign. I had no doubt they'd have tried to kill him before, but they hadn't had the necromancy magic of the Blacks to aid them.

A breeze blew through the room as it filled with her air, washing over my skin and chilling me to the bone. She handed the knife to Della at her side, the faint sprinkle of rain falling in the room leaving tiny droplets within our spell circle.

The Yellow witch cut herself, the vines that had grown on the table filling with flames. They acted as a boundary, containing the fire that would hurt when I needed to place the blade back in the middle. The blood there burned, becoming one with the flames as the acrid scent filled the room.

The Red witch at her side turned to drag the knife across his hand, a wash of need spreading through us. Iban tensed at my side, but I forced myself to ignore him when he stepped closer to me. The magic of the Reds was potent, but it could not create what was not already there.

And it wasn't him my body sang for.

The White witch added her blood, the hum of the crystals drowning out all sound beyond our circle. The Purple witch finished the circle as Iban stepped out of the way, cast out because of his lack of magic. His displeasure at being excluded from the very plan he'd set in motion was palpable, but I hated the way he lingered at my back.

He'd need to be dealt with as soon as Gray was gone, the boundaries set very clearly. There was no future for he and I even without Gray in the picture.

Stars shimmered on the ceiling, falling to the circle and spreading amongst us as I stared in awe. The Purple witch handed me the blade, allowing me to take the final step in imbuing all our magic within the dagger.

I swallowed as I took it from her, staring at the burning pentagon. I pushed myself to move, guiding my hand to those flames. The fire licked at my skin, burning and leaving charred black cracks behind as I placed the knife upon the table. The pain was agony, searing down to the bone as I gritted my teeth through it.

To bear the power, I would need to give more of myself.

I withdrew, watching as my skin healed anew as I pulled my arm back toward me. Fresh pink skin replaced the charred black.

The blade rested in the flames, until slowly they faded. The dagger pulsed with golden light, absorbing that fire and the blood that burned with it. My vines retreated as I swept my hand over the table, summoning my bones back to me. They circled my waist all over again, returning home as the White witch gathered her crystals in the same manner.

I reached into the circle, wrapping my fingers around the hilt of the blade. The fresh heat of power scalded me, drawing a gasp from my lungs as I accepted the mantle. I felt it deep within me, the rumble of ancient power trapped in that blade.

I gripped it tightly, raising my eyes to stare at those who waited around the table. The Red witch leveled Iban with a stare, nodding as he turned for the door. "I hope we did not make a mistake in trusting you, Covenant," he said to me finally, his red eyes narrowed as he left the room.

"Let's hope it works," I said, watching as the others slowly filtered out. I took my seat at the table, waiting and rejecting all conversation from Della, Nova, and Iban. Eventually, they left me, too.

Until there was only me.

30

WILLOW

I moved on instinct.

It didn't feel as if my legs were attached to my body, and even though the blade was no longer clutched within my grasp, I could feel the echo of its power within me as the one who had placed it in the flames. When it was tucked safely into the messenger bag at my side, I made my way up the stairs slowly.

Students passed me, but I took the precious few moments I had to let myself feel the grief over what I had to do. Once I set foot in that room, there would be no ability to feel sorry for myself. There would only be my deception.

There would only be the task I'd come here to do, finishing the job that was always meant to be mine.

I could be the devil's wife, or I could be the woman who sacrificed herself to save the world from his corruption.

I knew the way he slithered under the skin of all those he touched, the way he could turn us against ourselves.

I knew how easy it was to fall for his lies, even knowing that he was everything that was wrong.

I rounded the corner, pausing outside our door. I drew in a few deep breaths, centering myself and pushing back my pain and fear. I hoped he would have the mercy I would not, the quick and easy death I would never get. His archdemons would make me suffer when they learned what I had done, and the rest of Lucifer's power would leave this world with me.

I forced a hesitant smile to my face, pushing the door open and stepping into the room. Gray lounged on the couch, a book on his lap as he flipped the pages. He looked so comfortable, so relaxed in the new home he'd created for himself here.

He looked up from his book, smiling when he saw me approach. He read the look on my face, misinterpreting it for awkwardness about my confession earlier.

Which was doing exactly what I'd planned, covering for the emotion that clogged my throat and kept me silent. My father had meant for me to be ruthless, for me to kill without thought or care and seduce with skill.

There was none of that left in me as I approached, stopping just in front of Gray.

I swung my messenger bag onto the back of the sofa, letting it rest there as Gray spread his legs and pulled my hips between them. His fingers brushed against the bones as he touched me, his thumbs working circles over me as he looked up at me. "There's no need to feel awkward, Witchling. It changes nothing between us."

I nodded. He was right.

My love for him changed *nothing*.

I smiled as he slid his thumbs beneath the hem of my shirt, sucking back a breath when he touched my bare skin. "You're humming with power," he said, leaning forward to inhale a deep breath of me. I stilled, waiting for the moment he realized that the power trapped within me wasn't entirely my own.

He said nothing as I took a step back, bending down to cup his cheek in my hand. I tilted his face up to mine, staring down at the angel before me. In this moment, he was far more the Morningstar than the devil, gazing up at me as if I were his entire world. I touched my mouth to his, kissing him gently.

Kissing him goodbye.

He groaned into the kiss, letting me place my hands on his

shoulders and shove him back. He fell against the back of the sofa, smirking up at me as I lifted the hem of my dress and slid my underwear down to kick them to the side. His brow quirked when I came to him, unbuckling his belt and unzipping his fly.

"Greedy little witch," he said, the laughter in those words making me flinch. I brushed it off as I straddled his waist, crashing my mouth to his more forcefully. I reached between us, guiding him to my entrance.

He was too big for the fact that I wasn't wet, the rush of need from the Red witch having faded with my stress over what I had to do. The pinch of pain grounded me, making me whimper into his mouth as I rolled my hips. Rising and falling with shallow thrusts, I let my body take over. It knew what to do, responding to the glide of his cock inside me and the press of his lips on mine. Gray groaned as I worked myself down his length, stretching myself open.

I angled my head, tangling my tongue with his. This was far more gentle than I wanted it to be; it felt far more like making love than fucking. Gray grabbed my ass in his hands, cupping each cheek as he let me set the pace. He supported me as I raised and lowered myself on him, moving slowly as I distracted him with my kiss.

Cupping his face in my hands, I poured everything I had into making him believe me. For one single moment, I wanted him to know that I'd meant my words.

I wanted him to know he was loved, even if I couldn't be selfish enough to choose us.

"Witchling," he murmured, his eyes staying closed when I finally pulled away. That nickname struck the wall I'd tried to place around my heart to do this, the surface cracking as I realized it would be the last time I heard his deep voice murmur it.

The last time he called me Witchling.

I stared down at him as his eyes fluttered open, releasing his face and placing my hands on the back of the sofa behind him.

I used the leverage to take him deeper, rolling my hips more fervently. He moaned my name, his cock twitching inside me as a sign of his coming release.

I moved slowly, angling my hand into the bag and pulling the dagger free. Leaning in, I took his mouth with one last kiss, the gentle brush of my lips against his making him feel like he was already a ghost.

I knew there were tears in my eyes as I pulled back finally, placing the blade at my side. He opened his eyes, his head tilting in concern as he cupped my cheek. "What's wrong, my love?" he asked.

My bottom lip trembled as I gave in to the threat of tears, unable to hold them back any longer. "I'm sorry," I said, gasping through the breath that didn't come easy.

I fought for it, trying to quell my panic at the confusion in his stare.

And I plunged the knife into his heart.

31

WILLOW

He gasped, the sound wet and ragged.

His brow furrowed as he looked down at the knife protruding from his ribs, angled just right to get to the fleshy organ beneath. He looked back up at me, the hurt in those eyes drawing a strangled sob from me.

"I'm sorry," I said again, twisting the knife to take as much of his heart with me as I could.

He wheezed, sputtering beneath me. I pulled the dagger free, tossing it to the side as his blood poured free from the wound without obstruction. It pumped onto the sofa, staining the beige fabric with his life. "Why?" he asked, his voice hoarse and rough. I couldn't bring myself to separate from him, to leave him on the sofa.

I didn't want him to be alone.

I'd needed to deceive him for this to work, so why did his question make me feel even worse? "You know why," I said, shaking my head as I stayed with him.

His blood continued to spill, his vision going unfocused. He raised a hand to my face, his palm stained with his blood. He cupped my cheek, the wetness of it smearing against my skin. "I love you," he said, the steely resolve in that voice taking me aback. There was none of the weakness that I would have expected of a man close to death, only a firm warning wrapped in warm words.

He loved me, but that didn't mean I wouldn't suffer for what I'd done . . .

I turned my gaze down to his wound, to the stain on his shirt, and realized that the flow of blood had stopped. My eyes flashed back to his, the calm fury in his gaze more terrifying than any outward rage could have been.

I pressed my hand to his wound in a panic, sinking my fingers into the slit in his shirt. There was no stab wound, only fresh skin covering what I'd done.

If it hadn't been for the puddle of blood staining the couch, I might have thought I had imagined it all.

I scrambled back, wincing when the movement pulled him free from me. He watched me go, sitting on that sofa as I stood in the living room. I didn't bother to run, knowing I wouldn't get far before he sought his revenge. I wouldn't allow anyone else to get caught up in his anger.

Gray tucked himself back into his slacks, standing smoothly without any hint of pain.

"Gray," I said, before clamping my mouth shut. There was nothing I could say, nothing I could plead.

I'd tried to fucking kill him.

And I'd failed.

"Have I been that horrible to you?" he asked, approaching me slowly. Jonathan hissed and retreated beneath the couch, leaving me to my fate.

"That's not—"

"That's not what, Willow?" he asked, his anger pulsing off him. "Why you tried to fucking kill me?"

"You used me!" I screamed, wincing when he jerked back. He'd thought we were beyond what he'd done to get us here, but I didn't think I was capable of moving past it. "And we both know you will do it again."

"You're right," he said, nodding his head. "I used you to get what I wanted, and then I tried to do *everything* I could to make it up to you. I would never hurt you again. I would never do *this*. I would never throw us away."

"Don't you understand? It was never about us!" I yelled, taking a step back as he approached.

"Always the fucking martyr," he snapped, his words sinking inside me. I'd been raised to be a martyr, raised to sacrifice myself to get the bones my father couldn't get for himself.

I didn't know who I was without that purpose.

"Let me spell it out for you, Willow. This was *always* about us," Gray growled, taking slow steps toward me. I had no choice but to retreat into the bedroom, looking around the room as he followed me. He gripped the door, swinging it shut so that it slammed behind him. I winced as I thought of my friends waiting to hear from me, wondering if they'd feel the way the very school seemed to vibrate with the force of it. "You wanted to get rid of me, because you're too weak to *choose* me."

"You're going to *break me!*" I screamed, the shrill sound shocking even me as it clawed its way up my throat. I froze in the center of the bedroom, refusing to retreat any farther. I'd given him enough ground, backed myself into a corner. He could hurt me; he could kill me, and there wasn't a thing I could do to stop it.

I'd deserve it after what I'd done. My guilt pressed down on me, but I forced myself not to think of it. He'd done worse.

"You naive fool," Gray snapped, and my mouth dropped open in shock. "You were broken long before I found you."

I blinked at him from across the room, everything in me going still. "You're wrong," I said, clenching my teeth in my anger. I wanted to hurt him, wanted to stab him again.

"I didn't have a heart when I hurt you, and it was the most miserable experience of my existence. *You* have a heart, Witchling, and you would rather murder the man you love than accept that you care about someone!" he yelled, his voice rising.

"Oh, fuck you," I snapped, striding toward him. Determined to get past him, I made my way for the bedroom door. "I admit that I care about plenty of people in my life. They deserve my love, unlike you."

"Is that why you keep them at arm's length? Is that why you can't even say you *love plenty of people* in your life?" he asked, his voice mocking as it poked at all the little holes in me where that love should have been.

I cared. I protected.

But I'd only loved my mom and Ash.

And now they were both gone.

I shook my head, ending the argument by simply not giving him an answer. There was nothing I could say when we both knew he was right, but it didn't fucking matter. I hurried for the door.

"We aren't fucking finished," Gray snapped, wrapping his fingers around my arm. He gripped me tightly, pulling me close to glare down at me.

"We never even started," I said with a scoff, yanking on my arm until he had to choose between bruising and releasing me. Where he might have once let go to avoid hurting me, he held me tight.

"You're terrified of the fact that you love me. You spend every day petrified that I'll do something to hurt you again," he said. I shoved at him, pushing him back and tearing my arm from his grip forcefully. I turned away from him while he caught his balance, racing for the door all over again.

My fingers wrapped around the knob, pulling it open. Gray's palm slapped against the wood, slamming it shut as I spun to face him. I punched him in the stomach, aiming for the wound I'd made between his ribs. He grunted, wrapping his fingers around my throat and shoving my back into the door.

He held me there, his thumb and fingers squeezing just tightly enough to give me his warning. "Enough, Willow."

"Do it," I growled, making his brow furrow with my command. "Just fucking kill me already."

He loosened his grip on my throat, keeping me still as he sighed and leaned forward. Resting his forehead against mine, he paused for a moment. I tensed when he touched his mouth to my forehead, releasing me and pulling me away from the door.

He moved into the living room, and I had no choice but to follow when he picked up the knife I'd used to stab him. I felt the press of its magic the moment he touched it, certain that he'd decided to be done with me already. "You want me dead this badly?" he asked, staring down at the knife as he turned it in his hand.

I couldn't answer, my mouth filled with sand as I watched the sorrow play across his face. "Gray," I said.

"Answer me. Do you want me dead? Do you really hate me so much that you would rather go through your life and never see me again?" he asked. I rubbed my hands over my face desperately, trying to rid myself of the tears that I couldn't seem to stop.

Gray turned the blade as he came toward me, pressing it into my hand. My fingers wrapped around the hilt, but it wasn't his chest he guided it to.

It was mine.

"This blade was created to kill me, make no mistake, but it's not my weakness, Witchling," he said, releasing my hands and leaving me standing there and holding the knife to my own heart. "You are."

"What are you saying?" I asked, sniffling as he put distance between us.

I wanted more of it, and I wanted him to hold me all at once. That was the conflict of our love—the constant push and pull of two people who shouldn't work, but somehow did.

"I'm saying that your mistake was stabbing *me*. That blade was made for you," he said, forcing me to drop my gaze to the tip of the knife where it touched me.

"What does that—"

"I bound our lives together when I brought you back, Willow.

If you die, I will follow," he answered, the words sitting between us as he waited. Waited for me to choose. "And this is how you die."

The martyrdom I'd been raised to want, or a life with him at my side.

"They sent you here knowing you would very likely die," he said. I couldn't even muster the energy to argue, because we'd all known the odds were not in my favor. Success meant death, and none of them had any reason to believe that Gray cared enough about me to spare my life after an attempt on his. "You are worth so much more than a fucking sacrifice, Willow. I've failed you if you don't know that."

I moved the knife in my hand, watching as he flinched toward me when he thought I would plunge it into my own heart. "You would let me do this? Even knowing you would die, too?" I asked, needing the answer to his question like I needed my next breath.

I couldn't wrap my head around it, couldn't understand how we'd gotten here. This was a precipice, and I knew I would never be the same once he opened his mouth.

The sincerity on his face broke whatever remained within me. "Nothing here has any value without you. You're my home," he said, unable to take his eyes off mine. I held that stare, waiting for him to continue. "They would gladly sacrifice you if it meant the world survived, but I wouldn't. I would never walk this plane again if it meant I had you at my side in Hell."

I looked down to the knife in my hand, staring at it. It felt like the symbol for everything I'd thought I'd known about myself, for the woman who pretended to be strong to hide the fear of hurt and abandonment.

They would sacrifice me to save themselves, but he wouldn't. It might not have been the freedom I'd thought he'd give me; it might not have been the choice I'd hoped for, but it was mine all the same.

Just having it made everything so clear I winced.

I pulled the knife away from my chest, holding it out to the side and dropping it so that it fell to the floor beside me.

Gray was upon me the next instant, pulling me into his arms as my legs caved beneath me. "I'm sorry," I whispered, letting him lift me off my feet. I wrapped my arms around his head, holding him tight and frantically trying to get closer.

He carried me into the bedroom, laying me across the bed gently and shoving my dress up my thighs.

Laying his weight on top of mine, he drove inside.

Coming home.

32

GRAY

One of these days, Willow would learn to accept that she was allowed to want something for herself. It didn't make her selfish to put her needs first occasionally, because she would *never* be like me. She would never put herself over the world around her or over what was best for her Coven on a regular basis.

She whimpered as I drove inside her, her emotions tearing her in two. Willow had never before been so at odds with herself, not when all defiance had been stripped from her by the abusive piece-of-shit father I wished Charlotte hadn't taken from me.

I would have given almost anything to make him suffer slowly. I'd have buried him alive, just to dig him up and force him to fight for his life or spend the evening on his knees.

I shoved the thoughts away, focusing on the silent tears leaking from Willow's face. It was as if she couldn't stop now that she'd started, her own horror over her actions turning her into a mess. I wanted the strong witch who'd come to Hollow's Grove back, wanted her to find her way back to the person she'd been before I added my manipulation to the mix of betrayals she'd suffered through her life.

My wife needed a purpose to drive her forward, something to keep her focused so that she didn't spend her entire day stewing and thinking about the possible heartaches coming her way. I'd deal with it in the morning, give her the thing she needed more than anything.

After I found whoever had helped her spell that knife and killed them for it.

I crashed my mouth against hers, moving within her to distract her for the time being. She wrapped her arms and legs around me, clinging to me like I was her lifeline.

But I wasn't, and she needed a reminder of something she'd always known before.

Just because she wasn't alone anymore didn't mean that she needed me. I was sure enough to admit I needed her far more than she'd ever need me. Where I couldn't bear the thought of a life without her, she'd been willing to tear me from her soul.

The thought was enough to bring my anger back, a growl rumbling in my throat as her legs tightened and tried to hold me to her. She was soft and pliant in my arms, almost making me regret what I would do to remind her who we *both* were.

I wanted her to be mine. I wanted her to open for me and welcome me with waiting arms.

But I *never* wanted to lose the witchling who was more than willing to bleed me when I pissed her off.

I pulled free from her body, shoving her arms and legs off me as I maneuvered myself to the end of the bed. Willow's eyes widened as she pushed up, leaning on her elbows as she stared down at my hard cock pointedly. I was far from done with her, and she seemed to realize she was in danger the moment she glanced up to the empty mask of my face.

She turned, scrambling toward the opposite end of the bed and trying to shove her dress down to cover herself. I'd have torn it off her body if I didn't want her to wear it into the throne room when I was done with her, a pointed display of my victory.

Willow was covered in my blood, and by the time I was done with her, I'd make sure that every man in that room knew I'd filled her with me, too.

I grabbed her hips, pulling her back toward me. Her knees slid across the covers, her nails gripping the fabric as she fought to get hold of something solid. I yanked her to the end of the bed, sweeping her knees out from under her. When her body draped over the edge of the bed, her toes barely touched the floor, leaving her to strain to support herself. Her thighs tensed with the effort as she squeezed them together to keep me out.

I chuckled, leaning my weight over her. My cock nestled into the crack of her ass, leaving me to make shallow thrusts against her as I fought to grab her by the wrists. Yanking them behind her, I pinned them to the small of her back and trapped them between our bodies. "Did you really think you would get off that easy, Witchling? After what you did?" I whispered, watching as she shuddered.

There was that delectable mixture of fear and anger on her face as she turned to glare at me over her shoulder, wrenching her arms to the side as she tried to fight me off. If I'd been anyone else, she probably would have succeeded.

My witchling didn't even recognize her own strength for it to require any effort for me to restrain her.

I repositioned her wrists, pinning them with one of my hands. I loved the curve of her shoulders as they arched back with her arms, the curve that it gave to her body making me wish I could run my tongue along her spine.

I did just that, using my free hand to brush her hair out of my way as I went. She shivered beneath the touch of my tongue, goose bumps of pleasure breaking out all over her skin.

I reached her neck finally, toying with the delicate skin where I would have bitten her if I'd still had fangs. I gave in to the temptation anyway, sinking my teeth into her flesh hard enough that she cried out and struggled beneath me. Determined to leave my mark on her, I bit down harder while she struggled, holding her still as I bruised her throat.

I kept my mouth there, enjoying the taste of her injured flesh against my tongue. The hand that didn't hold her pinned shoved her dress up to gather at the center of her back and out of my way. Then I trailed my touch down to her thighs, slipping between them. She was wet despite the roughness of my bite, her body responding to the pain that she was only beginning to appreciate. She ground her hips as I brushed against her, slipping two fingers into her easily.

With my teeth at her throat and her hands pinned behind her back, Willow fucked herself on the fingers I offered, taking everything I would give her. I smiled against her as I took my fingers away, replacing them with my cock and driving into her. She cried out, bucking against me to meet my thrust as I gripped her around the back of her knee. I lifted her leg to perch that knee on the very edge of the bed, opening her wide as I released her throat finally.

Her neck was red, the distinct mark of my teeth purpling already. It wasn't a protest or argument that left her mouth as I slapped a palm down against the flesh of her ass, watching it bounce as I pounded my cock into her.

"Harder," she moaned, tilting her hips for me to give her what she wanted.

"Such a good fucking witch," I murmured, slapping her harder. Her ass turned red beneath where I'd struck her, my handprint looking fucking perfect against her flesh. "You want me to punish you, don't you?"

She whimpered, the sound going straight to my balls.

This woman had been fucking made for me—every goddamned part of her.

"Gray," she said. My name had never sounded more reverent than when it came from her in the throes of passion. Her pleas were far more beautiful than any of the souls who prayed to my father, far more stunning than any of the condemned who begged me for mercy.

She made me a god, and her body was my altar.

"Answer me," I said, driving deep. I paused at the end of her, letting her feel the head of my cock in the deepest parts of her pussy. She flinched back slightly, the bite of pain mixing with her pleasure as her gaze softened. She sank her teeth into her bottom lip, her eyes closing in shame as she admitted to the dark edge of her desire.

"Yes," she said, her voice trailing off. I pulled my hips back, moving inside her slowly as she finally opened her eyes. There was determination in that stare as she shoved aside her feelings of shame, the vibrant, defiant woman refusing to be told what she should and should not want from me. What she did in the privacy of our bed was no one's business but our own, and she couldn't know that nobody else would know she became my perfect little fuck toy the moment I touched her.

That knowledge was mine alone, and I would burn out the brain of any who ever thought of her this way.

"I want the words, Witchling," I said, holding her gaze. I wouldn't act if she didn't want it, if she weren't strong enough to admit her desires and ask me to fulfill them.

Willow and I both knew she needed my punishment to wipe the slate clean between us. She craved it for herself as much as I did.

"I want you to punish me for what I did," she said finally, the words making my cock twitch inside her. I groaned, shoving down the need building in my balls.

It wouldn't be her pussy I finished in tonight.

"Make it go away," she pleaded, allowing me to lower the leg I'd propped on the edge of the bed. I moved it, watching as it tensed while she strained to reach the floor.

"I can't say no to you, my love. Not when you beg me so prettily," I admitted, slapping my hand down on her ass again. She moaned, rising up to meet my strike. I chuckled, reaching for the nightstand drawer. "You're going to hold still, or I will tie you down. Do you understand me?" I asked, knowing that what I would do to her required careful precision.

I wanted it to hurt, but I didn't want it to hurt her so much that she never craved this from me. Her trust was a careful balance to maintain, giving her just enough without crossing over the line of her limits. She nodded her acceptance, flinching immediately when she heard the bottle cap open.

"What is that?" she asked, straining to look over her shoulder. I kept the bottle out of sight, low enough that she couldn't see it. Tipping it over, I let a few drops drizzle onto the base of my cock. I used her body to spread it through her, gliding in and out of her pussy as her eyes widened and her mouth dropped open.

The elixir had been spelled with the magic of the Reds, an enhancer that I'd created just for her. I'd known this day would come eventually, my desire to take all of Willow and make her mine far too strong for me to ignore. I'd known she'd be hesitant to give me this part of her, and she'd have been a fool not to be.

She whimpered as I fucked her in long, slow glides, her pretty face twisted in ecstasy. "Please," she begged, practically writhing on the bed. She wouldn't be able to hold still once she took me in her ass, not with the way her poor pussy would be neglected.

The elixir would last for hours, and it was my full intention to bring her down to the throne room when she was desperate for my cock. In an ideal world, I'd let her punishment be being forced to sit on it without moving while the Coven watched.

I released her arms for the moment, watching to see if she obeyed my order to hold still. She moved a fraction, catching herself and stilling when she realized what she'd done. I chuckled, knowing that the next few moments would end with her tangled up in vines so tightly that she couldn't move at all.

I drizzled the elixir onto my hand, focusing on my fingers before setting the bottle on top of the nightstand. My fingers were wet when I touched the spot where Willow and I were joined, rubbing those fingers against my cock and giving her more of the magic that would make her insatiable.

She came when I slid two of them inside her alongside my

cock, stuffing her full of me. Her arms unwrapped from her back, gliding down to grip the bedding in her fists as she moaned, the long and low sound going straight to my cock.

So fucking tight.

I moved inside her, pumping my fingers in an opposite rhythm and reveling in every moment of the friction. Willow bit the bedding, her strangled groan meeting me as her dark lashes fluttered. I pulled my fingers free while she was in the throes of her orgasm, slipping them higher and touching them to her ass.

She stilled, her eyes flying wide as she released the bedding and pushed up onto her arms. The wood frame of the bed burst into vines at my command, spreading along the floor and the bed to reach Willow.

A vine wrapped around each of her ankles, spreading them shoulder width apart and holding her steady as I pressed my wet fingers against her hole. "Gray!" she protested, her voice turning shrill as those vines grew and covered her back, pinning her down to the mattress and gathering her arms. She fell to the surface, her breasts pressed tightly against it as the vines wound around her, acting as the rope that would keep her right where I wanted her.

"It wouldn't be a punishment if you wanted it, love," I said, dragging my free hand down her spine. I grasped the vines, ignoring the pinch of pain from the thorns and using them to hold on as I fucked her pussy. She clenched around me, her body swollen and needy in spite of her trepidation.

Trussed up like this for me, she made the perfect feast.

I pressed my fingers tighter to her as I moved my hips. They moved in shallow pulses, the lubrication from the elixir easing the way as her body reacted. "Relax," I murmured, the softness of my voice directly contradicting the way I'd trapped her here.

Willow responded anyway, letting her eyes drift closed as she blew out a slow breath. Her body followed, her ass unclenching and allowing me to slowly glide a finger into her. She was hot and tight, gripping me like a vise with my cock in her pussy and a finger in her ass. Using shallow thrusts, I slowed down to an easy pace.

My cock and finger moved in tune, one making her enjoy it while the other opened her up for me. I lined up a second finger, sliding it in beside the first as she groaned long and low. "You like that, don't you?" I asked, chuckling when Willow narrowed her eyes at me where I watched her face.

As much as fucking her ass would be about me and taking what I wanted, I wouldn't do it at the expense of her never letting me do it again. I intended to spend my life inside her, and that meant fucking her wherever and whenever I wanted.

Even in her pretty fucking ass.

"Fuck you," Willow snarled, but her words lost their venom when I spread my fingers apart, making her eyes go lazy.

I drove deep into her pussy, stilling there as I worked my fingers inside her ass and spread her the best I could. Grabbing the elixir bottle off the nightstand, I drizzled more down between her cheeks, dragging a third finger through it before I pressed that against her. "Working on it, Witchling," I said, chuckling beneath my breath when she focused on her breathing.

The third finger slid inside, her ass resisting the intrusion more than the first two. I worked them apart, prepping her for my cock. It would still be a struggle for me to fit inside her the first time, but I had no doubt Willow could take it.

She could take anything I gave her.

When my third finger was settled as deep as it could go, I moved within her pussy again. The wetness of her against my cock was obscene, the noises of her pussy filling the room. I leaned forward, touching my mouth to my mark on her shoulder blade. She shuddered at the contact, the scrape of my teeth against it making her wiggle beneath me.

I slid my fingers free slowly, taking care not to hurt her as I righted myself. Staring down at her pussy spread wide to accommodate my dick and her ass waiting just for me, I felt the first true contentment I'd had in centuries.

Who needed Heaven when I had my wife's body ready and waiting for me?

I moved my hand down between us, gripping the base of my cock as I pulled out of her pussy slowly. It clenched around air as I left, fighting to cling to me as I abandoned her. She moaned in need as I rubbed it over the thin flesh between her holes, guiding it up to her ass and drizzling more of the elixir on myself.

She tensed as I slid my clean hand beneath her hips, touching my fingers to her clit and making small circles. "Take a deep breath," I said, my voice soothing as I angled myself and pressed the head of my cock into her. She winced, her body spreading wide as I applied slow, steady pressure.

Her breaths were shallow, the pain threatening to consume her past the pleasure. I moved my fingers more quickly, bringing her back to the brink of an orgasm and then slowing down just before she could come for me. "You come when you take my cock in your ass. Not a moment before," I said, pushing forward.

Willow stopped breathing, her pants ceasing as she focused on gathering air in her lungs. She let out a deep sigh, her body relaxing enough to let me in with her exhale. I slid inside, the head of my cock popping through the ring of muscle that had been determined to keep me out. Willow's mouth dropped open into a silent *oh,* my free hand moving to draw soothing circles over her hip.

I groaned as her ass choked my cock, inching forward and then withdrawing. I never let the head leave the haven of her body, taking each shallow thrust to gain another inch of her for myself. "You're so fucking beautiful," I said, slapping her ass. I felt the jiggle of it against the side of my cock, and used her moment of shock to thrust forward in one last firm glide.

My balls nestled against her pussy, slapping against her swollen flesh and drawing a moan from her. "I'm never going to stop fucking your tight little ass now, love," I said, pulling back slowly. She winced as I dragged over every inch of sensitive flesh within her, pushing forward more firmly than before. I studied her face as pain flashed over it, circling my fingers just enough to watch her retreat from that ledge and move back into pleasure.

She was the instrument, and I was the conductor. Our song was one of pain and ecstasy, but it was ours all the same.

My hips slapped against her ass as we found the pace that worked for us, my balls smacking into her pussy as my fingers toyed with her clit. Willow fought off her orgasm, trying to deny the pleasure that she felt from this.

"You fucking love my cock in your ass, you dirty fucking witch," I said, chuckling as her ass tightened around me. Her eyes fluttered closed, her orgasm taking her as I drove deep. I focused my attention on her pussy, circling her clit with my thumb as I angled myself and slid three fingers into her.

Her mouth opened with a cry, her ass tightening like a vise. I moved through it, using her grip to find my own release. My heat filled her, the sting of it scalding her insides as Willow went limp against the bed.

Her breathing steadied, her body sated for a brief moment before the elixir could take hold again.

I pulled out of her ass slowly, watching as she winced, and headed for the bathroom. Cleaning myself up, I grabbed a cloth and wet it for Willow. The vines retreated as I walked back to her, using the cloth to clean her up. Even without the vines, Willow never moved on her own.

I grinned as I lifted her, turning her to lay her on her back with her legs dangling over the edge of the bed. I spread them wide, staring down at her and the wet mess I'd made of her pussy. Leaning forward, I dragged my tongue through her.

She moaned immediately, her eyes opening to stare at me between her legs.

She smirked as she raised her arm, burying her hand in my hair and angling me in her desired position.

It was Willow's turn to take what she wanted.

33

WILLOW

I waved my hand over the Tribunal room doors as we approached, the gears immediately turning to allow me entry. The room was empty as we stepped inside, all signs of the carnage that had occurred the last time I'd set foot in the circular room erased.

I turned to Gray, taking in the disheveled state of his clothing. His shirt was torn where I'd stabbed him, the distinct slit of my blade as it had sunk into his skin. His torso was covered in blood, and I knew if I touched his slacks they would be crusty with dried blood.

My own black dress that I'd worn was stiff from his blood. My body felt abused, the space between my thighs sore from the way he'd fucked me.

I could still feel him inside me, the unfamiliar ache doing nothing to appease the need the elixir still caused.

"What are we doing here?" I asked, spinning in the center of the room.

Gray's eyes darkened, reading between the lines of my words. I'd have much rather been in the privacy of our bedroom, maybe the shower specifically.

Gray took my arm, guiding me up to the throne of the Covenant on the dais. He sat me in it slowly, staring down at me as if he truly appreciated the sight of me in a position of power. It was such a stark contrast to men like my father and Itan, who could not stand the thought of a woman being placed as their equal. "You're going to summon the Coven," he said, reaching down to cup my cheek. He ran his thumb over my bottom lip, tugging it away from my teeth and sinking the tip into my mouth.

A growl rumbled in my throat, making him tilt his head to the side with a smirk. "Dirty girl," he said when I bit him, pulling his thumb back. He sucked it into his own mouth to soothe the hurt, staring down at me intently. The bastard knew exactly what kind of torture every moment was for me right now, that the idea of facing my Coven in this moment was horrific.

I could barely sit still.

"Why would I summon the Coven?" I asked finally as Gray leaned into my space. He grabbed my hand in his easily, maneuvering it to the arm of the throne so that I could rest my palm against the thorns. He pressed it down firmly, the thorn cutting through my flesh to the bone. I winced, a startled gasp of pain coming through my parted lips.

He repeated it with my other hand, impaling me upon the thorns. My blood seeped into the bones and roses, centering me in my seat of power. Susannah and George hadn't summoned the Coven, only ordered Tribunal members to join them. Under the rare circumstances they'd done so since I came to Crystal Hollow, they'd sent a messenger to collect people.

I hadn't understood at the time, but as my blood swept down the vines and sank into the lines on the floor, I did.

They hadn't had the ability to summon the Coven this way, because they'd never been meant to take this seat.

It had been Charlotte's by right.

Susannah and George had merely occupied it in her absence, and they had no blood to spill.

The thorns pressed through the other side of my hands, sticking out between the bones on the back. I gritted my teeth through the pain, watching my blood travel into the circle at the center of the room. Each chair fed from the blood I provided, sending out a call until the room was filled with the magic of all my people.

Our people, I corrected myself. The witches were Gray's creations just as much as the demons and Vessels were, something he'd done for selfish gain—but done no less.

"We are summoning the Coven to show them their assassination attempt failed," Gray said, making me turn my shocked stare up to him. "If they think that you did not even attempt to do it in the first place, they will never be loyal to you."

"So you think the solution is to make me look like a failure?" I asked, huffing in indignation. If I failed in my first task as Covenant, what did that say about my ability to lead?

"You did not fail. You did exactly what was asked of you, down to being able to stab me in the first place. *Their* plan failed, and they will pay for sending you to your death," Gray explained, stepping out of the way. The gears of the Tribunal room moved in the distance as the first of the witches responded to my call. He moved to stand beside my throne, leaning his weight into the side of it with a cocky grin.

"You cannot punish them for what they attempted without giving me the same fate," I said, turning to Gray. It wasn't fair that they should suffer when I didn't, not when it had been me to deliver the blow.

"Watch me," Gray growled, the warning in those words shocking me.

"Some of them are my friends," I admitted, waiting for him to condemn them anyway. I could seemingly forgive him for most of his wrongs, believing they came from the right place, but if he killed Della and Nova there would be no coming back for us.

"Which ones?" he asked, sighing in aggravation as a witch waited by the entrance. I didn't recognize her, and she certainly kept her distance until more familiar faces arrived.

"Della, Nova, and . . ." I trailed off, knowing that the next name would infuriate him. I'd made it clear that I would not allow Iban to touch me again, and instead I'd schemed with him to kill my husband. I didn't consider him a friend anymore, not in the same way I did Della and Nova, but I didn't want him to die for his role, either.

Fuck.

"Say it," Gray said, staring down at me. He already knew the answer, knew the one name I would say that would give me pause.

"Iban. Iban was the one who found the dagger and the book," I said, swallowing my nerves.

"So he was the one who knew you would die doing this?" Gray asked, his lethal words oddly calm. Cold washed over me as I thought of his warning to Gray before he'd tossed him over the stairs.

Someone will use me as his weakness.

"He wouldn't," I said, shaking my head in objection. "If he'd known, he would have just told me to kill myself, Gray. It doesn't make sense."

"That may be for now, but there's nothing stopping him from putting the pieces together," he argued, turning to face the group that stepped into the room. Our conversation was over with enough witnesses that they moved close enough to hear us, filling the room slowly.

It was a steady stream from there, most of the Coven having come in their sleep clothes to obey my command. Della and Nova entered the room together, their gazes landing on my hands that were impaled by the throne. I took the opportunity to raise them, pulling the thorns through my flesh without sparing a glance. The pain was agony, but I forced my face into a stoic mask as I stood. Every eye in the room fell to my hands as gold light shimmered over the wounds, healing them as I turned my attention to where Gray waited.

He pushed off the throne slowly, stalking toward me and coming to stand at my side. I didn't miss the gasp at the sight of his bloodstained shirt, or the way those who had known about Iban's plan glanced between us.

Shocked to see me breathing, I realized, swallowing down my distaste.

I'd let myself be manipulated again, so lost in the notion that it was my responsibility to fix what I'd done. I would never stop being a pawn until I started acting for myself, abandoning all thought of the goals of others and doing what was *right*.

I would do what was right for me from that point on.

Gray captured my chin with his fingers, turning my face to meet his eyes. Whatever he saw there made him nod, an approving smile tipping up the corners of his mouth. The expression nearly stole the breath from my lungs, far more intimate than anything he'd done to me in the privacy of our bedroom.

He wore his approval and pride openly on his face, leaving no question for anyone watching our exchange that he'd forgiven me for what I'd done.

"We tried it your way," Gray said, looking through the members of the Coven who had gathered. "You sent my wife to do what you were too afraid to attempt on your own. As you can see, she was vicious enough to stab me." He chuckled as he said the words.

I hadn't *just* stabbed him. I'd twisted the blade in his heart, determined to shred it into pieces that would never heal.

I blanched at the recent memory, the feeling of his blood soaking my hands mixing with my own blood that dried on my skin as he spoke. When I was a child, all I'd wanted was a peaceful life in a home by the woods, surrounded by gardens like my mother's.

This could be my home, but I knew I would see it drenched in the blood of those who opposed me long before I had the peace I wanted.

"Yet here you stand," the Purple witch said as she stepped forward. Her eyes glimmered like stars, a warning in her gaze as she was bold enough to speak. Identifying herself as one of those

Gray would see as a traitor, even knowing what the consequences would be. "And she is alive and well."

"Of course she is," Gray said, his words spoken through clenched teeth. His lips peeled back as he continued, the brutality in that expression making the Purple witch flinch back slightly. "She is my wife, and just because you were so willing to sacrifice her for your own foolishness does not mean I am."

"She knew what she was risking," the Purple witch said, raising her chin as she turned her eyes to me. She waited for me to speak, for me to save her from the fate that would be waiting for her. I couldn't intercede on her behalf, not when I, too, had started to question how much I wanted to give to protect someone who would willingly send me to my death.

If the roles had been reversed, I would not have been so quick to allow someone to die for the greater good. I didn't have that in me.

We were not the same.

"I did," I agreed, clasping my hands together in front of me. "That doesn't mean it should have ever been asked of me."

She scoffed, turning to look at Iban where he lingered in the middle of the group. He stepped forward, wringing his hands and stopping at an appropriate distance with only a glare from Gray. His brown eyes stared up at me on the dais, his expression pleading.

But for the first time when I looked at him, I didn't see the friend I'd thought would have my back. I saw someone who had seen my weakness and the walls around me, playing them against me to achieve what he thought this Coven needed.

"We've had *centuries* of conflict between the witches and the Vessels," I said, speaking not to Iban but to the Coven. He opened his mouth as if he might interrupt me, but I silenced him by holding out a hand. "Have you not had enough?"

"What would you know of our centuries of strife?" an older

White witch asked. "You've been here for five minutes, and endured only *one* Reaping. You know nothing of our history."

"You're right," I admitted, nodding my head. "I did not grow up here. I have not spent my lifetime immersed in the hatred the way that you have, but I was raised to come here and destroy the Vessels, regardless of the cost. If I am willing to set that aside for peace, why aren't you?"

"Because I'm not fucking the bastard who is responsible for it!" she yelled, resulting in a murmur of agreement.

"That bastard is also responsible for you having magic in the first place," I said, taking a step down the dais. I approached her, stopping in front of her and leaning up into her face. "Perhaps you'd prefer he take it back."

She blanched at that, the same way any of the witches would when faced with the thought of not having their magic. Somewhere along the line, it had become who we were, the only way we identified.

There was more to us than the magic in our veins.

Gray stood to the side, allowing me to interact with the Coven and their rebellions. I had more appreciation for him in those moments than ever before, in his willingness to step aside and let me fight my own battles. If I was truly to replace the Covenant, they would not gain respect for me if he interfered at every turn.

I didn't miss the archdemons making their way into the back of the room, lurking quietly in preparation for the moment when Gray had to deal with his penance himself. Just as he hadn't interfered now, I would step back and allow him to do what was necessary for his people.

Even if it meant punishing those who had once stood with me and sacrificed me like a lamb.

Juliet moved through the crowd, making her way to Della and Nova and grabbing them each with a calm hand. She led them from the room while they looked back at me, and I sighed in contentment. At least they were safe, spared from what was to come because of Gray's unwillingness to make me hate him all over again.

"You don't deserve to fill the Covenant's shoes," the Purple witch said, the sneer of disgust on her face one that I would have hated to see at one point.

Now it only filled me with resolve as I pinned her with a glare. "The Covenant didn't wear shoes, so I find it difficult to imagine I cannot fill them," I said, thinking of the way their bones had clacked against the floor with every step. Gray snorted from the dais, the sound warming my soul. "But if the legacy they left behind was the destruction of the very magic that we claim to love, that's not a legacy I want any part of."

"Sweetheart, this Coven has operated on tradition for centuries," Iban said, glancing around the room when Gray growled a warning at Iban's unwanted endearment.

"Has it?" I asked, furrowing my brow. "Centuries of tradition demanded blood magic and sacrifice to give back what we took from the Source. This Coven lost its way decades ago, and I will see it returned to what it should have been."

"That's all well and good, but you cannot expect them to approve of you if you stand with him at your side!" Iban said, his voice rising as he stared at me. He looked more like his uncle in those moments than he ever had, the contortion of his features in anger making him appear cruel and spiteful.

"I don't need their approval, though I expect it will come in time," I said, taking a few steps up the dais. I took my seat, perching on the throne as I stared at Iban. "Why don't we discuss what is really driving your anger, Iban? Jealousy doesn't look good on you."

He pursed his lips, glancing to his side as attention turned to him. "You can claim whatever you want, but the good of the Coven should come first. Ally with him, fine, but he can never do the one thing you are required to do for the sake of the Source.

You cannot allow your lines to end with you, and he can never give you children!"

I flinched with the whiplash the change of conversation gave me, fully acknowledging that his desperation made him grasp at any straws he could. I'd considered it briefly once upon a time, but no matter what he thought my obligation was to my Coven, I didn't want kids right now. That was a tomorrow problem, for a woman who wasn't sure she'd even live that long.

"Can't I?" Gray asked, making everything in me still. I forced myself not to look at him, focusing on my breathing and keeping my face a blank mask. I couldn't allow my thoughts to show on my face, not when those watching me were looking for cracks in our marriage.

"Vessels cannot sire children," Iban said, but his voice was far less sure as I turned to look at Gray's arrogant face.

My husband smiled as Iban blanched; the reality of the situation hadn't occurred to any of us. We knew next to *nothing* of Lucifer Morningstar, and even less of the archdemons he'd brought with him. "Ah, but we both know I am no Vessel," he said simply.

Everything in me froze, even as I forced my expression into one of indifference. I swallowed, trying not to think about the number of times we'd had sex. I'd taken the tonic to prevent childbirth monthly, keeping my period at bay for as long as I could remember.

I was safe.

But I didn't know if my husband knew that. I didn't know if he was aware of the steps I'd taken to prevent pregnancy in the event that a man took what I didn't offer. My world was harsh and brutal, and I hadn't known what situations I might find myself in once I came to the Coven.

I'd never been more appreciative than now for my paranoia.

"Would the child be a witch? Or nephilim?" one of the Devoes asked, stepping forward. He was calm, collecting the information as his brain worked through the options at our disposal. "A nephilim child would not continue the legacy of our founding houses."

"There's no way to know for sure," Gray answered, returning the man's calm, collected attitude. "But I am also the only being alive who can create new witches. I can merely bestow the power of a Green and a Black to mortals of my choosing should Willow's and my children prove to be too powerful to fill the role."

I held in my startled gasp, hating that we sat negotiating with the potential of children I didn't even know if I wanted. I kept quiet, trusting that Gray knew what he was doing. I would argue with him later, when the prying eyes of the Coven were no longer scrutinizing every move we made.

"And what would you expect in return for such a bargain?" the Devoe asked, quirking his brow.

"The Coven will embrace Willow as you promised the night you bowed to her, and when the time is right, she will open the seal permanently and allow our people to come and go between our lands as they please," Gray said, and I barely stopped my sigh of hurt.

Another motivation, another goal that we hadn't discussed.

"We'll discuss it privately," the Devoe said, lifting his chin.

"I would expect nothing less," Gray said, coming to my side. He took my hand in his, lifting it to his mouth to press a soft kiss to the back of my hand. It soothed my hurt for the moment, allowing me to push through this show so that I could tear his throat out in private if I pleased.

"You cannot be okay with this," Iban said, forcing me to turn my attention back to him. "The girl I knew would never allow—"

"The girl you thought you knew did not exist," I said, my voice soft as I delivered words I knew would hurt. It was my own fault that Iban had twisted our relationship into more than it was. I'd used him to make Gray jealous, and allowed him to kiss me when I'd known my heart belonged elsewhere. "Because she was something you created in your mind. The real Willow does not live for your approval or make choices based on what you may think of them. Accept this or don't," I added, crossing my legs and settling into my chair fully. "You and I are done either way."

Iban sighed, his shoulders dropping as he stared at me. I hoped he would have the sense to walk away, to realize that a public forum like this was not the place for us to hash out the details if we wanted to preserve any semblance of a friendship. "I'm disappointed in you," he said, shaking his head.

The petty part of me couldn't let him have the last word, not when it could make me look weak when I needed to look strong. "Then call me your queen of disappointment, and I'll add that to the list of things I don't give a fuck about," I snapped, immediately regretting the harsh words. I just wanted to go back to our bedroom, take a shower, and take care of a much more pressing urge than Iban's wounded ego.

"Enough. Name your coconspirators," Gray said, stepping up to me. His eyes bore down into mine, the command in that gaze forcing me to shove away my thoughts of remorse. Gray had seen it rising in me, I realized, and stopped me from taking back the harsh reprimand that I suspected Iban and I both needed.

I was no longer his equal in the eyes of the Coven, and he needed to learn to respect the new boundaries of our friendship if we were going to have one.

"I don't know their names," I admitted, but my eyes wandered to each and every one of them.

So many people I was responsible for, and I couldn't even name them as I sent them to their deaths.

I closed my eyes when Gray turned his attention to the person I'd isolated as the leader of the charge. "Then you will," he said, nodding his head. Beelzebub and Leviathan moved, pushing through the crowd to each take one of Iban's arms in their grip. They lifted him from his feet, carrying him out the doors of the Tribunal room as Gray followed after them. He turned at the last moment, his gaze coming to mine with an order that I would obey even if it took everything in me not to challenge him.

I would demand the same retribution if one of his own wronged the witches.

"Nobody leaves until I have the answers I need."

34

GRAY

Leviathan and Beelzebub dragged Iban into one of the nearby classrooms, dropping him to the floor in the center of the desks. The man stumbled to his feet, glaring at me as Beelzebub stepped aside to allow me to pass.

"I have to admit, you made her turn her back on you far earlier than I expected," I said, taking a few steps until I stopped just in front of him. "I'm almost glad you survived your little fall the other day. It was worth it to see you crash and burn all on your own. I thought I'd have to wait years to be rid of you, but you made this so painfully easy."

He paled as I took another step, throwing his hands up to defend himself even though I hadn't moved to harm him. "You can't hurt me. She won't forgive you for it," he said, his rational brain trying to cling to his only hope.

"She watched me take you somewhere private," I said, my nose wrinkling in irritation. The dried blood on my shirt was rubbing against the surface of my skin in a way that felt irritating. I wanted to be done with this business so I could get Willow into the shower and tend to her needs while removing all symptoms of her betrayal from my body. "What exactly do you think she believes is happening?"

"She's not ready to watch me die," Iban said, shaking his head. Even if Willow had distanced herself from her former friend and admitted he was out for his own interests, she still didn't want him dead. From the moment he first betrayed the girl he hadn't even met, locking her into an arrangement with no care for her own feelings, he'd acted with one purpose in mind.

Serving himself.

He would only keep proving that to her with every breath he took, driving her deeper into my arms. A woman like Willow would suffocate in a marriage that was just as much about control as it was doing what was expected of her.

She needed to defy expectations, to thrive with the man who appreciated her tendency to stab first and ask questions later and to hide her vulnerabilities with carefully barbed words.

"Who said anything about killing you?" I asked, tipping my head to the side. I had no intention of ending Iban's life, not when his life would offer so much more suffering. "I want the names of the witches who participated in spelling that knife."

"And if I don't give them?" Iban asked, standing taller.

I barked a laugh, blinking and embracing the swell of starlight that consumed the room. We plummeted into pitch darkness aside from the twinkling lights that gathered on his skin, tiny pinpricks of burning fire that scalded him where they settled.

He patted at his bare arms, frantically attempting to brush them off and wincing back from the burn that moved to his hands.

"You will," I said simply as Leviathan tipped over a vase on the desk. Water poured over the wood, allowing me to gather it into a ball that I brought to Iban's face with only a thought. He paled as the water covered his nose, consuming his mouth.

His chest did not move as he fought to hold his breath, determined not to allow me to drown him. I held his gaze, patiently waiting for the moment he realized he could not fight me. Men like Iban were so self-serving, there would be no denying his instinct.

He grumbled, the sound coming through the water as bubbles.

Only when he finally inhaled and choked on the water did I release it, allowing the rest to fall to the floor in a puddle at his feet. "Did you have something to tell me?"

He sputtered for breath, sucking back a deep lungful of air. "Are you going to kill Della and Nova? Because that is who you'll have to punish if you want to rid the Coven of all those who opposed you," Iban said, spitting out the remaining water.

"No, because unlike you, I believe the two of them only acted because they thought it was what Willow wanted. They were willing to stand beside her if it was her choice, and they will stand beside her as she works to unite the Coven with me. The others just wanted to get rid of me, and you and I both know it," I said, stepping forward to grab him around the throat.

I squeezed the sensitive flesh that I'd damaged with the water, offering a final warning. I'd burn pieces of him next, watch the flesh melt from his legs until he gave me what I wanted.

He dropped his gaze, his voice a hoarse whisper as he spoke the first name.

The rest followed shortly after.

"I'll let you in on a little secret," I said when he'd finished, leaning in so that the words were a whisper between us. "I already knew who spelled that dagger. I can *feel* their magic, even if I don't know their names."

"Then why?" he asked, the grumble one of confused defeat.

"I wanted to watch you break, and know you were willing to give them up to save yourself some pain," I said, standing and adjusting my clothes. "I wanted you to know that even in this, you put yourself first."

I strode into the Tribunal room, leaving Iban in the classroom with Beelzebub and Leviathan. Making my way past the witches gathered, I moved to lean down and kiss Willow gently.

"I'll see you in bed," I said, watching as she raised her brow in disbelief.

"You can't expect me to just walk away," she said, arguing when I'd known she would. As much as I wished she would respect my wish to see her safely tucked away where she couldn't witness my brutality, I understood why she needed to see it.

Her actions had contributed to their deaths. The least she could do was bear witness.

"Very well," I said, turning to face the crowd. Satanus stood at the doorway, blocking the exit from any who might have tried to escape. "Blair Beltran, Uriah Peabody, Kass Madlock, and Teagan Realta, step into the circle."

The four stepped in, looking around as they realized there were two witches missing from their scheme who would not endure the same punishment. Under any normal circumstances, Della and Nova would have suffered the same fate.

The Realta witch turned her glare to Willow. "Wait a minute, you little fucking—"

I clenched my hand into a fist, pulling on the power I'd instilled within them through their bloodlines. They sputtered, clutching at their chests as the magic clawed its way up their throats. The Realta suffocated on her own magic, falling to her knees as her hateful words caught in her throat.

Another of the Realta witches stepped forward, moving to intercede in her family member's suffering. Willow held up a hand, cutting through the room with a burst of air that rippled like a tornado. It moved between the woman and the Realta who suffered, creating a barrier the cosmic witch couldn't breach.

My wife got to her feet, her shoulders relaxing with her sigh as she leveled the one who would have interceded with a glare. The other witch banged against the wall of wind, her fists scraping with the force of the air. She pulled back as Willow held her ground, staring at the witch who now led the Coven with wide eyes.

They'd seen her use her necromancy and earth magic, but this was the first moment Willow revealed the extent of just *how* like the previous Covenant she had become.

Loyal to none, the magic of all the houses flowed through her veins. She was the perfect witch to lead them, with no ties to family to make her behave in a way that wasn't fair.

"They wronged Lucifer, and they wronged me when they sent me to kill Him," Willow said, her voice coming out loud and clear. I yanked my hand back, tearing the magic free from those witches who had been so willing for her to die.

It seemed only fitting that what they valued more than anything should become a part of her.

Instead of allowing the magic to curl back into me, returning to the home it had spent far too many centuries separate from, I let it crawl along the floor. All four of the witches knelt as it pulled free from their mouths, spilling upon the floor as they gagged. It slithered insidiously, the varying colors mixing into mist that moved over the tile slowly as it approached the dais.

Willow's brow furrowed as it swirled around her, entwining around her body and wrapping her in its embrace.

It touched the center of her chest, pressing at the line I had once drawn there to make her believe I would take her magic from her. Even though the wound had long since healed, Willow's skin peeled away from the thin line to reveal a golden shimmering light within her where all her magic resided.

The mist moved into her slowly, a long ribbon of smoke that made her back arch until all of it returned to where I really wanted it to go.

My home, and the home of all that mattered to me.

Willow's eyes flashed with light as her wound healed over itself, her stare landing on mine as I smirked at her. I didn't give her time to question my decision, spinning and swiping out with a mass of night-tinted air. It split through the center of the circle, cutting the heads from the four magicless witches kneeling and thinking their punishment had been delivered.

Even Willow gasped as their heads rolled to the floor, their bodies collapsing to the side. In the crowd of onlookers, somebody screamed in grief that made Willow clench her teeth.

Her nostrils flared in irritation, but she recovered quickly and spoke to the Coven. Keeping the peace, as any decent leader would do in a time of strife.

"His justice is met, and I expect that he will be just as swift to allow me to take our own vengeance should any of the Vessels or demons wrong the witches in such a way," she said, the challenge for fairness playing out with the perfect audience. She delivered her message to those who were loyal to me, announcing that she would come for them if they touched what she considered hers.

I grinned.

There was my favorite witchling.

"I wouldn't have it any other way, Covenant," I said, dropping into a bow that would have been mocking if it were to anyone other than Willow.

For her, I'd spend my life on my knees if she asked it.

35

WILLOW

I moved through the bedroom, Jonathan twirling around my feet. I groaned my frustration as he meowed at me, constantly getting in the way. It took every ounce of balance I had to prevent me from landing flat on my face regularly.

My foot connected with him, but the cat showed no sign of irritation.

He didn't hiss the way he normally might have to show me his displeasure.

I furrowed my brow, staring down at the black cat for a moment before I bent down to scratch his neck. My hand went through him, moving to the other side as everything within me tensed.

"I'm impressed," a male voice said, forcing me to stand quickly and spin to face him. He waited in the doorway, his form alone enough to fill the gap that would have normally led to the living room and office beyond it.

If his body hadn't been enough, the white feathered wings that spread out beyond him would have done it.

His face was so similar to Gray's that it hurt, hitting me like a punch to the gut. He was clean-cut, his hair appropriately trimmed and his features kind. His lips tipped up into a smile that felt more false than any of the mocking ones Gray had given me during his deception.

I took a step toward him, swallowing as I realized who he must be.
"Michael," I said, my voice as apprehensive as I felt.
"Willow Hecate," he said, purposefully ignoring my married name.
"Willow Morningstar," I corrected him pointedly, raising my chin.
He chuckled, taking a step toward me. He moved until he was far
too close for comfort, even in the realm of dreams where no normal
being could touch me. I didn't know what magic he had, or if it was
similar to his twin brother's, but Gray had managed to mark me in
a dream once.

"Not in the eyes of God you aren't," he said, his lips peeling back
farther. The teeth behind them were perfectly white and straight,
unassuming and dull. Yet there was something about him that made
me wonder if he was even more ruthless than Gray, his righteousness
a weapon to be wielded.

I shrugged, moving to the window to look out over the gar-
dens. They were dark, without the illumination of the starlight
that normally twinkled in the lanterns overhead. "I've never put
much stock in what your God thinks of me," I said, turning back
to face him.

Staring at him was disarming, his eyes the same shocking blue that
Gray's Vessel had possessed. I'd once thought I'd miss the blue of that
stare when I lost it to the gold and the realization of what he was, but
staring at Michael, I couldn't help but realize he was nothing but a
pale imitation.

"I wouldn't expect someone like you to care. We both know where
you will go when you die, Witch," Michael said, the word far more
malicious than the affection Gray usually gave me.

"Is that any way to speak to your sister-in-law?" I asked, smiling
at him and channeling the attitude that Gray had so openly em-
braced in me. Michael only looked down his nose at me as if I weren't
worth the dirt on his pretty white shoes.

"You are no sister of mine," he snarled, stepping farther into the
illusion of the bedroom he'd created in my mind.

"Then why don't you get to the point and tell me what the fuck

you want so I can go back to sleep?" I asked, meeting that snarl with one of my own.

He scoffed. "You are everything He said you would be," he said, drawing a smile from me.

"I'm just glad my reputation precedes me," I said, waving a hand to tell him to get on with it.

"You have the ability to open the Hellgate again," Michael said. I raised a brow at him, crossing my arms over my chest. "He wants you to do it, and to bring all your kind and Lucifer's family back where they belong."

"My kind were born here," I said, uncrossing my arms and clenching my hands into fists at my side. "This place is just ours."

"You are abominations that never should have existed. You've sold your souls to the devil, and you should go where all who choose his embrace belong," Michael said, standing taller. He puffed up his wings as if his size might intimidate me.

"What's in it for me?" I asked, tipping my head to the side as I studied him.

"He does not deal with the damned," he said, a warning in the calm fury of his voice.

I stepped closer, taking his blue tie in my hands and straightening it as I looked up at him from between my lashes mockingly. "And what if I do not want to be a heathen? Would He accept me into Heaven then?"

He took a step back, revulsion on his face from the threat of my touch. He'd been solid even in the dream state, touchable and tangible.

Able to be killed in theory.

"Of course not. Your soul is tainted by your use of the Source," he said, and I understood the words very clearly.

"I do not use the Source. I am part of it, and He cannot stand that, can he?" I asked, my laughter filling the room. "You mean to tell me that any good acts I might commit will never matter? There is no heavenly embrace for me?"

He raised his chin, his indignation clear as he watched me. "You cannot change what you are."

I grinned. "Thank you, Michael," I said, turning my back on the archangel and moving to play with the petals of the rose I kept on my nightstand. I couldn't touch it, my fingers filtering through it, but it still served its purpose and left me feeling fortified.

"For what?" he asked, that deceptively handsome face twisting in confusion.

"Giving me the excuse I needed to just do whatever the fuck I want from now on," I said. I closed the distance between us, that magic of life flowing over my skin like a whisper of what was real. "Tell your father I said fuck you, messenger boy."

I placed my palms against his chest, meeting solid flesh as his eyes flew wide. I shoved him back, forcing him through the open bedroom door. The archangel stumbled back into the darkness, fading from view as quickly as he'd appeared.

I turned,

And I sat up in bed, glancing to my side to find Gray sleeping fretfully beside me as if he could sense his brother's presence. Reaching out, I stroked the petals of the flower I'd touched in my dream. They crumbled to ash beneath my touch, the life I'd taken fading from them.

I curled back into bed, vowing to replace the roses in the morning.

I had a feeling I'd need them.

36

WILLOW

Gray stepped into the room the next morning, startling me awake. A pair of gray sweatpants was slung low on his hips. There was a breakfast tray in his hands, an ornate wooden thing that was carved immaculately and definitely hadn't come from the school dining hall.

I adjusted the bedding around my waist as I settled in more comfortably, staring down at the variety of fruit and pastries he'd put onto plates for us.

"Good morning, my love," he said, leaning forward to touch his mouth to my forehead gently. The touch was so tender and sweet that I hated to break the moment, stunned into silence by the thoughtfulness he'd shown in bringing me breakfast.

"You didn't have to do this," I said, reaching for a glass of water. I took a few sips, letting it cool my throat, which felt too warm. I didn't know what to do with this version of Gray, with the kind gestures that were so out of character compared to what I had gotten used to.

"I wanted to," he said, reaching for a strawberry. He bit into the fruit slowly, my eyes tracking the movement of his mouth around the plump flesh. I was ashamed of the way I reacted to something that should have been so innocent, but there was one realization that was more important than my own hormones.

"I don't think I've ever seen you eat," I said, the observation making him chuckle.

"I don't need to, but that doesn't mean I can't," he said, finishing off his strawberry and depositing the stem onto the tray. "I like ripe fruit in particular."

"Don't be disgusting," I said, rolling my eyes as I reached for a chunk of pineapple.

I popped it into my mouth, chewing slowly as I used the time to consider how to broach this conversation. I didn't normally care if what I said pissed Gray off or led to a fight, but this new ground where we were attempting an actual relationship made me uneasy.

Normal couples didn't *want* to fight.

Were Gray and I even capable of peace?

"Just say it, Witchling," he said, raising his brow as he watched me chew. I flushed, irritated with the way he seemed to see right through me. He always knew when there was something on my mind, and I wished I had the same ability to read him.

"Why didn't you say anything about you being able to have children?" I asked after I swallowed.

He took a seat on the bed, leaning back on one of his arms as he settled in. There was an ease to his posture that told me he'd known this conversation was coming after his revelation the night before. "I know you're taking the tonic," he said, surprising me. I hadn't taken it in front of him, because it had always just been a part of my morning routine on the first of the month. "It didn't seem like we needed to have a conversation about it in the meantime. Not when our relationship was so complicated as it was."

I paused, hating that our history meant I had to question him. I needed to know the truth, because I knew exactly what he was capable of. "So you didn't keep it from me in the hopes I would stop taking my tonic thinking we were safe?"

Gray chuckled, shaking his head. It wasn't a mocking laugh

like I would have expected, but one that coated my skin in warmth. "No, Willow. When I want you pregnant, I'll make you perfectly aware of my intentions." He picked up one of the berries, but instead of raising it to his own mouth, he guided it to mine. The tip pressed against my lips, and I spread them open slowly to allow him to offer me a bite. With his intoxicating stare on me, I couldn't help the heat that prickled the back of my neck.

I chewed and swallowed, holding his gaze. "When *you* want me pregnant? What about what I want?" I asked, feigning indifference even though his answer mattered to me very much. I'd spent my life knowing the Coven would see me as nothing but a breeder, something to continue a legacy. His words the night before had struck the fear in me that I'd escaped one person who wanted that for me only to jump into the fire with another.

"Trust me," he said, taking my hands in his. He leaned in, the sincerity in his gaze shocking me into silence. Whatever I'd been about to say faded away, so lost to that somber look on his face. "Children are a gift, and I would never force you to have them if you didn't want them. Not everyone is fit to be a parent, and a lot of the ability to be a good mother comes from the *desire* to be."

My throat burned with the threat of tears, thinking of my own mother, who had wanted me more than anything. She'd loved me, really loved me, in spite of the challenges I'd presented her with and the man who hadn't seen her as anything but something to use.

"Even if I were to decide I don't want them at all?" I asked, watching as the pain of that possibility played over his face. If there was one thing I knew to be true, it was that Lucifer Morningstar craved a family of his own more than anything.

His had abandoned him, forcing him to start a new one. He wanted one that couldn't leave him, that wouldn't walk away just because they didn't agree with something he did.

He wanted unconditional love, and that innocence came from the love of a child.

"Even then," he said, surprising me as he composed himself. "As long as I have you, I can be okay with that decision if I need to be."

I smiled, my expression feeling softer than it normally did as I leaned forward and kissed him gently. "I think that was quite possibly the perfect answer."

He grinned against my mouth, returning my kiss with a soft peck. "I meant it."

I pulled back, letting him see how much I meant every word. "I know you did. That's what made it perfect."

37

WILLOW

Gray and I went our separate ways after we'd gotten ready for the day. He went to his classroom that he insisted on holding on to for the time being, and I found myself wandering outside toward the gardens. In light of our conversation that morning, I needed to ground myself in the earth.

I needed the reminder of my mother, the reminder of the joy my family had brought me.

I hadn't let myself consider the possibility of kids before, but did I really want to never claim that for myself? I'd have been lying if I said my ideal world didn't involve bringing Ash to Crystal Hollow when we somehow found a way to calm the dissent between the archdemons and the Coven.

The Choice would no longer be necessary for him, not when I'd already fulfilled the destiny the previous Covenant had been trying to prevent.

The flowers surrounded me as I walked through them, swaying toward me in the hopes that I would make an offering. I held out an arm, allowing the stems to wrap around my forearm and tighten until they drew blood. They retreated after only a taste, slinking back into the garden beds. The wounds around my arm were like a delicate rope, the skin shimmering and healing before my eyes. There was something so reassuring about the familiarity of the gardens taking what they needed, reminding me that through all the changes, one thing held true.

This was where I belonged.

I ran my fingertip over the petals of a flower, letting the texture of it sink inside me. The gardens had flourished with life since I'd arrived, a return of something that never should have left. Michael flitted through my mind, and I couldn't help the surge of guilt I felt not telling Gray about his brother's interference. He'd told me there was no place in Heaven for me, that my soul had been sold to the devil from the moment of my birth for the way I corrupted the Source.

But this didn't feel like corruption. This felt like harmony, like two halves of one whole that should have always been united together.

Not with Gray, but with the earth that was mine and the Source that I could reach out and touch with only a thought.

I smiled, feeling the cool breeze floating off the water as it reached me in the garden. The cliffs in the distance were covered in mist, the prisms of the crystal bays below hidden from view. Before those cliffs lay the cemetery that was now mostly empty, only the Green witches buried within it but freed from their coffins.

I stepped toward that ground unwillingly, my feet taking me toward that other half of my heritage. I felt the pulsing magic of the Greens spreading through the earth there, the ground above their burial site a mass of wildflowers and fresh green grass that wouldn't stop growing.

The magic of those who came before me had finally been returned to where it belonged, and I stepped up to the edge of the cemetery to pay my respects. One day, I'd find a way to return my mother's body here so that she could be a part of her hometown as well.

For now, I sat at the edge of the cemetery, sinking my hands down into the blades of grass. The magic of both death and life pulsed in the earth here, carrying through the soil to touch my skin. I heaved a sigh of relief at the magic that spread through my body, clawing at my throat and holding me captive.

But unlike when I'd first touched my necromancy, I did not fear it any longer. It had become another part of me, joining with all the other magic I needed to get comfortable with.

So I sank down into it, feeling the breeze on my skin. I spread that magic out farther into the earth, touching the natural springs buried deep in the ground and feeling the wash of cold over my body. The sun in the sky warmed me against that chill, the brightest star burning even in daylight as the cosmic side of my magic stretched up and out. The crystals at the edge of the cliffs felt hard and unyielding, casting a prism of colors over my vision. There were the faint burning embers of a flame within the torches that had mostly faded out in daylight, flickering against me like the warmth of a hearth.

The magic of the Reds was harder for me to tap into, the magic I'd grown up using coming from outside my body. The Reds' magic came from within just as much as from within the bodies of those around them, but I sank into that place of longing that came whenever I thought of Gray. Of the feeling his hands on my body gave me.

The moment that desire sparked to life, I sucked in a ragged breath. Touching all the parts of the Source at once, I tasted the magic of creation itself. It poured down my throat like a rhythm of the seasons, a pattern that had been there since the dawn of time.

My eyes drifted closed, my breathing slowing until I wasn't sure I was even alive or if I had become one with the Source. It was a part of me, drifting through my body and touching every corner. I couldn't imagine what it felt like to be Gray, to have lived with this feeling for centuries and still be trapped away from all of it.

I opened my eyes at the snapping of a twig, *feeling* the crack like it was one of *my* bones.

The Cursed stepped out from the woods, forcing me to rise to my feet slowly. There were more of them than I'd thought as they stepped into the light. Their figures were just as horrifying as I'd remembered, the slow, unnatural movement of wolves walking on two hairy but human legs striking deep into my soul.

I could save them, Unmake them the way I had Jonathan, but I knew in my gut that I needed to lay my hands on them for that to work.

There were eleven of them, and I could not possibly fight them all off at once.

I looked around them as they moved, observing the way they spread out through the cemetery. They didn't come particularly close to me, most of them keeping their distance, except for the one who stopped a few feet away.

I widened my stance, planting my feet shoulder width apart. The magic of the Source flowed through my veins, and I'd spent many, many years fighting for my life in the cages designed to weaken and belittle me.

The Cursed closest to me stood there, tilting his head forward silently. The move was distinctly submissive, and I studied him as I took a few steps forward.

The ruthless brutality that the Cursed had shown me in my first escape attempt was gone as all the others did the same, mimicking his posture as I came close enough to touch. I swallowed, meeting the intensity of his stare. He made no move to touch me, remaining perfectly still, and I wondered if he *wanted* me to free him. If they somehow knew of what I'd done for Jonathan . . .

I reached up a trembling hand, touching it to the side of his face. His fur was rough beneath my palm, coarse where I wanted it to be smooth.

His eyes drifted closed as I tried to call to the same black magic I'd pulled on to free Jonathan.

What answered was different, stronger, with a mind of its own. The Source of all magic rose up in me, entwined into one living, breathing magic that demanded the sacrifice it had been offered. I tried to pull my hand back quickly, removing myself when the Cursed's eyes flew open wide. All at once, the others mimicked the motion, panic in their faces as if they, too, felt the pull of whatever I'd summoned.

The Cursed in front of me grasped me by the wrist, holding me still so that I could not take my hand away. "Stop," I whispered, but he nodded as if he understood what was coming.

But I didn't.

The Cursed's legs twisted into the roots of a tree, anchoring him to the ground as he yowled in pain. Still, he did not release me. Not even when branches burst free from his torso, splattering his blood and flesh all over the greenery that followed. Leaves budded on the branches that came from him as he finally released me, sending me stumbling back to fall onto my ass.

His body faded from view entirely, swallowed by the hedge that formed in a circle. It moved to the next Cursed, until one by one it swallowed them all whole. Bursting free from their bodies, the maze that appeared in front of me was far too familiar.

I walked around the perimeter, wincing when I took in the sight of each head of the Cursed where they remained mounted at the tops of the pillars that formed the maze. Their eyes were blank and unseeing, their lives given to the Source, which surged anew with their offering. I hurried, running the full circle of the maze. There were three openings, three paths that I knew would go to the center if I could get a bird's-eye view of it.

I knew because it was the same symbol I'd branded onto Gray's chest when I marked him as mine.

I stumbled to a stop in front of the entrance that had appeared before me, staring up at the dead wolfish face of the Cursed whom I had touched.

I swallowed back my fear, the trepidation of what the Source was trying to tell me.

I stepped into the maze.

38

GRAY

I faltered in my steps as I walked around my desk, glancing over at the window to stare at the courtyard beyond. Willow was nowhere to be seen within it, but I knew she'd found a place to call upon her magic and ground herself once again.

My witchling could be shaken, she could bend, but she never broke.

I smiled, a chuckle of laughter slipping free. Leviathan stepped toward me as my students began to file into the room. "Crafty little fucking witch," I said, shaking my head as I turned to face him.

"What's your wife done now?" Leviathan asked, his own amusement matching mine.

"She touched the Source," I said, feeling the magic on my own skin in response to hers. In the past, Willow had used the magic in her veins to call the Source to her. This time?

This time she'd shoved her hands wrist-deep into it, taking for herself and letting it slither inside her.

"Is that even possible?" Leviathan asked, turning to look out the window. He, too, searched for Willow, knowing she would be either in the courtyard or the gardens if she was touching magic so thoroughly. Those were the places where she'd have felt the most comfortable delving into the unknown.

I smiled fondly. "It would appear even the Source cannot say no to my wife," I said, turning to face the students who had gathered. There were less than I expected on any given day, some members of the Coven deciding that they no longer wanted their children to attend a class with the devil.

That was their prerogative, but the students would not be full members of the Coven until they graduated from Hollow's Grove. I realized the irony and hypocrisy in that statement, considering they were led by a witch who hadn't completed a single year.

Part of me wished there was someone who could have sat on that throne until Willow graduated, giving her the opportunity to attend school like any other. I told myself that we would have a conversation later, letting her know we would find a way for her to continue with her education if she so desired.

The other part of me wanted nothing more than to kneel before her and encourage her reign of terror.

"She is a menace," Leviathan said, but it was a quiet reprimand that sounded more like that of an affectionate older brother. There was no threat to me in the way he looked at Willow, only admiration for the woman who had made his presence here possible.

If only Beelzebub was as amicable toward her. The demon who had killed her was still frustrated with her very existence, even if the witch he wanted to court was friends with Willow.

Poor Margot.

The witch didn't stand a chance.

"Should you stop her?" Leviathan asked, raising a brow. Toying with the Source came with risks, but that was normally when someone tried to force their way in. The magic that coated my skin as an extension of Willow wasn't malicious; it was the welcoming warmth of a familiar embrace.

It recognized her and invited her to join it.

"No," I said, shaking my head as I picked up a piece of chalk and began scrawling notes on the chalkboard. "Let her play. The Source will tell her when she's wandered too far."

39

WILLOW

I wandered through the maze, ignoring the way the hedges reached out to touch me. They weren't looking for blood; that need had been satiated by the Cursed. They just strained to touch my bare skin, brushing leaves and flowers against me.

All the earth was alive, but this was different.

This felt like it held secrets.

I moved along the path, following it as it wound through the greenery. The ground beneath my feet felt strange, foreign in a way it never had. It wasn't the earth I had known all my life, almost as if this maze existed between realms.

A place all its own.

I rounded the corner yet again, half expecting something to jump out at me. What met me instead were the glimmering wings of butterflies as they fluttered down the path. One landed on my hand, the glowing blue wings so much like a crystal that I stared at it for a moment before continuing on my way. The magic in this place coated the air, surrounding me like the depths of the ocean after I'd plummeted to the bottom.

I felt it in my lungs. Felt it in my stomach and my mind.

I was it, and it was me, and as I walked to the center circle, I understood where I had wandered.

Into the heart of the Source itself.

40

WILLOW

Iapproached the three statues of the Cursed that waited in the center of the circle, laying a hand on the one closest to me. He pointed to the circle they formed, guarding it like sentries as they looked out at each of the three paths. One lay to my left, the hedges in that path older. They were the thorned, twining branches of death. Jutting toward the path as if they might cut any who entered, they were a relic from the past.

To my right the maze grew with the brightness of spring. The path was littered with flowers, the hedges bright, new green and budding where mine was the green of a mature plant.

I looked down onto the pedestal at the center, my brow furrowing at the symbol of the triple goddess looking back at me. The full moon in the center was surrounded by two crescents facing out, the arches curved slightly to point toward the two paths I had not taken.

Movement to my left sent me reeling, spinning back from the triple goddess and what I could not understand, to face the figure moving through the thorns. She emerged from the path, donning a black dress that covered her arms and fell to the ground, dragging over the grass as she made her way toward me.

She was exactly as I remembered her, her face so like mine even now that she had been gifted the truest of deaths.

"Charlotte," I said, my voice barely above a whisper. Tears stung my eyes, even as I understood it was foolish to be so happy to see her. I'd only met the elder Hecate witch once, but she'd held my hand when I needed it most.

She smiled sadly, crossing the distance between us to stand on the side of one of the crescents. "Willow." Her voice was soft, as fond as I remembered my mother's being when I'd had a nightmare and crawled into her bed at night as a little girl. Charlotte reached over the triple goddess, cupping my cheeks in her hands softly. "I told you I would always be with you."

"How is this possible? How am I here?" I asked, looking around the maze.

Her smile widened. "Clever girl, you've already figured out where you are?"

"I can feel it," I admitted with a nod, raising my hands in front of me. They reminded me of Gray's eyes, of the golden magic that shimmered within me when I healed over a wound, but in this place, my skin seemed to glow with it.

"You are here because you submitted yourself to the Source," Charlotte said, tracing the shape of the crescent moon closest to her with her pointer finger. "Just as I did when I gave my life to save yours."

"But I'm not dead," I said, glancing back at the entrance of the maze. I'd been alive when I entered, and the thought that I would have unknowingly left Gray, after everything we'd gone through . . .

He'd be dead, too.

"No, you are not dead, Willow. My purpose in life was to strike my bargain, to lead to the price that Lucifer demanded. Lucifer believed that your purpose ended the moment you opened that seal, until that dream when He decided He wanted to keep you anyway," she said, taking my hand in hers. She touched my fingers to the moon at the center of the triple goddess, a spark of power flickering against me when I touched it. "But I knew you had to live. That was why I made Lucifer promise to make sure I was always with you. So that I could be there in the end to protect you."

"I don't understand," I said, drawing my hand back from the triple goddess.

"Lucifer is as much a part of the Source as you and I, as are His father and His siblings. Long ago, God submitted himself to the Source to gain its trust and power to create life. But he has since turned his back on those creations in his own greed for worship. He deviated from the Source, taking enough of its power with him to make any fight impossible. He used his influence to make people turn their backs on the old ways and traditions. With every person who abandoned it, with every witch who neglected it, the Source weakened. Your job is to give that power back, so that we are strong enough to fight God's army," Charlotte said, her voice going distant. She stared at the empty place where the other crescent moon waited, the budding life waiting there as we were.

"The angels," I said, nodding along. My memory of Michael was so vivid, his assertion that the witches should be condemned something he truly believed.

Charlotte nodded. "They carry the power God stole within them. We carry the power of the Source, directly from her. We are not the same, and we will not be demonized for touching what was forbidden to us in the Garden of Eden," she said, pulling an apple from the pocket of her dress. She tossed it to me, forcing me to catch it in two hands as she stepped away from the triple goddess.

I stared down at the red apple in my hands, the forbidden temptation pulsing with magic.

"How did Lucifer come to access the Source directly, if His father turned his back on it?" I asked, turning my stare to her.

"The devil is not the only one who knows how to *use* people, sweet Willow," Charlotte said, staring down at the triple goddess. "Destiny speaks of three women who will change everything. Of the three women who will bring about the new order."

I exhaled, staring down at the triple goddess symbol with new understanding.

The Maiden.

The Mother.

The Crone.

I swallowed, turning my gaze to Charlotte. "I have done my part in striking the bargain that enabled Lucifer to walk this earth alongside you. But the balance *must* be maintained," she said, her eyes gentle as I stared into the familiar purple of them.

"As above, so below," I said, my words sounding distant. My ears rang, warning bells going off in my head.

"The devil is no longer in Hell, and that means the time has come for someone to *tear* God out of Heaven," she said, the cruelty on her face so similar to the hatred I had felt when Michael had told me *nothing* I ever did would be worth forgiveness.

I'd be condemned, merely for daring to touch power he didn't think I had a right to have.

I swallowed, uncertain I wanted the answer. "Me?" I asked, watching as Charlotte's soft smile broadened into a grin of pure satisfaction.

"No, Willow," she said, reaching to cross the distance between us. She rested her open palm against my stomach, her fingers curling around it meaningfully. "*Her.*"

41

WILLOW

I stumbled back from her touch, shaking my head. "I'm not pregnant," I said, pursing my lips together. The thought that all choice might have been taken from me, when I'd already decided that I could want it . . . someday . . . seemed impossible. Coming to terms with the future didn't mean coming to terms with it *now*.

"No, you're not," she said, and my lungs heaved with my relief. I wasn't ready.

No matter what decision I'd made earlier, given this warning, I wasn't sure I ever would be.

"The Maiden *will* come," Charlotte said, her voice sympathetic. "You've already decided you might want children one day. This changes nothing," she said, those words so in tune with the thoughts I'd already had in my reflections.

Always with me, even in my head at times, it seemed.

"Does he know?" I asked. The thought that this all came so quickly after our discussion about children didn't sit right with me, but the Source wrapped itself around me, the touch distinctly soothing as I stared at the springlike path of the Maiden.

The path my daughter would one day walk when she submitted herself and her body to the Source.

"No. Even Lucifer does not know the price the Source will ask of Him," Charlotte said, taking my hand in hers.

"The price?" I asked, my confusion making my brow tense. The maze trembled around us as Charlotte guided me away from the triple goddess. Her concern was evident as she glanced back down my path. That warm, soothing touch of the Source against me had shifted into something darker, an edge of fear prickling along my skin.

"Your daughter will lead the fight one day. She will be the weapon that allows for us to right the world to what it was always meant to be," she said, pushing me toward my path.

"I'm not ready to be a mother," I said, watching as she moved toward her own path. She glanced back at me, her eyes knowing.

"I know. The Source has waited for centuries. It will wait a thousand more if it must," Charlotte said, stepping into the mouth of her path. "Time has no meaning to something that is older than all measurement." There was no goodbye as she disappeared from view, taking the path provided for her and her alone to escape.

I hurried down mine, racing along it as the walls trembled beside me. It was as if the Source itself were under attack, as if someone were battering at the walls and demanding entry. I didn't want to stop to think about what could have caused it to tremble.

My lungs heaved as I ran, determined to make my way out before whatever retaliation was building. My feet carried me as fast as they could, rounding the corner to the entrance that called to me. The area outside it was blurred, but I sprinted toward it.

I leapt out of the maze as it collapsed around me, tossing me through the air as I fell for the ground that I never seemed to find. My arms flailed, the wind of my plummet billowing my hair out behind me.

Falling. Falling.

I landed in my own body and sat as I had before the maze appeared, staring back at the cemetery where it had formed. There were no pillars that the Cursed had formed, no severed heads resting upon hedges. The ground in front of me was flat and even, a mix of grass and wildflowers covering the gravesites of the past generations of Brays and Madizzas.

As if the maze had only existed inside my head.

I pulled my hands off the ground, flinching back from the severing of the magic I'd immersed myself in. Staring down at my hands in shock, I never saw the branch swinging into the side of my head.

I felt the pain, my temple exploding into agony the moment it struck. The stick cracked in half as I tumbled to the side, forcing myself to roll onto my feet as I turned to face the person responsible. The witch who stood before me was young, a member of my legacy class.

There was a group of six standing behind her, each having gathered branches of their own. My body felt battered as I came back into it, my arms covered in bruises and scratches I hadn't felt at first.

How long had they stood there, beating me as I dreamt of the Source?

It hadn't been the Source that was under attack in the vision I'd thought was reality.

It had been me.

I stood as straight as I could manage, glaring at them with disdain. My body swayed to the side, feeling like I might fall over. The Source reached up to grab me, a gentle cradle supporting my weight as my vision swam.

The first witch swallowed as she tossed her cracked branch to the ground, and I turned my attention to the others.

I blinked, sending out the call with my magic. The Source skittered along the ground, crawling like an insect until it touched those branches. Twisting into knots, they turned on those who wielded them and jabbed toward their hearts.

One witch squealed as she dropped hers, the others following suit as they looked at me.

"Fine," the male witch said, cracking his head to the side. He wore the white robes of the crystal witches, his muscles bulging from them and hard as stone. "No magic then."

He surged forward, sprinting to close the distance between us. My body snapped into that place of muscle memory and adrenaline, moving to the side to avoid his attack. I cracked my elbow down against his spine, sending him crashing toward the ground as I turned and caught the next witch with the heel of my palm in her throat.

Her hands grappled for purchase, her nails scratching the surface of my skin before she collapsed to her knees and sputtered for breath.

I stepped past her, gliding forward on sure feet. The magic in my veins fueled my body, making me feel invincible in spite of my injuries. In all my years fighting in the cages my father put me in, I'd never felt such rage.

I slammed my fist into the next witch's spleen, driving my knee into her nose when she bent over in pain.

Two of the others turned to retreat back to the school, but I committed their faces to memory. It would not be Gray who meted out their punishment this time.

It would be me.

"How pathetic," I mumbled, turning back to face the first male witch, who got to his feet. He looked to the other one, who had yet to attack, waiting as they glanced between each other. "Beating on a woman when she's daydreaming." The disgust in my tone was evident, leaving little doubt as to what I thought of them and their bravery in attacking me.

I took them by surprise, running toward the big one. He reached out as he spun away in an attempt to escape, giving me his back. I hooked my arm around his stomach, grasping him and using him to shift my weight up. He stumbled as I got my legs around his neck, clasping him tightly and switching my weight to his other side to throw him off balance. Holding his head tightly between my knees, I used my legs to pull him forward and flip him over, slamming his back to the ground beneath me.

He groaned as I vaulted to my feet, stalking forward to go for the other male witch, who held up both hands as if he weren't a threat. As if he hadn't seen a woman in a moment of weakness and decided to use it against her.

I had no tolerance for bullies.

I stalked forward, crossing over the discarded witches I'd left on the ground before me. Summoning the magic that existed just at the edge of my fingertips, I called to the dead within the ground beneath us.

The earth shook, the ground splitting as the witches who had dared to lay their hands upon me scrambled to their feet. The bony hands of the Madizza and Bray witches emerged from the earth, crawling out of the dirt and righting their bones to stand tall.

Making my way back to the school, I didn't speak a word as the dead descended on those who had wronged me, and I certainly didn't watch as they tore them into pieces.

The sounds were detail enough.

42

WILLOW

The Tribunal room waited for me, the throne atop the dais calling me forward. I would summon the Coven, knowing that those who had escaped would not be able to resist the call of the Covenant. If they remained in Crystal Hollow, they would be forced to come and answer for their crimes.

They'd be forced to answer to *me*.

I stalked across the center circle, my irritation driving me forward. I was so tired of the divisive bullshit within the Coven. If what Charlotte had told me was true, we needed to find a way to come together. We were all part of the same plan, two sides of the same magic. But we couldn't do that if we were so at odds with one another that we killed each other in darkness.

The thought that we were meant to be opposing one another was a lost cause. Charlotte might have made a mistake in setting this all into motion, in opening the world up to a war that would tear it in two. Only time would tell. But we couldn't go back and change that we'd taken those first steps. All we could do was accept it and follow through.

I'd nearly reached my throne, my body pulsing with agony as the adrenaline of the fight started to flitter out of my system. Everything throbbed, my head swimming with both rage and dizziness.

Michael stepped out from the Covenant's private rooms that I had not had any interest in claiming for myself. The reminder of the ancestor who had nearly ruined everything was too much for me to bear as my private space.

I stopped in my tracks, staring at the archangel in front of me. For a moment, I wondered if I'd walked straight into another vision, the pain inducing the dreamlike state.

No.

This was no dream.

He didn't move toward me, but I was not dumb enough to think that I would be strong enough to fight the archangel on my own. Michael was Gray's twin, his equivalent by heavenly fire.

"Hello, Willow," he said, the smooth accent of his voice polished. I hated the way his face was so similar to Gray's, despised the way he could be so similar to the man who would never allow anything to hurt me and so *wrong* all the same.

Spinning, I made my way back to the doors of the Tribunal room. Alarm bells rang in my head, the knowledge that *this* was no dream settling over me. I should have told Gray about his twin's visit in my dream, but I hadn't been able to find the words in light of the conversation we'd had that morning.

There was enough heaviness between us. I hadn't wanted to add to it.

I slammed into a male chest as I spun, familiar hands grabbing me around the waist and steadying me.

Iban stood behind me, his face somber as he held me still. My hands landed on his shoulders as I righted myself, his fingers curling into the fabric of my shirt.

White-hot pain erupted in my belly, searing me from the inside as he held my gaze. The apology in his eyes meant nothing as I stumbled back a step, staring down at the familiar white bone handle where it protruded from my stomach.

My confusion settled over me, not understanding how Iban had the knife that Gray had locked away in his vault for safekeeping. The archangel at my back chuckled as if he could hear the spinning thoughts, and I realized *that* had been the night Michael visited my dream.

My eyes rolled back in my head, weak hands reaching for the blade. The magic of the Source cleaved me in half, pulling more of my magic into the blade and leaving me drained. I stumbled to the side, my fingers wrapping around the hilt as Iban caught my hands in his and turned me to face Michael. He pinned my arms at my sides, holding me prisoner when I could barely find the strength to stand.

I felt totally, helplessly human and knew I would never be right again so long as that blade remained planted within my body.

"I'm sorry," Iban murmured, the words a twisted reminder of what I'd offered to Gray when I'd done the same to him. He'd worked with Michael somehow to plan this.

There was no doubt in my mind that it had been his intent all along. He'd needed me to spell the knife, manipulated me so that I would do it thinking I was ridding the world of Lucifer.

He knew it would fail. And he knew he'd use it to kill me.

"How could you?" I mumbled, shaking my head from side to side to shake off the weakness plaguing my soul. "You're betraying your own kind, and he has *nothing* to offer you." I knew that as much as Michael did, what with the pathetic chance he'd given me to do the same.

I was beyond salvation because of what I was.

"I gave up my magic for a family. I never corrupted the Source like you did. I can repent," Iban explained, tripping over my feet as he guided me toward the seal on the ground at the center of the circle.

"You fucking fool," I snapped, falling to the glass pane of the mirror. The gateway to Hell had filled with stone, cutting off the view I knew of below. Iban let me fall, my body settling against the odd mix of glass and stone.

He covered my body with his, laying himself atop my back

where I knelt on hands and knees. I grimaced, flinching away from his touch even in this.

His hand wrapped around the hilt of the blade, twisting it within my belly so that a fresh squelch of blood dripped down onto the surface of the mirror.

An offering.

I reared back, struggling against him as he lifted me off the glass as the stone melted away, giving me a bird's-eye view into the pit of Hell.

He grasped each of my hands in his, wrestling with my weakened body. I couldn't fight, couldn't do anything as my life and magic faded into that blade.

Iban guided my hands to the border of the mirror, slamming them down onto the face that was mine. The magic latched onto me immediately, taking even more from me than I had to give. I winced back, attempting to sever the connection.

The seal held fast, sucking me deeper as the glass shattered.

And the gate to Hell opened once more.

43

GRAY

Ten minutes earlier

I picked up the textbook off my desk halfway through the class. "Turn to page one ninety-three," I said, thumbing through to find the page myself. We'd made our way past the history of the bargain that created the Coven in the first place already, but I wanted to discuss it from a different vantage point. Beelzebub and Leviathan waited at the back of the class, their presence unnecessary, but Beelzebub was always with me if he couldn't be with Margot.

It was as if the bastard couldn't function being alone anymore.

"We discussed the bargain I made with Charlotte at the beginning of this class," I said, setting the textbook down. "But we did not discuss it from my point of view. Now that the truth is out, I thought we could take some time today to address any questions you might have."

Leviathan raised his brow, his perpetually intrigued face not matching the enormity of his size and the intimidation that came with it.

"Why are you even teaching this class? Don't you have better things to do? Witches to eat?" one of the students asked, his face flushed with fear as he spoke.

"First of all, there's only one witch who is a part of my diet plan," I said, resulting in the startled laughter of some of the other students. "Second, I happen to be of the belief that our greatest achievements come in the undertakings of the generation that comes after ours. The best thing we can do for the world is give our children the chance to thrive. Knowledge is power, and it is the best gift I can give to you all in the changing environment around you," I said, shocking the one boy into silence.

The fear faded from his face slowly, his gaze dropping to my stomach. Blinding pain followed, making me stumble into the side of my desk.

I touched a hand to my belly, staring down at it when I pulled it away. Bright, viscous blood covered it, seeping from a wound in my stomach that I had no explanation for.

Beelzebub and Leviathan got to their feet, their expressions shocked as they stared at my abdomen. I met their gazes, already moving for the door.

"Willow," I said, my voice laced with the panic I felt. For her to be injured severely enough that it would affect me, for neither of us to be healing . . .

"Get the others," I said to Leviathan, watching as the massive archdemon burst out of the classroom.

I followed the tether of Willow's pain, letting it guide me down the stairs. I stumbled on the steps, the bond between us pulling from my magic to keep her alive. The Source slid through me, using me as a conduit to keep my wife alive, but I couldn't grasp it for myself in any way.

Willow needed it all.

Beelzebub and I moved in a flurry of motion, even when the bell rang and students piled into the hallway. I shoved them to the side, bleeding all over the floor as I made my way to her. I groaned, grasping the railing as the pain in my stomach twisted, tearing through my innards in an echo of what Willow suffered.

There was only one weapon that could have done this, only one knife that could hurt her this way.

It may not have killed me, but Willow's life slid between my fingers as I tried to reach her. The Source could only sustain her for so long. My only comfort, my only breath of relief, was that I would follow after her and be with her in Hell.

But she would never be the same once she was separated from the very earth that she loved so dearly.

"Gray, she may already be gone," Beelzebub said, his voice strained as he eyed the fresh flow of blood dripping down my pants to splash onto the floor.

I grunted, pushing past that horrifying thought. "I would be, too," I said, dispelling it with the only logic I could hang on to at that moment. "She's clinging to life."

"Where is she?" Beelzebub asked, knowing I could feel her. He eyed me as if I were weak, a hindrance to him reaching her in time.

I hated it. Hated that for the first time in centuries, I was vulnerable.

And it was the first time that mattered.

"The Tribunal room," I said, following the tether to Willow. Her pain was like an anchor, radiating through the darkened halls of Hollow's Grove. "Go!" I snapped, watching as he pumped his wings. He dove over the stairwell, flying to get to my wife faster than I could. Without my wings, the useless scars on my back all that remained of them, and with no power to claim for myself, I couldn't get to her as quickly as he could.

I just hoped he'd reach her in time.

44

WILLOW

I stared down into the pit of Hell. Demons made for the stairs en masse, but I knew they would never reach us. Michael retreated into the Covenant's private quarters, emerging with Margot at his side. She'd been gagged, her hands tied in front of her as silent tears streamed down her face.

I bucked against Iban, fighting through my weakness. He held me steady, his strength greater than mine. It was the weakest I'd ever been since childhood, and my body felt entirely at his whims. "You're going to be a good girl and stay put for me, Willow, or so help me, I will slit her throat and make you watch her die," Michael said, the warning slithering beneath my skin.

The thought of letting myself fall in came unbidden to my mind, the knowledge that if I were gone, no one could ever use me to open the door again.

Gray would murder me himself.

Margot shook her head, her nostrils flaring with her anger. Her strength stoked the flame of mine higher, an understanding passing between us. We would fight.

We would die.

But we would never give up.

I knew something that Michael didn't know. I knew why he was so desperate to get rid of me now. He didn't have time to waste, because one day my daughter would rise.

One day, my daughter would kill them all.

I stopped fighting against Iban's grip, letting him grow comfortable in the hold he had on me. I sank into that touch, gathering what little strength I had and preparing to use it against him. The Source lingered at my fingertips, but I didn't dare touch it until I was ready. Not with the way the knife felt like it had taken everything from me.

Not with the way the Source alone kept me alive.

"She shouldn't be breathing," Michael said, warning Iban as my eyes drifted closed. I was letting him see what he wanted to see in my weakening.

Iban stroked his hand over my hair, brushing it back from my face as he turned me slightly to look at me. "Sweetheart," he said, the delusion in his voice nearly making me lose my grip and attack in that moment. I wasn't strong enough to fight off Michael, and I needed to wait for Gray to reach me. I couldn't feel him, the pain silencing everything outside my body. But I knew he would come for me. "It's not too late for you to repent."

"You're even dumber than I thought if you believe that," I said, the words trailing off.

The Tribunal doors burst open as a male form flew through the air. Beelzebub landed in the room, staring at me and taking a single step forward. He paused as his gaze swept around the mostly empty room to assess the threat.

I knew the moment he saw Margot. Everything in him went solid, his body freezing as he was caught between his feelings for her and his loyalty to Gray.

I smiled at him when he clenched his jaw, nodding simply to communicate that I understood. He went for Margot, and I winced when Michael tossed her to the side. She tumbled toward the seal, unable to catch herself as she rolled.

"Margot!" I screamed, attempting to tear my hands off the

seal to stop her. "She's your friend!" I shouted, reprimanding Iban when he made no move to help her. He held me steady as she tumbled onto the seal, trying to catch herself with legs that she threw wide at the last moment. Her long legs were the only thing allowing her to hold on, but even those began to slip in the slickness of my blood.

She grumbled against her gag, the panic in her voice stalling my heart.

"MARGOT!" I screamed again, watching as her legs caved and slipped over the border of the doorway.

She fell into the seal, tumbling out of reach as I screamed at the top of my lungs. Beelzebub abandoned his fight with Michael, turning to meet my gaze as I silently pleaded with him. Shoving Michael off, he dove for the seal and slid through the hole, tucking his wings in tight to chase after my friend.

I watched in panic as he sped toward her, straining for her before she could hit the ground below. His wings unfolded at the last moment, wrapping her up in a tight embrace only seconds before they struck the red earth. He twisted his body just before they landed, taking the brunt of the fall and covering Margot with his wings. He hid her from sight, but it was him who sank into the earth below, denting it with the force of his fall.

Neither of them moved as I waited, turning my attention to Michael only when he took a step toward me. His face was pinched in fury, his hands sweeping out to create a vortex of air. The storm tore through the Tribunal room, gathering the blood that had seeped from my wound and pressing it into the floor and the throne on the dais. I felt the call of the Covenant spread through me, summoning the Coven to the Tribunal room where Michael would send them to Hell.

"Iban, it isn't too late to stop this. We can save Margot. We can save your family," I pleaded, staring down below and waiting for any sign of life from Beelzebub or Margot where they'd been swallowed up by the crowd of demons gathering to climb their way up the stairs that appeared to lead them out.

The Tribunal door flew open again, and I knew in my heart who I would find stalking into the room. He still wore his suit, having wasted no time in getting to me. The expression on his face was a mask of pure vehemence when he found Iban leaning over me, pinning me down, and the knife still stabbed into my abdomen.

A black ball of fur surged past him, darting between his legs. Jonathan raced toward me, leaping through the air. He shifted mid-leap, his body growing as his black fur lengthened. Smooth, fair skin peeked out from his legs as they lengthened. His snout curved out, his teeth elongated into fangs that hung out of his mouth. He shook his head as he landed on all fours, his paws enormous as he righted himself to stand on both feet, taking his Cursed form once again.

"Please, move," I begged, turning my attention back to Margot. I didn't know how much more time I could buy them to get out of there before I would have to succumb to the pain and death lurking just beyond the Source or fight back.

"Consort," Jonathan said, his voice startling me. It was deeper than his human form, mesmerizing in the way it felt like a growl.

"Save her. Save Margot, please," I begged, turning my teary stare toward him. With Gray here, I had to hope that together we would be able to close the seal.

But I couldn't do that until Beelzebub got her out of there.

Jonathan nodded his wolfish head, bowing low in a parting gesture. Losing him felt like losing a part of myself, but I couldn't just leave Margot to rot, either. "As you wish, Consort."

Jonathan leapt down into the pit, paying no mind to the drop that would have killed a human. He landed with bent knees, sprawling forward to lessen the impact, then curled his body to run on all fours below. I watched him fight to make his way to where Beelzebub still covered Margot's body with his wings—unmoving and silent.

"Michael," Gray said, forcing me to look away from the scene below. His amber eyes turned to his twin in surprise, pain flickering over his expression as he looked between us and connected the dots. I realized he probably hadn't seen his brother in centuries since his fall, what could have been a reunion turning terrible. "What are you doing?"

"He banished you to Hell. You have to go back," Michael said, his jaw clenching in something that I thought might have been remorse. Whatever had happened between them, whatever God had instilled in them, at one point they'd been family.

The closest family could be.

That didn't stop Michael from approaching Gray and wrapping his hands around his shoulders as my husband stared at him in shock. He tossed Gray to the floor, angling him to the hole in the floor. Gray fought back as he snapped out of his confusion, driving his elbow into Michael's stomach and cracking the back of his head against his face.

"The devil belongs in Hell!" Michael shouted, grunting through the pain as he aimed his fist for Gray's face. They fought, grappling with one another as Satanus and Mammon burst into the room to help.

Movement from below distracted me from the fight, the sight of Beelzebub unfolding his great leathery wings renewing my hope. He sat beside Margot, tugging her into his lap as he fought with her gag and unbound her hands.

She was alive.

He touched her face, cupping it in his grip so sweetly that I wondered if I needed to reconsider my dislike for the massive demon. She wrapped her arms around his neck frantically as he glanced above, getting to his feet with her in his arms. Jonathan fought at their side, swiping and biting at anything that moved too close. The demons were vicious, attempting to cut him down where he stood.

The burst of air that Michael sent through the room nearly sent me tumbling down into the pit, only the connection of the seal clinging to my magic keeping me steady. Iban held on to me, shifting the knife within my abdomen so that it slid a little farther out of my body.

"You could be free!" Michael shouted, and I turned to watch him fight with Gray. Satanus and Mammon were caught in his storm, lightning cracking through the tornado he'd formed with the wind. It dragged them across the floor, their hands clawing and grappling for purchase as it drew them closer and closer to the seal.

Gray fought, exchanging strikes with his brother that left both of them bruised and bleeding. Gray never reached for his magic, leaving the Source untouched.

Saving it for me, I realized, as it coated my skin in power.

Saving it because it was the only thing keeping me alive as my lifeblood dripped down onto the seal to keep it open.

"Send him back! You could be free, Witch!" Michael shouted again, twisting Gray in his arms. He wrapped his forearm around the front of my husband's throat, walking him toward the seal slowly.

I held Gray's amber stare, the fear there that I might forsake him far greater than what might wait for him in Hell. I held his gaze as I uttered words that were barely audible over the cyclone as it yanked Satanus and Mammon back into Hell. They disappeared down the hole, forcing Beelzebub to drag Margot to the side.

They'd never make it in time.

Still, I turned my stare back to Gray's. "I already am," I said firmly, speaking more for my husband than for Michael. If this was how it ended, if this was how I died, I wanted him to know.

I didn't regret any of it.

He'd shown me what it was to choose.

And I chose him.

Gray bucked against Michael's hold with renewed energy, jerking his head back as he threw his brother to the floor. Michael hurried to his feet as Gray shouted to me, his eyes communicating everything his voice didn't. "Now, Willow!"

I slammed the back of my head into Iban's nose, feeling it crack beneath the force. His hands lifted to grasp his broken nose, releasing me as I cut myself off from the magic with a scream of agony that tore the skin from my bones. Wrapping my ruined palm around the hilt of the bone knife buried inside me, I grasped it firmly and pulled it free.

Fresh blood swelled as I spun on my knees, sweeping my arm out in a single smooth arch.

The blade caught Iban across the throat, the thin line taking a moment to show the blood swelling free. He sputtered, staring at me before his gaze dropped to the slow trickle that fell onto his shirt.

I bit back my sorrow at what had become of us, awkwardly stumbling to my feet with the knife in my hand. Its power slid through me, sinking back into the place where it belonged at my center. Everything came into focus as I felt Gray, felt his own access to the Source strengthening as it stopped feeding through to me.

Gray kicked Michael in the chest with a fresh burst of gray magic, sending him staggering back. I shoved Iban's body into his path, sliding him through his own blood and watching as Michael tripped and fell backward. His arms struck out, catching hold of the edge of the seal as it tried to close without my magic to keep it open.

Even as it closed, I felt the pull on my power. On my soul as it demanded a life.

It would all be for nothing if I couldn't satisfy the cost.

I grabbed Iban, shoving him on top of Michael's body as Gray stepped on his brother's hand where it gripped the seal. Michael dropped, his body sagging beneath the border as Iban fell into the pit. His body exploded into a mass of blood and flesh the moment he passed through, the sacrifice completed. Glass covered the pit, cutting through Michael's fingers and severing them from his body as the seal closed over my friend and my familiar, who were still trapped below. A demon struck out, landing his blow with three slash marks across Jonathan's chest as I watched. My familiar shifted into his feline form, racing for Margot where Beelzebub roared his rage and the demons quivered.

I fell to the glass on my knees, staring down at Margot below as her fear-filled gaze looked up at me. She held Jonathan to her chest, my cat bleeding but alive as his violet stare met mine, too.

Stone covered glass.

And they were both gone.

45

WILLOW

I clawed at the stone, desperate to dig through. My nails scratched at the surface, blood leaking onto the seal as I moved to the border and prepared to latch my hands onto it.

"No!" Gray shouted, diving toward me. He wrapped his arms around my waist, yanking me back from the seal as I struggled in his grip. My blood leaked free from the wound that wouldn't heal, sliding down over my side.

Gray held me steady as he flipped me to my stomach on the Tribunal room floor. "Let me go!" I screamed, thrashing in his grip. Even now, my body felt so fucking tired that it took everything in me. It was only adrenaline that kept me going, the Source refusing to let me go.

"You're no good to her if you're dead!" he shouted, turning me to my back. He raised his wrist to his mouth, biting himself and tearing through his skin with dull, humanlike teeth. I winced as his flesh parted, ripping open to drip down onto my face.

He pressed his wrist to my mouth, slamming it against my teeth harshly enough that I felt my lips bruise beneath the force of it. I shook my head from side to side, rejecting the blood from his torn arm.

Still, he pressed it into my mouth, forcing my lips to part. His blood slid through the gaps between my teeth, touching my tongue. The taste of him was as exquisite as ever, exploding over my tongue and tasting like pure, undiluted magic. I knew now it was the Source flowing through him, the taste of all things life and death that existed within him.

I grasped his arm, pulling him closer as the blood poured down my throat. Unable to stop, completely enraptured by the magic rejuvenating me, I knew I would drink from him until he had nothing left to give.

I was vaguely aware of voices as Gray spoke with someone else, the deep tenor of the other man's voice familiar. I couldn't be bothered to look as I drank, warmth spreading through my side as it finally healed the damage from the knife.

The bone knife I still clutched tightly in my hands.

"Witchling," Gray said, cupping my cheek finally. He tried to drag his wrist away from my mouth, but I held fast, sinking my teeth into his skin in my refusal.

He chuckled as another male came, grasping my hands and wrestling them away from his arm. Gray tore his arm free, leaving my lungs heaving as I watched him fall back onto his ass. He clutched his arm, the wound healing slower than it should have.

Leviathan helped me sit up, guiding my back up off the floor with a gentle, brotherly touch.

My eyes immediately went for the seal, a strangled sob catching in my throat when I realized I would have to tell Della and Nova that Iban was dead and Margot . . .

Fuck.

"Look at me," Gray said, his face filling my vision. He put himself between me and the seal, capturing my face in his hands. "Beelzebub will *never* let anything happen to her. You understand me?"

I nodded, grasping onto that logic with everything I had. I didn't know Beelzebub well enough to know if I could trust him or if he would be an ally or a foe, but what I did know was that the way he looked at Margot would have to be enough for now.

"She is to him what you are to me, my love," Gray said, touching his forehead to mine. "We'll get them back when we can."

"We'll have to. We'll need them when the price of you being here comes crashing down on us," I said, hanging my head. Charlotte said he didn't know what his price would be, and I believed her from the way he studied me.

"What are you talking about?" Gray asked.

"The Maiden. The Mother. The Crone," I said, watching as Gray's face paled. He shared a look with Leviathan, his eyes wide when they finally came back to me. "We upset the balance by bringing you here, and our daughter will be the one to make it right."

"Charlotte was the Crone," Leviathan said, understanding dawning on him while Gray stared at me.

"And you're the Mother," my husband said, his hand dropping to touch the wound on my stomach.

"Not yet, but I will be," I admitted.

Gray shook his head, his denial rising immediately. "This changes nothing. If you don't want children, we will not have children. It is that simple," he said, standing and pulling me into his arms. He lifted me from the ground, moving to the Tribunal room doors as the Coven stepped inside.

Leviathan waved us on, signaling that he would deal with the witches for the time being.

"But the balance," I argued.

"Fuck the balance. I'll watch the world burn before I allow it to force you into something you do not want," he said. Gray's headshake sank inside me, soothing the frayed edges of my soul. Tonight I would grieve for the friends I'd lost.

Tomorrow, I'd find a way to move forward.

46

GRAY

I took Willow into the bathroom, stripping her out of her clothes. She didn't move as I tended to her, staring at the wall as if it might hold the answers to her problems. She'd long since stopped crying as I gave Leviathan instructions on how to deal with the Coven members flooding into the Tribunal room, taking her to the privacy of our rooms so that she could break in peace. Moisture gathered at the bottoms of her eyes, but she never let those tears fall as I tore her shirt up the middle and stripped it off her.

My fingers went to the new pink skin on her abdomen just above her belly button. Trembling as I grazed the wound, I watched her flinch back from the touch. Her eyes went wild, her body physically recoiling as she snapped out of her trance.

She was in shock, her body working to protect her mind from what she'd experienced. "It's just me, Witchling," I said, raising my hands in front of her. I waited for her eyes to settle on mine, for her subtle nod as recognition flared in her stare.

"It's my fault," she mumbled as I hurried to strip off her pants, pulling them down her legs. Her skin was far too cold to the touch, like ice compared to the comforting warmth she usually offered. "If I hadn't spelled that dagger . . ."

"Don't you dare," I snapped, hating the way she flinched from the violence in my tone. "You do not need to carry the weight of the world every time someone fucks you over. Sometimes people just do shitty things. He tried to sacrifice you and everyone he knew. It is *his* fault."

Willow nodded, stepping into the shower when I gestured her in. I watched through the open door as she stood beneath the cascade, letting the water flow onto her face. Her eyes closed, her lungs heaving at the sudden warmth. She turned, tipping her head back to allow the water to rinse out her hair, her body slick and wet even before she wiped the water from her eyes and reached for the shampoo.

She paused, looking at me suddenly where I stood. "What are you doing?" she asked, her voice painfully soft. "Aren't you coming in?"

I paused, considering her state and weighing my choices. I could be honest with her, communicate my needs and give her the choice, or I could allow her to just grieve in peace. "I can't," I said, thinking only of her.

"But you're covered in blood," she said, glancing down at my own bloodstained clothing.

"I'll shower when you're done," I said.

"Gray," she argued, her brow furrowing. Her bottom lip trembled with a flash of vulnerability, her arms wrapping around herself.

I strode forward, stopping only when I lingered just outside the shower door. "I almost lost you," I said, the confession pulling from the deepest part of me. I hadn't wanted to admit how close Willow was to death when she finally managed to tear that dagger from her stomach, but I'd felt the call of the afterlife coming from her.

I'd seen the reaper waiting in the shadows.

"You didn't," she said, the gentleness of her voice striking me in the heart. She'd nearly died, and still she worried for how it affected *me*.

"But I almost did, and if I come in there with you, all I'm going to want is to feel you in my arms. To remind myself that you're still here, because if you weren't . . ." I trailed off. Even knowing I'd follow her to Hell, I knew the Willow I loved would be gone.

She'd never be the same after her death. Never be the same living through her first day in Hell.

But I couldn't tell her that, because that would only admit to everything Margot was experiencing while Willow showered the evidence of the night from her body.

"What makes you think I don't want you to remind me that I'm still alive?" Willow asked, the gentleness of those words conflicting with the heat of her stare.

"You're grieving," I said, shaking my head in denial. I wouldn't take advantage of her.

Not like this.

The moisture in her eyes fell finally, her face twisting. It left me with no choice but to surge forward into the shower, gathering her in my arms. The water soaked my clothes, making them cling to my skin as Willow wrapped her arms around my neck. She yanked me down to her height, capturing my mouth with hers.

It was a soft demand, her need for touch communicated in the frantic grip of her fingers at my nape.

I stripped my shirt off, tossing it to the bathroom floor behind me. The squelching noise didn't force me to take my lips away from my wife, refusing to sever our connection as I unbuckled my belt and shoved my pants down my thighs.

I separated from her only long enough to peel the wet fabric from my calves, kicking them and my boxer briefs to the corner of the shower. Willow lifted one of her legs in tune with me as I grasped her behind the thigh, using that grip to lift her into my arms and guide her to the opposite corner. She braced a single foot on the ledge meant for shaving, offering support as she guided a single hand between our bodies.

There was no preamble or foreplay as she guided my cock to

her entrance, shifting her hand out of the way so that I could push inside her. Her forehead rested against mine, her breathing turning ragged as I stretched her open for me.

Willow clung to me as if her life depended on it, as if her very being needed the reminder that I was real.

Her breath tangled with mine, and I knew I would never take a single one of those breaths for granted. Her heart pumped against my chest, her pulse thumping in tune with my own. I felt every beat of that heart within me, striking deep into the Source with the pull of destiny.

"I love you," Willow murmured, her words spoken softly against my lips. She kissed me as I thrust within her, her body opening for me to make love to the woman I'd almost lost.

"Witchling," I moaned, the magic of the Reds coating my skin. Willow cupped my face in her hands, her eyes flashing with the power of the Source as she stared down at me.

"I choose you, every day," she said, those words the reassurance of everything I'd wanted to hear.

Everything I needed to be at peace.

I devoured her mouth with mine, angling my head to kiss her long and deep. I moved within her with slow, languid strokes, bringing her to pleasure slowly and giving her the reminder we both needed when we finally climaxed as one.

We were here. We were together.

We were home.

47

WILLOW

I walked into the Tribunal room, refusing to look at the seal for fear I would lose my shit. Only a day had passed since everything happened, and the loss of Margot was never more evident than when the Coven gathered in the room where I'd lost her.

The newly selected Tribunal members waited on their own thrones as I made my way toward the dais, their families scattered about the room alongside them.

Della and Nova waited on the dais to my right, dressed in pretty dresses that represented their houses. Their somber faces echoed mine, the missing witch felt even more heavily in light of the day that had come so quickly.

Gray stood at the center, dressed all in black. He'd worn a forest-green tie for me, and Leviathan stood at his side along with Asmodeus. We both knew that Beelzebub would have stood with them if he hadn't been lost with Margot.

We'd get them back. We had to get them back.

But first I needed to get stronger. I needed to be able to keep the seal open for long enough for them to escape, without risking my life. Who could I sacrifice in my place otherwise?

Maybe the next witch who dared to defy me would find themselves of much greater use.

I stepped up the dais, placing my hand in Gray's. His eyes

were warm as they landed on me, flowing down the soft lace lines of my black gown. The train that flowed out behind me faded into a sparkling emerald shimmer, a nod to my mother on the day that neither of us had been able to see coming.

"I have one last surprise for you, before you become mine again," Gray said, turning his attention to the Tribunal room doors. I turned, facing it as Juliet stepped into the room. The boy at her side clung to her for support, his brown eyes wide as they swept over the Coven.

I hiked up my gown, sprinting down the dais and uncaring for how it must have looked. Ash's eyes were wide as I dropped to my knees in front of him, wrapping a hand around the back of his head. I crushed him to me, absorbing the happy tears he cried with the fabric of my dress.

Pulling back, I touched his face and looked him over more thoroughly.

Even in just a few weeks, he'd grown.

Juliet had dressed him in a suit for the occasion, and a sobbing laugh clawed up my throat as I stared at him. "Low," Ash said, the sound of that little voice striking me deep in the heart.

"Hey, Bug," I said, smiling through my tears. I stood, taking his hand in mine, and immediately felt at home when I turned and found Gray's amber eyes staring at me.

He smiled, and Ash shocked me when he stepped up and tucked himself into Gray's side quickly. He answered my silent question, "We had some time while you were getting ready today."

I turned my stare down to Ash, wondering how he would handle the knowledge of all that had changed. "Are you—" I broke off, smiling as I realized I couldn't handle the answer if it were a no. I couldn't function if they couldn't stand one another. "Is this okay with you?" I asked, feeling more nervous in this moment than I had the day Gray had come knocking on my door, calling himself an invitation I hadn't wanted.

"I just want you to be happy, Low," Ash said, staring up at me with those kind brown eyes that had been the center of my universe for so long.

Now I had two.

I nodded, shoving back the tears long enough to smile at him. Leviathan came over, taking Ash's hand and guiding him to stand in Gray's line of groomsmen with him. The meaning wasn't lost on me, but I spoke through a clogged throat. "Please don't send him away again."

"He's right where he belongs, Witchling," Gray said, taking my hands in his.

I nodded, squeezing his hands back as he turned to face the windows. Golden light streamed in them, shimmering so brightly I had to squint.

The Goddess stepped through the glass, appearing before us in a dazzling display. She smiled at Gray, reaching across the distance to cup his cheek in her hand affectionately. One by one, the Tribunal leaders stepped up to the foot of the dais, laying symbols of their magic at our feet as an offering.

Petra and Beltran brought crystals of every color, the vivid greens warming my heart.

Realta and Amar brought jars filled with starlight.

Bray brought a single branch.

Aurai and Devoe each laid a windchime on the floor, the glass shards bumping against one another as they breathed life into them.

Tethys and Hawthorne brought a jar of water and a seashell.

Erotes and Peabody brought elixirs and love potions.

Collins and Madlock brought lanterns.

I took my hands out of Gray's, swirling them in a circle while I closed my eyes. A single rose grew from my palms, and I laid it down alongside the bone I had taken from Loralei's tomb earlier that day for the offering.

"Your beloved's Coven has made a lovely offering on her behalf,

Lucifer Morningstar," the Goddess said, her eyes full of mischief as she looked at her brother.

He smiled, never taking his eyes off me as he considered his answer. "You can have anything you want, Goddess," he said, taking a step closer to me. I stared up at him, his face so close to mine. "As long as I can have her."

He cupped my cheek in his hand, the warmth of that embrace sinking inside me.

"Then all I ask is for you to be happy, dear brother," the Goddess said, resting a hand upon each of my shoulders.

Her light sank inside me, filling me with warmth as Gray sealed our final bargain with a kiss.

A bargain for an eternity at his side.

A bargain for love.

ACKNOWLEDGMENTS

First, thank you to my readers, whose love for this series has made all of this possible. I couldn't ask for a better group to join me in this transition from indie to traditional publishing. If you'd asked me when I started my author journey, I never would have seen myself here, and I owe it all to you. This last year has been overwhelming and surreal in all the best ways.

To my babies, K and C. You are my dreams come true. Thank you for putting up with my deadlines, and for always inspiring me to see light at the end of the tunnel. Thank you for being my daily reminders that love conquers all, and thank you for giving me purpose and a reason to keep dreaming bigger every day. I love you more than anything.

To Monique Patterson and the team at Bramble, who took a chance on me and this story. Thank you for working to make me feel valued in this process and answering every ridiculous question. It's been an honor to embark on this journey with you.

To my girls—Kelly, Caitlen, Ashley, Arin, and Renae—who held my hand as this story consumed my every thought, and gave me a voice when I had no more words at the end of the day. Thank you for understanding me and standing by me, through thick and through thin, and for always, *always* being willing to tell me when something needs work.

To my agent, Josi Beck, for working to make this happen and

for always believing in me—even when I don't believe in myself. Thank you for having my best interest at heart.

To Angie, for listening to me when I don't even make sense anymore. For making me feel valued and heard, no matter what we're talking about. Thank you for your unwavering support and for making these books sparkle. I'd be lost without you and your ability to make sense out of my muse-addled plot ramblings.

To Bri and Sienna, for being my author besties and supporting me unconditionally. Thank you for being my rocks. I would never be able to survive this industry without you by my side.

To my mom, for being my original hype girl when the world told me I'd never be good enough.

To Sarah, for taking a chance on a dark romance author who dared to step outside her comfort zone.

To Cassie at Opulent Designs. Thank you for the perfect cover. Of all your covers I've hoarded over the years, this one just might be my favorite.

ABOUT THE AUTHOR

HARPER L. WOODS is the *USA Today* bestselling fantasy romance alter ego for Adelaide Forrest. Raised in small-town Vermont, her passion for reading was born during long winters spent with her face buried between the pages of a book. She began to pass the time by writing short stories that quickly turned into full-length fiction. Since that time, she has published more than fifteen books and has plans for many more.

When she isn't writing, Woods can be found spending time with her two young kids, curled up with her dog, dreaming about travel to distant lands, or designing book covers she'll never have enough time to use.